running full tilt

A NOVEL BY

MICHAEL
CURRINDER

Charlesbridge
TEEN

Published by Charlesbridge
85 Main Street
Watertown, MA 02472
(617) 926-0329
www.charlesbridge.com

Library of Congress Cataloging-in-Publication Data
Names: Currinder, Michael, author.
Title: Running full tilt / Michael Currinder.
Description: Watertown, MA : Charlesbridge, [2017]
Summary: Sixteen-year-old Leo Coughlin's life is increasingly stressful because his autistic older brother Caleb's behavior is becoming more bizarre and even violent, and their parents' marriage is falling apart—but Leo finds an escape in long-distance running, and in two new friends: Curtis, himself a potential state champion who teaches him the strategy of running, and Mary, his would-be girlfriend.
Identifiers: LCCN 2016043040 (print) | LCCN 2016050004 (ebook) |
ISBN 9781580898027 (reinforced for library use) | ISBN 9781632896490 (ebook)
Subjects: LCSH: Autism—Juvenile fiction. | Long-distance running—Juvenile fiction. |
Running races—Juvenile fiction. | Brothers—Juvenile fiction. | Parent and child—Juvenile
fiction. | Families—Juvenile fiction. | Friendship—Juvenile fiction. | CYAC: Autism—
Fiction. | Running—Fiction. | Brothers—Fiction. | Parent and child—Fiction. |
Family problems—Fiction. | Friendship—Fiction.
Classification: LCC PZ7.1.C866 Ru 2017 (print) | LCC PZ7.1.C866 (ebook) |
DDC 813.6 [Fic] —dc23
LC record available at https://lccn.loc.gov/2016043040

Printed in the United States of America
(hc) 10 9 8 7 6 5 4 3 2 1

Display type set in Bootstrap and Veneer Two
Text type set in Adobe Jenson Pro
Printed by Berryville Graphics in Berryville, Virginia, USA
Production supervision by Brian G. Walker
Designed by Susan Mallory Sherman and Sarah Richards Taylor

TO MY BROTHER, CHRIS, for inspiration. It wasn't always easy, but it was worth the ride.

I DID ONE FINAL STRIDE and positioned myself on the line. It was a staggered start that would break at the first turn. When the gun finally blasted, I got sucked into the flow. I had to protect myself, but I had to be aggressive, too.

Unlike sprinters, distance runners don't run in the solitude of their own lanes. They run in packs, with steel spikes sharp as steak knives attached to their feet. Inside a tight pack moving at close to four-minute-mile pace, the spikes like barracuda teeth slashing at calves and shins from front and back, elbows and fists box for position.

By the time we cut in at the first turn, it was clear nobody wanted to take the lead in this race. So it was a scramble of bodies as we broke from the bend, sixteen guys angling toward the inside rail, like bees making their way to the hive.

We completed the first lap in 61 seconds and change. I knew damn well that when the pack is crammed tight and you lose focus for even a split second—the amount of time it takes to blink—it's easy to get clipped. So when I went down, the first person I cursed was myself. Falling is a runner's worst nightmare, but I did the only thing I could do at that moment. I got back up.

I knew if I could catch the pack by the bell lap, I might have a chance. At that point in the race, every runner has crossed the pain barrier and is running on fumes. It all comes down to guts and will in the final sprint. I had three laps to go. If I could be there for the final hundred meters, I still had a chance.

That's the beauty of a distance event. If you make a mistake early on, you can still get back in the race.

Part One

1.

"LEO?"

"Yes, Caleb?"

"Who put butter on Monica's nose?"

"You did, Caleb."

I flipped over onto my back, put my hands under my pillow, and watched the headlights from a passing car hit the speed bump and roll across our bedroom ceiling. It was our last night in the house, and I wished to God my older brother would stop talking nonsense and just close his eyes and go to sleep.

"Morris is frozen cat?"

"Yes, Morris is frozen cat," I answered.

"THAT'S RIGHT!" Caleb exploded in laughter. "Leo, what car God drive?"

"What car God drive?" I asked.

"GOD DRIVE BROWN THUNDERBIRD FORD!" he said, laughing again.

My brother posed riddles, ones I never solved. I had no idea who Monica was, why our cat was frozen, or why God drove a brown Thunderbird. I just knew my brother refused to sleep, and since he never slept, neither did I.

Dad once explained to me that Caleb's birth was a difficult one and his issues extended way past just autism. Mom was in labor for twenty hours and an encephalogram later revealed a lesion in Caleb's brain that probably was caused by a lack of oxygen. All I understood was that Caleb's autism and cognitive delays meant that his brain made sense of the world in a different way than mine. When he saw, heard, touched, or experienced something, his brain was doing something totally different with that information than my brain. I didn't really get it at the time. I just knew there was something inside him that made him talk differently, walk differently, act differently, and obsess on weird things like train tracks, ceiling fans, and Greyhound buses.

Caleb loved to paint, so Dad used to buy him paint-by-number kits, and on nights when he was especially restless he painted in the den outside our bedroom by the light of the television.

Caleb didn't get the whole idea of painting by numbers. He grasped the part about finding all the squiggly shapes with the same number and filling them in with the same color, but he didn't understand that the codes were predetermined. So he produced this crazy art. One month he painted this series of seascapes where deep-blue water and white-tipped waves became bubbling orange lava flecked with flames. Green-faced-sailors with blazing-red eyes fought for their lives adrift bubbling molten rock.

Dad framed and crammed our bedroom walls with Caleb's art. My favorite was da Vinci's *The Last Supper*. It hung opposite my bed, making it the first and last image I saw each day.

Caleb's version included an orange-skinned Jesus with purple hair, and apostles in jet-black robes circling behind a brick-red table. It looked more like Hells Angels at a Sizzler steak house than Christ's final meal.

"Leo, what happen long time ago?"

"What happened, Caleb?" I asked him.

"Caleb put Morris cat in mailbox."

"Yes, you did, Caleb," I confirmed.

"Scare mailman. RIGHT!" Caleb's laughter filled our tiny bedroom.

"You scared the holy crap out of him," I assured him.

"NEVER, EVER DO THAT AGAIN!" Caleb shouted. "CALEB GET IN BIG TROUBLE!"

"It's time to sleep." I turned and flipped my pillow. "Good night, Caleb."

"Good night, Leo. God love you."

My brother said this to me every night, and I always wondered what he meant.

Did God love me, or him?

2.

WHILE I WASN'T EXACTLY THRILLED about moving, I couldn't wait to get out of Manchester. We lived in one of those St. Louis subdivisions that looked like it had been designed with Legos; everything looked the same. Our house was located on one of those dead-end streets with a little loop so there's only one way in, one way out, and everybody knows everybody's business.

Last April, Caleb crawled out of bed late at night and wandered into the Larsens' house, a few doors down. He didn't bother ringing the doorbell or knocking. Caleb just barged into their living room and started zinging Mr. and Mrs. Larsen with his bizarre random questions. He did the same to the Pirellos a couple of months earlier, only a little earlier in the evening.

When some seventeen-year-old guy cruises into his neighbors' house late at night wearing nothing but his pajamas, it's going to cause a hot mess in the neighborhood. Breaking and entering lands some people in jail, but Mr. Larsen was pretty cool about the whole thing and didn't even call the cops. Mrs. Larsen was a different story, though. She went off the deep end because Caleb freaked out her twin daughters, Nina and Lori, who were in my grade. She got the whole neighborhood riled up. That was the final straw. After Caleb pulled that little stunt, my parents decided to ditch Manchester for a new scene.

Mom and Dad weren't exactly sure how Caleb would deal with the move, but they did know that once they started packing up boxes, all hell would probably break loose. My brother liked things predictable. Major disruptions to his routines often triggered tantrums where he'd go ballistic. Caleb would bite his knuckles, smack his head, jump up and down, and scream nonsense. Sometimes he even hurt himself. One time a lightning storm forced Caleb's favorite pool to close down early, so he punched out a bedroom window and ended up getting fifteen stitches.

Mom's solution was to haul Caleb and me down to her parents' farm for the weekend while my parents moved house. I knew it was probably for the best, but it also meant I was in for a crappy weekend. The only difference between Grandma and Grandpa's farm and a prison labor camp was that some prisons actually paid their inmates. By the time Mom rescued us on Monday morning, I was ready to snap.

Our "new" house on Geyer Road turned out to be one of those old ranch homes that looked frail and tired. Its wood siding was scarred from peeling paint and crawling with ivy, the roof spotted with missing shingles, and the windows clouded and bleary with dust. The front yard, though, was enormous and teeming with life. Old oak and elm trees loomed above me; thick, snaky branches shaded the lawn, cooling and hiding me. The tangled chatter of birds and insects made me feel isolated, but it also chilled me out.

"So . . . what do you think?" Mom asked.

I could barely see the neighbors' homes through the trees. That was another plus.

"It's pretty secluded," I said.

"It is," she agreed. "That's what I like about it."

Mom led us up a mossy brick walkway to the porch, unlocked the front door, and gave Caleb and me the grand tour. The entryway opened into a living and dining room with a wall of windows that overlooked a large backyard bordered by a creek and forest. To the right was a long hallway that led to two bedrooms and a bathroom. To the left was the kitchen, which adjoined a large den with walls made of red brick and old wood planks that looked like they might have come from a barn.

The rooms were still cluttered with unpacked boxes and brown sheet paper, but for the most part things were already in place just as before: same tired green sofa, same old dining room table and matching cupboard, same rugs, same bookshelves and books, same kitchen table and refrigerator. Mom looked over the living room and sighed. "I was kind of wishing your father would have looked at this as an opportunity to upgrade."

Her comment was a dig at Dad, but I didn't take the bait. She and Dad had all this complicated history that I preferred to stay away from.

"Honest, Mom, the place looks great. And it seems to be working for him." I nodded toward Caleb and smiled.

Caleb plucked two ice cubes from the freezer, tossed them into a glass, and filled the glass from the sink like it was any other day.

"Where will Caleb and I be stationed?"

"You two have an entire floor to yourselves."

Mom led us downstairs into a dimly lit room that felt like a bear den. I scoped out the place—the old brown couch, television, and bookshelves were now parked next to a brick fireplace. With a little work, the room might make a pretty decent man cave I thought. There was even a door that opened to a small patio. Our bedroom was on the far side of the room, partly underground, the windows high on the walls looking out into the massive backyard.

"Not bad?" Mom asked.

"Not bad," I said, but thinking about sleeping below the surface of the earth kind of creeped me out.

I looked out the window and spotted an albino squirrel in a tree, pure white from nose to fluffy tail, scrambling from branch to branch as it chased a gray squirrel.

"That's Al," Mom said, laughing, and nodding toward the squirrel. "We saw him the other day. Your father named him." She gave me a little hug. "I'm going to head upstairs and do some more unpacking. I'll let you and your brother settle in."

I turned and looked out the window again, but the white squirrel was gone.

I emptied a few boxes of clothes and my books, then took a break and decided to check out the backyard, but the door wouldn't budge. I had to throw my shoulder into the jamb a couple of times before the hinges finally loosened and I could pull the door open. I stepped outside into a yard thick with trees. With a little oil on those hinges, Caleb and I would have our own private exit.

3.

FOR THE MOST PART, I spent my summer scraping, sanding, painting, cleaning gutters, sealing and paving the driveway—you name it. I rarely saw any neighbors, and the ones I did see were old people, the kind that walked hunched over and moved slowly.

I met up with Vincent and Ricky from my old neighborhood a couple of times that summer. Ricky and I had played CYO soccer together at St. Joe's since we were five, and Vincent was this weird kid that lived down the street who knew everything about birds. The three of us liked to hang out in the woods behind our subdivision, and Vincent would whistle, gurgle, and squawk birdcalls and make the trees come alive in song. I'd known them almost twelve years, but they didn't offer much of a reaction when I told them I was moving. When our car pulled out of our driveway for the last time, they flipped me the bird. I think it was their way of telling me they'd miss me.

By August I was nearly going out of my mind, hungry for the company of people my age. I always got a little nervous before the first day of school, but this year I was also the new kid, which meant I was walking into a new school, a different terrain, one with unforeseen hazards. I slipped on my most comfortable jeans, a new black T-shirt that wouldn't show pit stains, and my

Nike running shoes. I took a look at myself in the bathroom mirror and figured I looked okay enough to just blend in.

"You need to remember to smile a lot and introduce yourself to your teachers and classmates," Mom cheerfully reminded me at breakfast. "You have a tendency to present yourself as a grouch."

"Thanks, Mom," I said, cringing at the way she said 'classmates' like I was heading off to first grade.

Dad reached into his pocket and handed me a crisp ten-dollar bill. "Knock yourself out, son. Think of this as an opportunity to reinvent yourself."

"What's that supposed to mean?" I asked him.

Dad smeared a giant glob of jam across his toast with his spoon. "Relax, Leo." He laughed. "Don't take life so seriously."

"I'll try that, Dad." I grabbed my lunch and thanked them for their crap advice.

It was the typical first day of school. Most teachers reviewed their grading policies and expectations, distributed books, and maybe launched partway into a lecture. I was bored senseless and famished by the time lunch rolled around.

My route to the cafeteria involved threading my way down unknown hallways past unfamiliar faces. Just outside the library, I had to skirt five thugs harassing some poor scrawny kid I assumed was a freshman. The ringleader, a burly guy wearing a football jersey with the name GLUSKER plastered over numbers, had his victim down on his knees, hands behind his back, pushing a tiny peanut across the tile floor with his nose. Glusker guided the kid by nudging his ass with the tip of his Timberland boot along a parade route lined by laughing up-perclassmen.

I made a quick U-turn and navigated my way safely through the student lounge and into the cafeteria, bought a couple of cartons of milk, and sought refuge at an empty section of table. Dad had made me an enormous ham-and-Swiss sandwich on rye that was goopy with honey-brown mustard, just the way I loved it. I opened my novel, and within five minutes I was in a different world.

My bubble was soon popped, though, by the clank and clatter of five plastic cafeteria trays piled high with cheeseburgers and fries slamming against the Formica tabletop. I glanced over the spine of my novel to find myself in the unfortunate company of Glusker and crew. Fearing I might be the next guy rolling a peanut across the floor, I spun my body the other way, started cramming my sandwich into my mouth, and hoped that the three seats separating me from them would provide a safe-enough buffer zone. For the next few minutes, I heard nothing but raucous laughter and lewd remarks about the cafeteria ladies before one of Glusker's minions snickered, "Hey, there's Itchy." And that stopped their conversation.

"Get over here, Itchy. Now!" Glusker barked. "You heard me! Get your sorry ass over here!"

I figured Itchy was probably just some dude from their football team with ringworm or a bad case of jock itch. If Itchy was going to take the seat closest to me, I was going to scram. But when I snuck another glance, I realized Itchy wasn't their buddy. He was a custodian.

Itchy was a scrawny guy with slicked-back dark hair and small, deep-set eyes rimmed by dark circles. He pushed his damp mop around in jerky crisscross patterns over the cafeteria floor. The guy walked with a gimp, pausing every few seconds to feverishly scratch at a bald spot behind his right ear. After a few seconds of scratching, he stopped, shook his head, slapped his hand, and mumbled something to himself before resuming mopping.

"Itchy," one brute yelled. "Tell us about your summer."

"What did you do with all that extra cash you pocketed last year?" another said, laughing. "Take your girlfriends to Vegas?"

"I missed you this summer, Itchy," Glusker yelled. "It's hard to find cheap entertainment when you're not around."

Itchy continued to push his mop, his lips twitching like he was attempting to smile, but the expression on his face made me think he was confused and becoming agitated. I had nearly finished my sandwich and was about to bolt when one of Glusker's goons took a nickel from his pocket and tossed it on the floor near Itchy. The poor guy dropped the mop, got down on his knees, crawled on the floor, located the nickel, and put it in his pocket. Within seconds, another guy at the table started flicking pennies on the floor so that now Itchy was scrambling around searching for them.

Bullying was bad enough, but hounding some poor guy who didn't even realize he was the victim of a cruel joke was as low as you could go in my book. There were kids in the old neighborhood who sometimes made Caleb do stupid stuff like that just for kicks.

Pennies, nickels, and dimes were flying off the table at Itchy like a Fourth of July bottle-rocket attack. Confronting Glusker and company would be suicidal, but I had to do something. So I took advantage of the fact that their undivided attention was directed toward Itchy. I pulled a nickel from my pocket and slid it inside Glusker's greasy hamburger bun as I slipped away. Near the garbage bins, I dumped my milk on the floor, then tapped Itchy on the shoulder and guided him to the puddle I'd created.

I threw my sandwich bag in the bin and was about to make a safe getaway when I felt a hand touch my shoulder. "I saw what you did," a calm, soft voice informed me. It was a girl. Thank God.

I turned to face her. "Saw what?" I mumbled defensively. She had slightly mussed-up long blond hair that fell to her shoulders, and these round, glassy green eyes that looked through me. She was wearing tight black jeans and a white button-down shirt with a tank top underneath. Amazing.

At a loss for words, I offered her an awkward dumb smile, but she crossed her arms and gave me a harsh stare. "I saw what you did," she repeated. "He could choke on that."

Part of me was totally unsettled by this girl's looks, and part of me was thrown off balance by her giving me crap for taking on those pricks. "Are you kidding?" I finally asked. "Did you see what those morons were doing to that guy?"

She glanced back and forth between me and Glusker. I seriously thought my time was up, but she suddenly smiled. "Nicely done," she said. "What those idiots were doing was wrong on so many levels."

At that moment a loud howl of pain sliced through the cafeteria. "Holy shit!" Glusker yelped. "There's a frickin' nickel inside my cheeseburger! I think my tooth is chipped!"

I turned and looked at the girl. "Well, at least he didn't choke," I offered.

Glusker was close to completely losing it by now, glaring wide-eyed at each member of his posse. "Which one of you guys did this?" he yelled.

"It might be a good time to make your escape." She laughed. "You've probably used up all your good karma for the day."

"I think that's a good idea," I agreed.

She turned, then glanced over her shoulder once more and flashed that sweet smile. "By the way, I'm Mary."

I opened my mouth to respond, but my tongue got all swelled up and nothing came out. Maybe I was focused on making a quick exit? Or maybe I was just chickenshit? I had to face the fact that I'd had enough guts to take on those dudes but couldn't find the nerve to tell this girl my name.

4.

BY LAST PERIOD, ALGEBRA 2, the novelty of the
first day at a new school had worn off. I was restless and just
about crawling out of my skin. My elementary school teachers
had told my parents I was hyperactive, but my parents had
scoffed. Compared with Caleb, I was a sloth.

After I finally located my gym locker and got dressed, I
headed outside and made my way to the track. The football
players were already on the inside field in full combat attire,
doing drills to the beat of claps and shrill whistles. Even for late
August, it was still blazing hot. Blanketed in pads and helmets,
they barked the number of each and every jumping jack and
push-up. Coaches stalked the chalked lines and got in the grille
of anyone slacking. That sport wasn't for me.

I'd decided I was going out for cross-country this year.

Looking across the football field I spotted a group of scraggly,
undernourished-looking guys in shorts and worn T-shirts
clustered in a section of bleachers lining the sidelines and track.
Behind the railing, they looked like those POWs you see in
old World War II movies. I figured they must be the cross-
country team, so I threaded my way across the field, climbed the

bleachers, and tried to drift in without being noticed. Some guys were doing some light stretching, but most were just sprawled out across the empty benches.

"You new here?" The voice came from behind me.

I turned and faced a tall guy with long blond hair pulled back with a headband stretching his hamstrings on the top guardrail. Compared with the others gathered around, this guy actually resembled an athlete, like he could be a wide receiver on the football team. He looked like a runner—lean but strong, with these thick veins in his arms and legs that swelled under his skin.

"I'm Leo."

"Curtis," he said, extending his hand. "What's your story, Leo?"

"Just moved from Parkway Central. I'm a junior."

He scratched his chin thoughtfully as he looked me up and down. "And what makes you think you have the talent to join this elite group of athletes?"

"Uh ...," I stammered, unable to read the guy. I wasn't quite sure if he was some smart dude who actually spoke this way, or if he was just messing with me.

He nodded toward a scrawny guy curled up in the fetal position in the shade below the first row. "Lighten up, Leo. I'm just giving you crap. I'm captain of this pathetic outfit," he told me. "Ever run before?"

"Not cross-country. Played soccer until now. I just started running this summer."

"How much?" He grabbed his ankle and contorted his leg behind him.

"Every day. Not sure how far, but every day."

He glanced at the other guys. "Well, you're way ahead of these buffoons," he said with a sweep of his hand. "Some of these athletes," he shouted, pointing toward two, "like Rosenthal and Rasmussen, could be respectable runners if they possessed even a shred of discipline." He then nodded toward the others. "The rest of this sorry lot," he said, shaking his head, "also have potential. Maybe if they'd put in their summer miles like they were supposed to, this team wouldn't be such an embarrassment."

"We prefer to come into the season well rested," Rosenthal replied calmly. Rosenthal was a tall, ridiculously thin guy with a mop of black hair. He was wearing long black basketball shorts and an oversize tank top that left every bone in his rib cage visible. Rasmussen was shorter, with slightly more muscle on his bones. He had buzzed blond hair and wire-rimmed glasses. Both appeared unfazed by Curtis's insults.

"You gotta be a glutton for punishment if you want to excel at this sport!" Curtis shot back.

"That sounds unhealthy if you ask me, Kaufman," Rosenthal said.

"I think *warped* and *twisted* are better words for it," Rasmussen added. "Burpee, Stuper, and I prefer to follow Rosenthal's summer training regimen," Rasmussen continued. "Twelve hours of sound sleep, two daily servings of Imo's pizza washed down with Coke, and a minimum of four hours of video games. Call of Duty, Madden, Grand Theft Auto, Resident Evil—we encourage variety."

Burpee and Stuper, I assumed, were the two guys seated next to Rasmussen who were slowly nodding their heads, perhaps too wiped out by their day to engage. Like Rosenthal, they were tall and gaunt and looked like they hadn't seen sunlight in months.

"Pitiful!" Curtis muttered in disgust. "You must embrace the monotony!" he screamed before pointing across the field. "Gentlemen, at attention! Our fearless leader has arrived."

A gray-haired hulk of a guy was marching toward us, carrying nothing but a clipboard. He was over six feet tall, with a thick neck, a barrel chest, and calves the size of bowling balls.

"Leo," Curtis said, "allow me to be the first to introduce you to Coach Archibald Gorsky."

The guys rolled up from their lounging positions and sat up straight.

Gorsky came to a halt at the foot of the bleacher stairs and scanned the group. "Gentlemen," he bellowed, before looking each of us in the eye. "I hope you've all had a restful summer and you're now prepared to get back to work."

He proceeded up the stairs, the bleachers shaking and rattling with each step.

"Gorsky's a good guy," Curtis whispered. "He actually has a degree in engineering, but he chose to apply his science to athletics. He'll give us a five-minute speech, send us out for our workout, then head over there and toss his shot and disc," Curtis said, nodding opposite us toward a large fenced-in field beyond the track. "If he's not there, you'll find him in the weight room pumping iron."

Gorsky covered all the typical first-day-of-practice details—attendance policies, deadlines for physicals, practice times, reminders about diet—and then gave a lengthy lecture about hydration and monitoring our urine for color and clarity. His clipboard circulated and we wrote down the usual crap.

Finally, Gorsky announced the day's workout: "Today we'll begin with our standard distance run."

A few guys groaned.

"That's correct, gentlemen. We'll start with the superblock." He laughed. "For those of you new to the team, I advise you to pair up with a veteran so you don't get lost. When you're done, meet me over there," he said, pointing to the shot put and discus rings. "I'll see where you're at and tell you what's next on the menu."

Guys stood up slowly, shook their legs, and made their way down the bleachers, past Gorsky. "Get a good drink of water before you head out," he yelled.

I followed Curtis down the steps. Gorsky placed his hand on Curtis's shoulder and stopped him. "Are you healthy, Kaufman?"

"Better than ever," Curtis told him.

"Didn't overdo it this summer?"

"Relax, old man," Curtis said, laughing. "I stuck to the plan."

Gorsky released his grip on Curtis's shoulder and gave him a pat on the back. "That's my boy," he said.

I followed Curtis along the track circling the football field. "Superblock?" I asked.

He broke into a slow jog. "The superblock is a running route you will soon learn to love and appreciate if you decide to pursue this fine sport," Curtis explained.

I looked back and saw the rest of the guys lingering at the water fountain, pretending to stretch. "Do you mind if I run with you?"

He raised an eyebrow. "Well, young grasshopper, that depends if you can keep up."

By the time we left the parking lot, Curtis had already picked up the pace. "To tell you the truth, most of the time I go solo. The rest of the guys don't train during the summer," he informed me. "I live for this, Leo."

His pace was quick, but I kept up.

"Run with me as long as you can," Curtis said. "If you get tired, you can wait for those guys to come along, and they'll show you the way back."

We ran another two hundred meters before I looked over my shoulder and saw nobody in sight. Soon enough Curtis and I ascended the first hill and coasted the descent. I loved my solitary runs, but it was kind of cool running beside another person and talking.

Curtis told me about some of the guys on the team, what the season would be like, and Gorsky's typical workout regimen. "He's pretty old-school," Curtis explained, "but his stuff works." Curtis signaled with his hand to turn at an intersection. He also increased the pace.

We approached another hill, one of several he had promised. "Tempo okay for you?" he asked.

I was pushing, but it felt manageable. "I feel all right."

He looked over his shoulder at me and smiled. "Do you mind if we pick it up a notch?"

"I can try."

Curtis increased the pace even more, and I felt myself start sucking desperately for air, but I hung with him. He asked why I came out for cross-country, and I made up this load of bull about how I was tired of playing on lousy soccer teams.

"Wise man," he said. "It's not like we've got a great cross-country team here, but aspects of this fine sport can still allow one to thrive as an individual."

Though I had put in some miles this summer, Curtis was on a different level. The hills and pace began taking their toll on me, making my legs burn and become heavy. By the time we made the turn onto Price Road, my lungs were screaming for more air.

"What's your last name, Leo?" he asked me.

"Coughlin," I gasped.

"Okay, Coughlin," he said casually. "Let's see what you've got."

He started hammering. The next hill nearly finished me for good, but I had a slight downhill to recover. "That hill's a beast," he confirmed. "I'm impressed."

When we made the turn onto Clayton, I spotted a gas station up ahead. "I think I need to stop for water," I panted.

"No water," he told me. "You're going to feel this same way toward the end of a race. Ten more minutes and you're done. Now's the time you need to embrace the pain."

"I think I embraced it a couple of miles ago," I gasped.

The next ten minutes were the longest of my life. "This is it," he assured me as we ascended another huge hill. "Once we get over this baby, it's over."

It hurt, and when we got to the bottom of the hill, it sure as hell wasn't over. We turned right onto Warson Road and still had another half mile he'd forgotten to mention. It was flat, but it was an eternity. That's where he left me in his dust.

I staggered back to school a minute behind him, bent over in pain.

"Stand up and put your hands above your head," he encouraged me. "It will get more air into your lungs." He helped me stand and patted me on my back, and I started to feel a little better.

"Mind if I get some water now?" I asked.

We stopped at the drinking fountain outside the gymnasium, and I gulped until my insides cooled.

"What do you think, Leo?" Curtis asked.

I lifted my head from the fountain. "I'm wrecked," I huffed, then continued guzzling water.

Gorsky was retrieving his discuses and shots when we returned to the track. He looked at us and flashed a smile. "What have we here, Kaufman?" he called out. "Someone who can finally keep up with you?"

"This is Leo," he told Gorsky. "The guy can run. At least, he could today."

"Leo," Gorsky repeated, studying me a moment. He turned and walked back to the shot ring, glancing over his shoulder this time at Curtis. "Kaufman, I don't suppose the rest of your teammates ran this summer?"

Curtis shook his head.

Gorsky nuzzled the shot against his bulging neck. "How

many times have I told them: cross-country is a summer sport. Unless you train in the summer, the season's pointless," he said to us as he positioned his massive body to throw.

We watched the small cannonball explode from his body and land with a thud in the grass. He chucked it pretty far for an old guy. "I tell them, but they never listen." He sighed.

Gorsky launched two more shots while we stretched against the fence, and then he trudged out to retrieve them. With his back to us, he issued final instructions. "Run eight strides at three-quarters sprint speed," he ordered. "Then call it a day."

"We'll see you tomorrow," Curtis yelled.

"Lift those damn knees on the strides, Kaufman," he ordered. "And remember to drink plenty of liquids."

After we'd finished I was walking like a zombie toward my bike, wondering how I'd ever make it home, when Curtis pulled up beside me in his car. "You're telling me that you never ran before this summer?" he asked me.

"Not really," I told him.

"I call bullshit, Coughlin," he said, smiling. "We hammered today, and I can sense you've definitely run."

When I finally got on my bike, my legs could barely crank the pedals. That workout had nearly killed me, but I loved the intensity and could feel myself craving more. If that was a typical workout, I could hardly imagine an actual race.

5.

I DIDN'T EXACTLY LIE TO CURTIS—I actually *had* started running that summer—but I didn't tell him the whole truth, either.

As it turned out, Caleb wasn't crazy about our new house at first. Shortly after the move his temper tantrums escalated to a whole new level. And he began directing them at me. His violent outbursts had me running out the back door on almost a daily basis.

In hindsight, Caleb had sent out plenty of signals even before the move—twirling the stick he always carried with more intensity, curling his fingers into a fist, biting his knuckles. I guess I should have known he was tightly wound and it was only a matter of time before he exploded. I really just didn't know what to do about it. Mom and Dad didn't seem to have a clue either, or maybe they were completely in denial.

"I need for you to keep a lid on things around here for a while," Dad told me at the beginning of the summer.

"What exactly does that mean?" I asked him. It was one of Dad's signature phrases that could refer to any number of things.

"Just keep an eye on your brother. We're new in the neighborhood and we don't need any incidents."

"I'm on it," I assured him.

While Caleb was certainly capable of taking care of his basic needs, particularly managing his enormous appetite, Mom and Dad were still a little apprehensive about Caleb's transition. Basically they wanted an extra set of eyes scoped on him over the summer in case he did anything especially inappropriate to freak out our new neighbors.

Dad had recently started paying Caleb for doing different jobs—sweeping the garage, pulling out the dandelions and crabgrass, or clipping the high grass around the trees and shrubs. When Caleb finished his assignments, he created his own jobs and negotiated a fee that Dad paid him in one-dollar bills. Caleb kept the cash neatly stacked in the top drawer of his dresser next to his socks, and he spent a portion of it on maintaining a stash of candy he kept hidden in a paper bag in the cabinet beneath our bathroom sink.

Lately Caleb had been using the rake to comb and thatch the front yard, a new obsession. One morning when I headed upstairs for breakfast—Mom was working early shifts at the hospital, and Dad liked to be the first one to the office, and I usually got up after they'd left for work—I saw that he'd already created twenty small piles of dead grass, twigs, and dirt clods. He would rake a small patch of grass for a minute or two, pause, and talk to himself, then plop on the ground and arrange the dead blades into neat little mounds. He would leave those piles in the yard until Dad got home, as concrete evidence of his labor. Based upon the number of piles I counted, I figured he'd already been hard at it for a couple of hours that morning.

I was reading the sports section when I glanced up and noticed Caleb really getting riled up—jumping around, his rake and garden fork discarded on the ground. He'd abandoned his piles and was now skipping around the yard, pounding one fist through the air and biting the knuckles on the other. It wasn't exactly the way I wanted to start my day, but I figured I'd better step outside and try to calm him down.

I approached him cautiously; he was thumping himself hard on the forehead. "Caleb, that can't feel too good," I told him. "Why don't you come inside and take a little break? You're going to hurt yourself, buddy."

He sat down, whacked the ground a few times with his fist, and eventually resumed picking through his grass piles. God knew what was making him angry this time, but he seemed steady for the moment, so I went back inside. I scanned the list of jobs Mom had left for me on the fridge. Vacuuming was easiest, so I started in the den.

That's when Caleb blasted into the room. "HOW MUCH MONEY LEO GET VACUUMING?" he yelled.

"I get an allowance, Caleb," I told him. "Flat rate. I do whatever I'm told and get my salary on Fridays."

"HOW MUCH LEO GET?" he shouted. He was talking faster now, and I realized he was really agitated.

"I told you already," I said calmly.

I had my back to him and was removing the plug from the socket when he smashed into me from behind. I smacked my head against an end table and collided with the wall. The lamp fell over and the bulb shattered. Before I knew it, he'd flipped me on my back and pinned my shoulders with his knees. He slapped my head with one open hand and started pounding the other side of my face with his fist. Then he grasped my throat with his right hand and started trying to jab his left thumb into my eye. I kicked and punched, but Caleb was built like a linebacker. I fought to grab a handful of his hair with one hand and his ear with my other, and I pinched and pulled with everything I had before he finally screamed and released me.

I rolled out from under him, tore through the kitchen, and tipped a chair in his path. I dashed downstairs toward the door to the patio, with Caleb in pursuit. If it wasn't open, I was screwed. Luck was on my side, though, and I was across the grass and into the next-door neighbor's backyard before I looked over my shoulder to catch my breath. Caleb was no longer chasing me. He had stopped in our driveway and was jumping and skipping around, hitting himself.

I decided it was best to keep moving. I watched my sneakers disappear under me, and after a while my body found a rhythm, my breathing evened out, and I relaxed a bit. I wondered what I'd done to set Caleb off. Caleb occasionally lost control of himself, but this was new territory as far as I knew. It was the first time he'd actually gone after a person instead of a window or a wall, and that person happened to be me. As mixed up as I was when running that morning, I wondered if it was better me than some other person.

I ran for a long time, making a loop along the major roads before heading back to the house. When I finally got home, Caleb was sitting calmly in the front yard, picking through the dead grass. He smiled and laughed as he talked about God and the Thunderbird Ford. I approached him tentatively.

"Hi, Leo," he said when he saw me.

"Hi, Caleb."

"Where Leo go?" he asked me.

"I had to take a little break," I explained, keeping my distance.

"Caleb good worker. Right!" Whenever my brother followed with "Right!" I understood that the preceding statement was actually a question—one he meant for me to affirm.

"Caleb is a good worker," I confirmed, wondering if maybe I was really the crazy one.

I studied my eighteen-year-old brother, sitting in the yard in the midst of another obsessive monologue, assembling more piles of dead grass and twigs. Caleb was a good worker all right, but when he lost control it was time to bolt.

"Are we cool?" I finally asked.

"TAKE CALEB SWIMMING!"

Crap. That, of course, was also on my list of duties for that day, and Caleb knew it. There wasn't a snowball's chance in hell I was going to get out of taking him to the pool.

"Have you calmed down?" I asked him.

"YES! Take Caleb pool!"

I took a moment to consider the possible consequences if I didn't. "All right," I decided. "Be ready in fifteen."

I was still a bit rattled when we got in the car, so I kept silent. I spent the twenty-minute drive listening to Caleb laugh and chatter away about God and rocky road ice cream.

The Mid-County Y was Caleb's home away from home. It had both an indoor and an outdoor pool, which kept Caleb happy all year long. I really didn't feel too much like swimming; I did a few laps, then sprawled out on a deck chair. Usually I sunk myself into a good book while Caleb swam, but today I couldn't focus. Instead I watched Caleb in the deep end as he jumped off the high dive, like he did every time we came to the pool. Again and again, he'd bound off the diving board high into the sky, laughing maniacally and screaming nonsense, then midair he'd do this crazy corkscrew spin. He'd hit the water with a tremendous splash and disappear until he finally needed a breath. Some kids laughed, others stared. Caleb's pool antics mortified me when I was younger, but I no longer gave a rip. It really made him happy.

Usually we'd hang out for only a couple of hours at the pool before I told him we needed to get going, but after the day we'd had I let him swim until he came out on his own terms. I wanted to make good and sure he had calmed down.

I told Mom and Dad about what had happened that morning, but Dad pretty much blew it off. "My big brother and I used to fight all the time," Dad said, and laughed, casually scooping from the salad bowl. "He used to beat the living daylight out of me sometimes."

Mom at least casted me a worried glance, but she didn't say anything. She also seemed kind of checked out.

The next day, Caleb went for a repeat performance. This

time I was folding laundry. He took me by surprise when he jumped me, but I managed to pull his hair, knee him in the groin, and take off running. This time I ran even farther. It took me longer to find a running rhythm, to settle down.

It happened again the next day when I was washing the windows.

And the day after that I decided to lay off the chores altogether, since that seemed to be his trigger, but he still came at me. At least this time I saw him coming and had a head start.

Before I knew it these attacks were a regular pattern and I was running every day, sometimes more than once. When Caleb lost control, I had to get away. I really didn't have much choice but to run, and I had to run far, because I had to give both of us enough time to cool off. When I got home I usually took him to the pool, where he'd unleash his energy and we'd both return to some semblance of normal.

I used to think that all that stuff I heard about a runner's high was legend, but it's actually true. I found if I ran far enough and hard enough, I actually got an amazing buzz like I was floating outside myself, looking down on my body running on earth, like a red-tailed hawk soaring high above. When that feeling kicked in, the pain and fear disappeared. Sometimes I felt like I could run forever.

One morning Mom posted a letter from the new high school with information about the upcoming year. She'd circled the information about fall sports: football, soccer, golf, cross-country.

Running seemed to be calling me, so I signed up for the cross-country team.

That's the part I didn't mention to Curtis after our first practice. I figured he didn't need to know that I'd started running because my brother scared the hell out of me.

6.

"GEEZ, MOM. CALEB'S STARTING TO make our front yard look like some kind of ancient burial ground," I commented as I dove into my third bowl of Cheerios. Those couple of weeks after I joined cross-country, Mom told me I was devouring food like an elephant with a tapeworm.

I was watching Caleb crawl around the front yard on his hands and knees, having an intense discussion with himself. He was obsessed. Bit by bit, he was scalping our lawn, making one mound of debris after another. Caleb labored before and after school, plucking each and every blade of dead grass, little twig, and dirt clod by hand.

"It makes him happy," she said. "Those little mounds he builds are kind of like your Cheerios."

"Not quite the same," I corrected her, before slurping the last soggy bits from the bowl.

As I headed out the door for school, Mom stopped me. "Why don't you invite one of the guys from the team over for dinner?" she asked.

"Really, Mom? Don't you think that might be kind of weird with the sacrificial graveyard out front? I'll think about it. Are we having cheese pizza or fish sticks?"

"Your choice."

Our family abandoned the church a couple of years ago, but Mom still harbored some residual Catholic guilt and clung to a few traditions like no meat on Fridays.

"You know I've never been a big fan of fish sticks. That's Caleb's thing."

"So I'll doctor up some cheese pizzas and plan on a guest?"

I gazed out at Caleb hacking up the yard and told Mom again that I'd think about it.

———

Curtis believed in a daily dose of intense focus and effort. He called that portion of the workout "red miles." I called it pain. The first ten minutes of our run were conversational. He would give me the rundown on what I needed to know about life at Ladue: the best-looking girls, a few thugs to avoid at all costs, and a couple of locations on campus where various sordid events had transpired. But after those first ten minutes, he jacked up the pace and things got serious.

By the time we crested the first hill that Friday, I was suffering. I told Curtis to go ahead, and I staggered along until the pack of Rasmussen, Stuper, Rosenthal, and Burpee pulled up beside me.

"So Rasmussen is our winner!" Burpee announced, raising Rasmussen's arm in victory.

"Winner of what?" I asked.

"We placed a bet the other day on how long it would take before you crashed and burned trying to hang with Kaufman," Stuper explained.

"The guy hammers," I gasped.

"No kidding." Rasmussen laughed.

"Kaufman's been running twice a day since ninth grade," Rosenthal offered up.

"He's a freak," Burpee said, as if it were widely accepted fact.

"Not to mention he took five APs last year," Stuper added.

"Kaufman is one intense freak," Burpee repeated.

"How does he do it?" I asked, suddenly feeling like a fool.

"There is rumor of steroid use," Rasmussen said with a raised eyebrow. "Or perhaps he's bionic."

"Come to think of it, the bionic theory might explain the way he speaks," Burpee suggested.

"Why *does* he talk that way?" I asked.

"Kaufman is a man of mystery," Rosenthal said to me.

The rest of the run was grueling, but when we finally finished, Curtis was waiting in front of the school, stretching under the shade of a tree.

"Look what we found during our run today, Kaufman!" Stuper yelled as he and Rasmussen grabbed my arms and pretended to haul me.

"Another one of your roadkill victims," Rosenthal said, laughing. "Someday you're going to be charged with manslaughter."

I looked at Curtis and shook my head. "I feel like total dog meat."

He laughed. "You're doing fine, Coughlin. Third week is the worst. Hang in one more and it'll get easier."

We headed onto the track, where Gorsky dictated the final portion of the workout: twelve strides a hundred meters in length.

We began each one slowly and increased the speed in increments, until we were going flat out the last thirty meters. My legs burned, but I could still hang with Curtis, given the short distance. The recovery was short, a ten-meter walk to and from the fence. By the time I'd completed my fourth, I was getting ready to blow chunks.

"Leo!" Gorsky bellowed. He waved me over and pulled a roll of white athletic tape from his equipment bag. "Give me your hands," he ordered.

I held out my arms, too exhausted, nauseous, and confused to question him.

"Now make fists and place your thumbs outward over your index fingers," he instructed.

I did like he said, so my thumbs were now pointing outward like some wayward hitchhikers. He taped my thumbs tightly around my fists so I couldn't move my fingers.

"Your arms flop back and forth like a rag doll when you run," he explained. "Go on back there and do a few more strides at full strength, but this time pump those arms of yours. Then come back and tell me what you notice."

I jogged back to the pack, my hands hanging outward, away from my hips. The guys were waiting for me, looking at my hands curiously.

"That's going to make going to the bathroom very problematic," Stuper decided.

"What's up with the bandages?" Rosenthal asked. "You look like a land-mine victim."

But as we accelerated into our next stride, it did feel different.

My arms pumped, drove forward, and provided power. By midway through that stride, I'd moved comfortably ahead of Curtis by five meters.

"What the hell?" he yelled from behind.

"Kaufman is finally getting his butt kicked," Burpee howled.

We did another, and I exaggerated my new arm swing and went even faster. "It's just a measly hundred meters, Coughlin. Anything farther, and I've got your ass!" Curtis shouted.

We ran the next two together, and I focused on my new arm swing. Gorsky had stopped throwing and was now leaning against the fence, studying us. We did four more before we jogged over to him.

"What did you notice, Coughlin?"

"I feel stronger," I told him. "Like my arms aren't just dangling from my shoulders."

"You run with more than just your legs, Leo. You need your arms, too," he explained. "When they're all moving in the same direction, and every part of your body is working together in concert, you run faster. It's that simple. We'll put that tape on your hands when you run for the next week and see if we can fix this little problem."

He picked up his shot and rolled it around in his palm. "Focus on your form and believe that what you are attempting to do is good for you, that it will make you a better runner. Learn the patterns, until it's innate."

"How come you don't tape *our* hands?" Rosenthal asked, offering his hands to Gorsky.

"The only place I'd put tape on your body is over that mouth of yours," Gorsky answered. He headed back to his shot put ring, but not before scolding Curtis. "You're pushing it too hard, Kaufman. I can tell by the length of your stride. You're your own worst enemy. If you don't back off, you're going to end up sick again." He blasted the shot once more. "That means rest, Kaufman," he said as the shot crashed upon the gravel.

"Relax, old man," Curtis told him. "I've got everything under control."

"I worry about you, son."

"No need to fret, Gorsky. I've learned my lesson."

At the bike rack Curtis helped me take off the tape. "What was that all about?" I asked.

"Ran myself into the ground last summer and fall and ended up with mono in October. I was running out of my mind, and then I imploded. Not fun." He pulled the tape off my hands, wadded it into a ball, and tossed it into the trash. "Hell, maybe I should tape my hands up to help me go faster, or just chop them off," he said with a chuckle.

I climbed aboard my old bike. "Believe me, you have plenty of speed."

"It's got to suck riding that bike home after running," he said to me. "You want a lift?"

"I thought you'd never ask. Give me a ride home and my mother will feed you dinner."

"What's the Friday-night special at the Coughlin house?" he asked.

"Pizza."

He took a moment to weigh the offer. "I'm in."

When I threw my bike in the hatch and climbed in, I suddenly realized I couldn't remember the last time I'd brought a friend home.

———

Curtis pulled into the driveway and immediately surveyed the yard. "What's up with all the little mounds?"

"It's a long story. I haven't told you about my brother yet." I gave Curtis a quick crash course on Caleb while we headed into the house. Before opening the door, I warned him that he was about to be interrogated.

Caleb met us in the front hall with his arms crossed.

"Good evening, Caleb," Curtis said, extending his hand to him. "I'm Curtis."

Caleb squeezed his hand briefly, crossed his arms again, and studied Curtis a moment. "CURTIS GRANDMOTHER DEAD!"

Curtis turned to me casually and whispered, "Was that a question or a statement?"

"That was a question," I whispered back.

Curtis turned back to Caleb. "Well, as a matter of fact, Caleb, both of my grandmothers have passed away."

"Caleb!" my mother shouted from the kitchen.

"GRANDFATHER STILL LIVING!" Caleb continued.

"One died about five years ago," Curtis explained. "However, my mother's father is still alive and kicking. Next question?"

"Caleb!" my mother yelled again.

Caleb scrutinized Curtis once more for a moment, uncrossed his arms, and marched toward the kitchen.

Curtis turned to me. "Have I been granted permission to enter the Coughlin premises?"

"I hope you don't think he's finished," I told him as we entered the kitchen.

"I'm up for the challenge," he said.

Mom was at the counter, making salad. When I introduced Curtis she was pleasant enough, but I could tell her mind was focused somewhere else. Mom asked Curtis twice within a five-minute interval what year he was in at school and how he liked Ladue. She invited Curtis to take a seat at the table with Caleb, then grabbed my arm and yanked me toward the sink. "Your father promised he'd be home an hour ago. I *know* he's playing golf with his buddies," she hissed. "But don't you worry. He'll be wearing his suit and pretend that he was just working late at the office—some 'unscheduled meeting' or something."

I nodded. "Sorry, Mom. Curtis and I can clear out if you want us to."

"Nonsense. We'll give your dad ten more minutes. If he's not home by then, we'll just sit down and enjoy this meal without him."

Enjoy? I thought. Not likely.

A moment later I heard the unmistakable thump of Dad's silver Chrysler tires rolling over the curb and into the driveway. I wasn't sure whether I should sigh with relief or prepare for the ensuing battle. It wasn't like I was worried about Mom and Dad having some big ol' knockdown, drag-out fight in front of Curtis or something. My parents didn't fight that way. It was going to be something less certain, and that might be way worse. My parents were skillful at getting underneath each other's skin. Mom took advantage of Dad's screwups in a passive-aggressive way. She cataloged his mistakes and exploded on him at the most inopportune moment and in the most unpredictable way.

Mom opened up the oven and pulled the pizza pans out with a thin dish towel, cursing under her breath when the second pan singed her fingers. Dad appeared just as Mom predicted—he was wearing his suit, but the knot of his tie was loose around his collar. He had a sheepish grin on his face like he'd already had a few.

Mom stood rigid at the cutting board with her back to Dad, slashing onions, her knife pecking against the cutting board. Dad placed his briefcase on the counter, then strolled over to Mom and kissed her on the cheek. "Hi, honey."

She turned the other cheek and nodded toward us. "*Your* dinner is ready," she announced.

I decided it was time for me to try and squelch the rising tension in the room. "Dad, this is Curtis," I said a bit too brightly. Curtis stood up from the table and they shook hands.

"Nice to meet you, Curtis," Dad said in a friendly voice. "Glad you can join us for dinner," he said, but Dad was also distracted by Mom's cool reception. He knew she was onto the golf game. "I bet after all that running, you boys are famished."

Dad removed his coat and tie, loosened his collar, and grabbed two glasses from the cabinet. He snatched some ice cubes from the freezer and poured some vodka. When he set a glass next to Mom, the chopping paused as she considered the drink. Then she nudged it away with the tip of her knife.

It's on, I thought with a slight heart skip.

Dad let out a loud sigh and owned up. "So I played a *little golf*, Elise," he confessed. "That's part of doing business. I'll slice the damn pizza."

Curtis raised an eyebrow. I winced.

Dad opened the counter drawer and pulled out a long knife. He chopped the two pizzas into quarters—a deliberate move to irritate Mom—placed the pizza trays before us, and took his seat at the head of the table.

When Mom put the salad on the table, she took one look at the pans and rolled her eyes. She snatched the knife and began sawing the pizzas up. Melted cheese, onions, peppers, and sausage bits clumped to the knife blade as Mom mangled the pizzas.

That set Dad off. He took a long, slow sip of his drink and considered his next move. I sat beside Caleb, and Curtis sat opposite us at the table, alone.

Caleb was the one who finally broke the silence. "CURTIS LIKE HONEY NUT CHEERIOS!" he announced.

Curtis looked up at me. I followed his eyes as they traveled from my father, to my mother cutting the pizzas, to Caleb, then back to me. He smiled. "As a matter of fact, Caleb, I do like a good bowl of Honey Nut Cheerios."

Mom finally finished hacking the pizzas, placed the knife on the counter, and sat down.

Caleb then resumed his interrogation. "CURTIS LIKE KELLOGG'S FROSTED FLAKES!"

Dad stood up and retrieved the knife.

"Okay, Dad," I interjected. "Curtis and I are big boys. We know how to use a knife and fork."

"Oh no, Leo. This is my pleasure. I'm just trying to help out your mother," he said mockingly. He leaned over one of the pizzas and, using the tip of the knife and a firm wrist, chopped at the crust to make the slices into sixteenths.

Beneath the tension, Curtis continued to answer Caleb's questions politely. "To tell you the truth, Caleb, I can't remember the last time I had Frosted Flakes." Curtis glanced at me, his eyebrows slightly raised. I rolled my shoulders slowly upward, shrugging an apology.

Dad placed the knife back on the counter and sat down again.

Now it was Mom's turn. She grabbed the knife and began cutting the pizza again.

How much could one pizza take?

Caleb began to warm to Curtis and his voice calmed. "Curtis like Cocoa Puffs?"

"Come to think of it, Cocoa Puffs are nice every now and then," Curtis answered.

"Raisin Bran?"

"Sorry, Caleb," he said, shaking his head. "Not a big fan of Raisin Bran."

Caleb quizzed Curtis about a few more cereal brands while Mom sliced the pizza. When she finished, there were thirty-two razor-thin slices of pizza before us. Mom put the knife down on the counter, sat in her chair, and glared at Dad.

Caleb was the one who finally stopped the nonsense. He

took the delay in action as a cue that it was finally time to eat. He held both hands up in the air and shouted, "SAY PRAYER!"

"Amen!" I whispered to myself. I glanced at Curtis, who mouthed "Jesus!" to me and hid a smile.

I grabbed Caleb's hand and reached for Mom's.

My father turned to Curtis. "Caleb insists that we pray before dinner," he explained. "It's a routine we've kind of fallen into."

Curtis took my father's hand. "No problem. Let's give thanks." He looked over at my mother and extended his hand to her, too.

Caleb began his unique version of the prayer aloud in a single note. "Blessed our Lord, for these our gifts, about to receive, from my bounty, through Christ our Lord. AMEN!" he shouted. "HOW MANY SLICES PIZZA HAVE?" Caleb asked my father in the same breath.

We dropped hands. "As many as you want." My father sighed. "There's certainly plenty here!"

After his second drink, Dad started to calm down and managed to ask Curtis a few polite questions, mostly the same ones Mom had already asked. Caleb ended the breakfast-cereal survey and then moved on to cataloging the makes, models, and years of cars Curtis's family had owned over the years. Curtis was patient with Caleb; his responses were upbeat and conveyed genuine interest. I even managed to coax a few words from Mom about her day.

As soon as we stepped out of the house, Curtis burst out howling. "So is that a typical dinner?" he asked.

I considered his question a moment. "I wouldn't say it's typical, but it's within the bell curve."

"That was priceless," he said. "Our family dinners are nothing in comparison with that."

"I hope not."

"What do you mean?" he said as he climbed into his car, still laughing. "That was good, wholesome family entertainment!"

"Let's say you experienced a slice of life in the Coughlin household," I said in defense.

"If that was just a slice," he answered with a sly grin, "I'm going to bet it was a very small slice."

7.

AFTER CURTIS LEFT I WATCHED some old *Seinfeld* episodes, then crashed, falling asleep as soon as my head hit the pillow. As luck would have it, that was the first time Caleb came after me during the night. He had trouble pinning me with his knees in the darkness, but he managed to slap my head a couple of times before going for my eyes. I got a knee into his crotch, pulled his hair, slipped from under him, ran across the room, and flipped on the lights. He was sitting on my bed rocking back and forth wildly and biting his fist.

I scrambled into my shorts, grabbed a T-shirt from the floor of the closet, snatched my running shoes, and made a run for it out the basement back door. I laced up my shoes by the side of the house, listening for Caleb's footsteps.

I took off through backyards and down side streets. It must have been the middle of the night. House lights were out and the streets were empty. I ran a few miles, until I relaxed and felt ready to deal. When I finally returned, Caleb was focused on a van Gogh *Starry Night* paint-by-number beside the television set. His painting made the sky look like it was raining fire.

He didn't even look up when I came in through the back door. "Sorry, Leo," he said to me. He had calmed down.

"It's all right, Caleb," I told him. It was no use mixing things up now.

"God not punish you?" he asked me.

I was thinking God should be on my side, but I paused and thought about his question a moment. "No, Caleb. God not punish you."

"Jesus love you?"

Where did he get this?

"Yes, Jesus loves you," I told him, and headed back to bed.

8.

I WAS SAVORING AN ENORMOUS BITE of my salami and cream cheese on an onion bagel when I saw the girl with blond hair standing at the salad bar. Mary.

Not that I have a photographic memory, but there was not a doubt in my mind that she was wearing the same black jeans as the last time I saw her, and I was fine with that. However, the white button-down shirt had been replaced with one of those long, button-down shirts that come down over girls' waists and turn into a skirt. The shirt's swirling pattern of green and black complemented her hair. Normally, I inhaled my sandwich in three or four bites. Today I involuntarily paused and gawked as she picked through a dodgy assortment of raw veggies with metal tongs.

Curtis followed my gaze from our lunch table to my target. "Her name is Mary Seisen. A junior like you," he informed me between bites of sandwich. "She's a little out of the box. I've known her since grade school." He took a sip of his Gatorade and nodded. "Interesting taste, Leo. Personally, I prefer brunettes."

Mary circled the salad bar, examining each item she placed on her plate.

"And if I'm not mistaken, she's single at the moment. I might be able to provide you with some assistance for a nominal charge."

"No, thanks."

"Whatever," he mumbled. He pointed at my face. "By the way," he said, "what's up with the scratch under your eye?"

"It's nothing," I mumbled. I kept my eyes glued on Mary and thought up a lie. "I took a shortcut biking home yesterday and got smacked by a tree branch."

"And who was holding the tree branch?" he joked. He continued looking at me with this expression on his face like something didn't quite add up.

"I was gassed after practice yesterday," I finally told him. "I totally spaced out on the ride home."

"You gotta be more careful, man."

I directed my attention back to Mary. She paid for her salad and took a few steps into the chaos of the school cafeteria, searching for possible refuge. That's when Curtis began frantically waving his arms like a lunatic. Mary acknowledged him with a nod and made her way toward us.

I tried to make a run for it, grabbing what was left of my sandwich and paper bag. "I have to get going," I told him.

"Sit your butt down and relax, Coughlin," he commanded. "Your lunch isn't over."

I did as told. I ran my hand through my hair nervously and wondered what I looked like.

Curtis stood up, wiped down the table surface with his napkin, and pulled out a chair for her as she approached the table. "Greetings, Miss Mary," he addressed her. "How are you on this fine afternoon?"

"Always the gentleman, Curtis," she said drily.

"Indeed," he said as he removed the paper napkin from her tray and placed it on her lap. "Would you like to see a wine list?"

"No, thank you. Instead I would like for you to stop speaking like a pompous, overeducated freak."

"My apologies, Mary. Growing up as the only child of two university professors who've made me attend frequent dinner parties listening to their peers endlessly pontificate has inevitably influenced my elocution. But I digress," he said, nodding toward me.

"It's annoying, Curtis," she said.

"Duly noted," he said insincerely. "Miss Mary Seisen, please allow me to cordially introduce you to my new friend, Leo Coughlin," he said.

She glanced at me and smiled. "We've met," she informed him.

I froze. Again.

"Mary and I have known each other since the fourth grade," he informed me. Curtis sat down with a huge, stupid smile on his face and resumed eating. I was cheap entertainment. He was enjoying that Mary clearly unhinged me. "So how was your summer, Miss Mary?" Curtis asked.

She nibbled on a carrot and pondered. "I was in Chicago for way too long with my father and his new wife. You'd think I'd have something in common with her. She's closer to my age than my dad's."

"Not the case?" Curtis asked.

Mary shook her head. "Let's just say she's something else altogether. But my dad gets this huge, dopey grin on his face whenever she walks in the room, so I suppose I'm happy for him." She looked at me again, giving me a thorough going-over with her eyes.

"Leo is a new arrival here," Curtis explained. "A transfer from Parkway Central, and more important, a new member of Ladue's elite cross-country program. He's quite a runner."

Mary looked directly into my eyes. "Why did your family move here?" Then she nodded at Curtis. "And how did he convince you to go out for that insane sport?"

I thought for a moment, hoping some words would come out that made sense. "The move mostly has to do with my brother, and that's actually a longer story. The cross-country part was my choice."

"What's up with your brother?" she asked, brushing aside a mushy chunk of tomato with her fork.

"Well, for one, he's autistic," I explained.

"Like Bill Gates autistic?" she replied casually. "Or like *Curious Incident of the Dog in the Night-Time* autistic?"

"Bill Gates's autism is pure conjecture," Curtis interrupted.

"Once again you're missing the point," she said, rolling her eyes at him before looking back at me.

"The autism is just one layer," I told her. "He's got a few other disabilities he's dealing with."

Curtis couldn't help himself. "Leo has quite an interesting family," he told Mary. "Maybe we can all go over there some night for pizza."

Thankfully, Mary ignored him as she poked at her salad. "So why did you have to move here on account of your brother?"

"Go on," Curtis said, motioning with his hand for me to continue. "You haven't told me this part yet."

I glared at Curtis. Honestly, I wasn't sure if he was laughing with me or laughing at me. So I just looked down at the table and tried to formulate a concise explanation.

"Let's just say that some of the stuff he pulled didn't always go over too well in the neighborhood where we were living," I told her. "Our house is a lot closer to his school now, and we don't have as many neighbors." I was now squirming in my own skin.

The bell rang and lunch was over. Curtis nodded and shrugged. "Personally, I'm glad you moved here, Leo," he said with an expression that sounded actually genuine. He stood and gave me a little slap on the back before departing. "Besides, your brother isn't the only one who's not exactly normal. I think your parents take the cake on that."

"Thanks," I mumbled, and got up to go to Spanish.

Mary tapped my shoulder as I turned to leave. "Nice to finally meet you, Leo." She smiled. "Again." Her green eyes drilled right through me.

This time I remembered Mom's advice and smiled back. "Nice to meet you, too," I said. I was too rattled at that moment to say much else.

9.

I COULDN'T GET MARY SEISEN out of my head. I was spacing out thinking about her during dinner when I saw Dad's headlights in the driveway. Caleb was too busy drawing train tracks in his mashed potatoes to notice Dad's arrival, and Mom was checked out again, not talking. She was pissed, maybe thinking Dad was coming home late again from work on account of golf or some other distraction at the office.

I figured I'd give her fair warning, since she had her back to the window. "Dad's home."

His voice drifted through the door behind me as he entered the kitchen. "Hi, guys." Dad sounded tired.

Mom looked up to greet him but didn't say a word. Her eyes grew huge, like she'd seen a ghost. She cast a quick glance at me and motioned with her head: *Don't look.*

I kept my shoulders and head square and focused on my salad, wondering what was going on this time. Two clinks signaled ice cubes hitting glass. More noise: the freezer door closing, the cap unscrewing from the bottle, liquid pouring. I cast a sideways glance again at my mother, who was still staring wide-eyed at Dad in disbelief.

I listened to the sounds of Dad's footsteps approaching the table, followed by the kiss on Mom's forehead. I peeked up at my mother once more as Dad sat down and began serving himself. She definitely wasn't checked out anymore.

"So," Dad said as he grabbed salad with the tongs, "who is going to tell us about their day?"

It was a loaded question, but I looked up.

I couldn't believe it. Dad had a toupee.

For my entire life, my father had had a deep receding hairline, one he attempted to mask by parting his long, thin gray hair on the left side. Tonight, his scalp was covered with thick silvery hair. Dad stared into my eyes, daring me to say so.

"Leo, you start. Tell us about your day." Dad served himself some green beans and cut into a baked chicken breast like it was a typical meal.

I looked at him. His face was the same, but the hair unsettled me. Dad sat with his knife and fork, cutting his chicken, a blank expression on his face, like this new hairpiece had been slipped onto his head without his knowledge.

Incredible.

My day? I thought. The day my father came home with a new head of hair? Having lunch with Mary Seisen? All I wanted at this point was to disappear, but instead I focused and tried to make eye contact.

"Well," I began. I looked up at him and felt my eyes darting back and forth between his eyes and his new hairline. "Today we began to learn about the impact of the Treaty of Versailles on Germany after World War I in Mr. Ohlendorf's class, but this kid kept whistling to distract Ohlendorf because the guy lectures and makes eye contact with the ceiling in the corner of the classroom." I looked back at my plate and pretended to cut meat from an already clean bone.

"That wasn't very nice," Dad said. "How about your day, Caleb?"

"DAD GOT HAIRCUT! RIGHT!"

I nearly lost it and spit out my food right when Caleb said it.

"It's not a haircut, Caleb," Dad stated matter-of-factly. "Did you behave in school today?" he asked in an attempt to shift topics.

"YES! LEAVE SCOTT BREWSTER ALONE!"

"I sure hope so," Dad said calmly. "I certainly don't want any more phone calls from Mr. Baims."

"STAY OUT OF TROUBLE!" Caleb assured him.

Mom looked up from her plate, but she wasn't going to say a word tonight. When Caleb burst into laughter, I figured that was a good time to excuse myself and make an exit. I washed my dish quickly and made a beeline to my room.

I fell asleep wondering about Dad. I thought about all those late-night Hair Club for Men infomercials with those guys and their before-and-after photos. There was always some guy doing a cheesy testimonial about his newly restored confidence and feelings about being a new man. One commercial even showed this guy who started bawling about how his hair restoration gave him his life back. I wondered how Dad felt about his new head of hair. I wondered what Mom thought about it too. Then I wondered if my hair was going to fall out. Mostly I wondered how I was part of this family where things just happened and nobody said a word about them.

When I headed up to the breakfast table the next morning, Dad had already left for work.

Mom said good morning, friendly enough.

"So what's up with Dad's hair?" I blurted.

"God knows." She buried her head in the morning paper, but I thought I detected a slight hint of a grin.

Like most things in our house, we'd never talk about it.

10.

IT WAS A LITTLE UNSETTLING not knowing when your older brother was going to try to take you down in the middle of the night. I didn't know what made it scarier: that he had a three-inch height and thirty-pound weight advantage, or that he wasn't working with a full deck.

My solution was to keep my old Little League bat nearby. At night I kept it wedged between the mattress and bed frame. When Caleb came at me in the pitch black, I gripped it high up the barrel like a club. If I smacked him on his back a couple of times, he usually rolled off me, and if that didn't work, I pinched and pulled his ears and hair. Usually that was enough to make him retreat. Sometimes he jumped around the room for a few minutes before settling back into his bed. Other times we were both so wound up that I had to head out for another night run. One way or another we always went through the same remorse ritual.

"Sorry, Leo," he'd say.

It was only at these times that his voice lost its robotic quality. He actually sounded like he was truly sorry, maybe even scared. Though it was dark in the room, I could see him lying on his bed on top of the covers, still heated with rage. When he spoke, he held his hands up toward the ceiling, and his thumbs and fingers clicked like marionettes in unison with his voice.

I was usually too angry to respond the first time he'd apologize.

"Sorry, Leo," he'd repeat.

I always caved eventually. "It's all right, Caleb."

"God not punish you, Leo?" he'd ask.

"You" was him, and for some reason he seemed to have a fear of God—even after we stopped attending church. How did someone like Caleb, who often struggled to understand the world around him, become so concerned about God—some abstract, invisible force that we barely mentioned in this house?

"God not punish you, Caleb," I'd assure him.

"God not punish you," he'd repeat each time, but now as a statement.

"Never hit Leo again. Right?"

"That would be great, Caleb."

"Don't poke Leo in eye," he'd say.

"Let's get some sleep, Caleb," I'd say.

"Good night, Leo."

"Good night, Caleb."

A few nights later, it would happen all over again.

I began to anticipate when Caleb was off-kilter. I would catch him with his back to me, shaking his hand in front of his face, or I'd notice the sudden skip to his step when he was walking across the room—some gesture that showed he was unsettled about something, that the fuse had been lit and time was ticking.

It could take place anytime: daytime, evening, or the middle of the night. So I began to keep my clothes on and my running shoes by the back door when I went to sleep. If I woke to find Caleb shaking both his hands frantically in front of his face, I was ready. If he bit his wrist or began to jump up and down, I knew it was time to slip out and run far.

I ran until the tension seeped out of my chest and shoulders. I ran until I felt my face relax and I no longer clenched my teeth. I ran until my fists unwound and my fingers felt loose. I ran until my anger was gone. I ran until I was alone with just the steady rhythm of my feet tapping the pavement, my breath a soft, steady flow of energy in and out of my lungs, and my sweat releasing the heat from my body.

I was alone, away from him, away from home. It was at times like this I'd feel the runner's high again.

By the time I returned, Caleb would be calm, like nothing had ever happened. I'd wipe down with a wet towel and crawl back into my bed, and I'd forgive him. I knew deep down that he couldn't control himself. It wasn't his fault.

11.

WHENEVER THERE WAS A PROBLEM in the house, Dad looked for a shortcut. One time we had a leaky ceiling pipe in the basement and he patched it up with Scotch tape. It fixed the crisis temporarily, but eventually the problem just got worse. Let's just say Dad's solution to my situation with Caleb wasn't much better than Scotch tape.

When I sat down for breakfast the next morning with a few raw scratches on my neck, Dad didn't ask me what happened. He just threw his fork down on his plate and pushed himself away from the table. "That's it," he muttered as he headed toward the basement door.

Mom slammed her fork down on the table. "Niles!"

"I suppose you're going to suggest I sit down and try to reason with him," he said sarcastically.

Mom got up, threw her plate in the sink, and left the room.

"That's right, Elise," Dad yelled. "Leave me to deal with the problem."

Mom's angry footsteps now pounded the floor in reverse. "Leave you to deal with the problem?" she hissed at Dad. "Which one of us spent the first six years of his life driving him back and forth across town from therapist to therapist? Which one of us stayed at home dealing with his tantrums? Which one of us was always scrubbing off those damn train tracks and buses he drew across the floors and walls?"

They just glared at each other for a long moment. I held my breath.

"What the hell do you suggest I do?" he finally asked.

She turned back toward their bedroom. "I don't know," she said, and sighed.

"I didn't sign up for this, Elise!" Dad yelled.

"I didn't sign up for this, either!" she echoed.

I was thinking I didn't sign up for this, either, but I opened my mouth and said something I probably shouldn't have. "Christ! Maybe we could start by building him his own bedroom," I mumbled.

"What did you say?" Dad was about to snap.

"Nothing."

"Walls aren't going to fix this problem, Leo. I know exactly what we're going to do. Tell your brother to get in the damn car. Now!"

Soon enough, Caleb and I were in the backseat of Dad's car, zipping down the highway toward the city. Caleb was oblivious that Dad was out of his mind. He was relaxing, twirling his stick and reciting the letters and numbers on the license plates of passing cars.

"I don't know where we're going or what we're doing, Dad, but I'm supposed to be in school," I reminded him.

Dad was still trying to calm himself after his spat with Mom. He drew a deep breath and exhaled. "Contrary to public opinion, Leo, life's greatest lessons aren't learned in school."

That favorite line of Dad's meant Caleb and I were in for something twisted.

When Dad took the Kingshighway exit, I saw the ten-story gray stone building and knew exactly where we were headed. St. Louis Children's Hospital sat high above the highway, its towers visible for miles.

Dad circled the hospital slowly along the neighboring streets before pulling into the parking garage. He snatched a ticket from the attendant at the tollbooth, then parked in front of the emergency room entrance.

We'd been here before.

I started feeling the sweat dribbling down my back under my T-shirt.

My father looked at Caleb in the rearview mirror. "You remember that place?" He pointed at the red neon sign above the entrance.

"YES!" Caleb answered.

"Did you like that place?"

"NO!"

Dad leaned over the seat and got face-to-face with Caleb. "You weren't too happy there, as I recall," he hissed. "Do you want to end up back there?"

"No!"

"Then quit hitting your brother," Dad told him.

"QUIT HITTING YOUR BROTHER. RIGHT!" he repeated. Even Caleb seemed anxious.

"I mean it," Dad said.

"MEAN IT!" Caleb repeated.

Dad turned back and stared out through the windshield at the hospital. "Jesus!" he screamed, whacking his hand on the steering wheel.

"MAKE GOD ANGRY!" Caleb yelled.

"You're making God and me freakin' angry," Dad said finally, sighing.

"Sorry, God!"

We sat in silence, and I started wondering who deserved to be committed to the hospital more—Dad or Caleb.

When Caleb started having these nasty outbursts four years ago and was hitting himself and breaking things, Mom and Dad brought him to Children's to get some help. But the psych ward was filled. So Caleb had to spend a couple of nights in the emergency room until a space opened. Sometimes they had to strap him down so he wouldn't hurt himself.

We camped out in the waiting room for three days next to other families with kids like Caleb stuck in emergency rooms. They were all waiting for a bed in the psych ward just like Caleb, except some of those kids were way worse. They saw things like blood on the walls and heard voices telling them to hurt people. Caleb never made it past the emergency room, though. We finally took him home when the insurance company told the hospital they weren't going to pay for another night.

We went back and forth that year a bunch of times, trying to get Caleb help at Children's. He saw different therapists, and he got more encephalograms to analyze the electrical activity in his brain. Caleb would be crying his eyeballs out and scream-ing, "SORRY! GOD NOT PUNISH YOU!" as Mom and

Dad hauled him inside the hospital doors. But it was the same old story: we never got past the emergency room. The psych beds were always full, and with people with bigger problems than Caleb's. He'd spend a night or two strapped to a bed, and once he got his meds recalibrated and he calmed down, the hospital told us it was time to take him home. The bottom line: Caleb's brain was a mystery.

Each time, we drove home and I listened to Dad go on and on telling Mom how "the system is broken" while Caleb sat next to me strung out on meds.

Eventually Caleb's monster tantrums slowed down.

Dad finally turned the key in the ignition, and I was thankful for the sound of the motor running. Before he put the car in drive, he turned around once more in his seat. This time he grabbed Caleb gently by the chin and looked him in the eyes. "Better shape up, Caleb," he said. He pointed Caleb's head toward the hospital. "I don't want to have to bring you back here." Dad's voice came out both gentle and fierce. I felt my stomach burn again as I was thinking I'd sort of caused the whole problem.

"No," Caleb half whispered.

Dad put the car in drive.

When he pulled up to the front of the high school, I unfastened my seat belt and reached for the door handle. "I did that for both of you," Dad told me.

I didn't know what I was supposed to say. Was I supposed to thank him? I shrugged.

"Have nice day, Leo," Caleb said.

"Have nice day, Caleb," I replied, like nothing had happened.

I closed the door to the car, waved to Dad, and headed into school, feeling the heat rising behind my eyes. Why did everything have to be so freakin' complicated?

———

In English, Ms. Liebner gave us a sheet of binder paper for a timed writing assignment. She asked us to write about a time when we were scared. I knew what I wanted to write about, but I wasn't about to put it down on paper. If Caleb came after me again at night, I wasn't going to tell Dad or Mom. Or anyone. It just wasn't worth it.

I didn't want to go back to Children's again either.

12.

CURTIS WAS SPRAWLED OUT on the ground in the midst of some bizarre stretching routine when I headed out to the track that afternoon. I was still processing the visit to Children's that morning, and I needed to run it off.

"How was another day in paradise?" he gasped as he pulled his right foot behind his rear end.

I wasn't about to give him a recap of my day, so I kept the conversation focused on life at school. "I have to admit it's a step up from Central," I told him. "It wasn't the best of times, but it wasn't the worst of times either. If I can figure out how to avoid walking through the student lounge, I'll survive."

"Wise man," he agreed. "I suggest cutting through the library. It runs parallel to the lounge."

Curtis seemed edgy. He stood and began pacing, contorting his body in strange ways, massaging his calves, and breathing deeply.

"What's up?" I asked. "You seem ramped up today."

"I'm always a little nervous before Gorsky's first interval workout," he told me. "It's an indicator," he explained. "Today you'll find out what kind of shape you're in. You're going to be in a world of pain, Leo." He laughed and continued stretching. "Start wrapping your head around that."

The other guys trickled onto the track, looking even more lethargic than usual.

"And what exactly is an interval workout?" I asked.

"Ohh, much to learn you still have, my young padawan. Just long distance a great runner doesn't make. Speed he must also have," Curtis explained in a surprisingly good Yoda voice. "Fully trained distance runner, with interval training as his ally, will conquer his competition."

"Pain, suffering, and near death you shall feel," Burpee said with a sigh as he joined us.

"Could someone please explain in plain English?"

Curtis lay down on the track, put his heels together so his legs stuck out like butterfly wings, and gazed up into the clear blue sky. "If I know Gorsky, we'll run 800-meter repeats. We'll go at a pace he sets, something a little quicker than what you'd run during a race. You'll get a short recovery between each one," he assured me.

"Running 800s sounds a whole lot easier to me than hammering out another seven miles with you."

"It's challenging in a different way," he said as he pulled his right leg behind his ass in another contorted motion.

"Final advice?"

"*Beware of the Dark Side.*" He stood, jumped up and down a few times, shook out his shoulders, and stretched his neck. "Don't try to be a hero and run too fast, especially at the beginning. Follow Gorsky's orders and you'll be fine." He nodded toward the distance as we walked over to join the team. "Overconfidence, overambition, pride—consume you they will," he warned.

Gorsky was marching across the football field, a clipboard in one hand and some large timing contraption in his other. It was the first time I'd seen him without his shots and discs.

"One more thing," Curtis said as he laced up his shoes. "I hope you didn't eat too much lunch."

Gorsky told us to take a seat on the bleachers and announced our agenda for the day, a confusing prescription of numbers, distances, times, and recovery periods that sounded like a foreign language. He then scanned the team, taking attendance. "Where's Stuper?"

"He had to go see a doctor," Rosenthal answered.

"Is he injured?" Gorsky asked, marking his clipboard.

"He's got a bad case of poison ivy," Rosenthal explained. "We were running in Forest Park the other day and he ducked into the woods to go to the bathroom. He wiped himself with it."

"Geezus!" Gorksy winced, sounding actually concerned. "Is he all right?"

"Yeah." Rosenthal went on. "At first he wouldn't tell his parents. He thought it was herpes because he'd just seen pictures of it in health class. But then we helped him connect the dots back to Forest Park."

"And reminded him that the only way you can get herpes is through sexual contact," Burpee continued.

"That's not entirely true," Curtis interrupted.

"It is in Stuper's case," Rasmussen chimed in, making the rest of us break into laughter and additional discussion.

Gorsky finally had to squelch the conversation. "That's enough, gentlemen! Report to the starting line in fifteen minutes ready to begin. And let Stuper's little problem serve as a cautionary reminder to you all: Leaves of three, beware of me! If it's shiny, watch your hiney!"

I joined Curtis as he headed out for a slow jog and asked him for a simpler explanation of the workout and, more important, what was in store for me in terms of pain and agony. "We're going to do a short warm-up, then a few strides, then run eight 800s, two laps," he explained. "Gorsky told you to run at a little over a five-minute-mile pace. I'll be running faster, so don't try hanging with me. At the end of each 800, you'll have a two-minute recovery. Keep moving during that time, a light jog down to the end of the track and back. Just breathe deeply and focus on getting ready for the next one."

"That doesn't sound so bad," I told him. "That's only four miles. What's the big deal?"

"You will soon find out, Leo," he said, laughing. "The workout really doesn't begin until the sixth interval. We'll see how you're feeling then."

I could hang with Curtis on most distance runs, so I figured it would be no problem keeping up with him for these shorter distances. We started the first 800, and those two laps felt like nothing, so despite the times Gorsky had prescribed, I locked in behind Curtis and ran with him. The first lap was a breeze, but on the second I began to labor on the homestretch. The pace was fast, much faster than any previous run we'd done, and by the end of the first interval I was winded. Curtis was breathing hard, but he was composed, his eyes and mind focused.

The two-minute recovery elapsed in a heave of heartbeats,

and by the time Gorsky was counting down the final five seconds of our short rest, I was still out of breath.

After the first lap I was gasping, and even though I hung with Curtis, I was toast by the end of the second 800. I spent the next two minutes bent over, clutching my knees, praying I wouldn't throw up lunch. I started the third interval and stuck with Curtis for half a lap before pulling into the infield and blowing out cafeteria lasagna, much to the amusement of a few football players.

I jogged slowly across the inside of the track, weaving my way through the field, avoiding football players colliding with one another, hoping I could make it to the starting line in time for the fourth interval.

"You're done for today, Coughlin!" Gorsky barked from the bleachers.

I waved Gorsky off and shook my head. I gave him two thumbs up, breathed in deeply, and spat out the sour residue of puke still lingering in my throat. I was determined to recover in what few seconds remained.

"Leo," Gorsky shouted. "I said you're finished. Off the track. Now!"

"Happens to every guy sometimes this does," Burpee gasped in Yoda as he stepped to the starting line beside me for the next interval. "At one point or another we've all tried to slay the dragon. You try to hang with Kaufman during intervals and you're guaranteed to lose your lunch."

Curtis's face was flushed, but he was still standing, tall and strong, awaiting the command from Gorsky to begin the next interval. Still fighting for air, I finally accepted I was done.

"Get over here!" Gorsky yelled.

I stepped off the track and slogged my way toward the bleachers and sat down beside Gorsky. As he waved his arm and gave the command for the next interval to begin, I felt like a failure.

"That's what you get for being a jackass," he muttered. "Had you followed my instructions, you'd still be running, and maybe even running with Kaufman by now."

I felt beat up for the second time in one day.

I watched Curtis glide across the backstretch. "Find your rhythm, Kaufman!" Gorsky screamed. He was midway through the fifth interval, looking stronger than he had on his first.

"How long have you been running?" Gorsky asked me. His eyes were focused on his clipboard, his pencil scribbling numbers.

"Since summer."

Our eyes followed Curtis around the back turn. "That guy you're trying to keep up with has three years' experience on you. He's one of the top runners in the state, Leo. The fact that you can hang with him on a seven-mile run is impressive, but I hope today's workout taught you that you're not quite on the same level as him . . . yet."

Gorsky patted me on the back, then redirected his attention to the guys still running. Compared with Curtis, the rest of the team was tragic. Rosenthal crumbled and flopped to the ground after each interval. Burpee staggered around in circles like guys in the movies who've been shot several times in the gut. Rasmussen was practically walking. The workout was now at a stage where Gorsky had Curtis on a separate program, taking off when Gorsky raised and dropped his arm. I sat and watched. I felt ready to get back out there and join him.

"I'm good to go again," I told Gorsky.

"No. You're done for today, Coughlin. Just keep watching and see if you can learn something," he said. "He's pushing himself, but he's able to sustain it for the entire workout. That's because he's got strength, and he knows his body. You'll get there, Leo. But not if you run like you did today. You need to respect the process."

Gorsky glanced back and forth between his stopwatch and Curtis. "Now get out of here. Go do a cooldown and get yourself ready for tomorrow."

After Curtis finished his last 800, I joined him to jog the trail on the periphery of campus.

"What did you learn today, Leo?" Curtis asked.

"I learned that you can kick my ass."

"What you lacked today was a little humility and respect. Give Gorsky his due. Listen and do what the old man tells you to do. Even better, listen to what I tell you to do," he said with a smirk. "Patience you must have, my young padawan."

"Enough with the Yoda," I told him. "Seriously, Gorksy just happened to mention that you're one of the best runners in the state."

"That is a fact, Leo. But I'm not interested in being one of the best," he told me as we began a slow jog around the campus. "I want to be the best. And to do that, I could use a little help."

"I'm not following."

"You've certainly got talent, Coughlin, and if you're patient, this could be an amazing year. For both of us."

I had no idea what Curtis meant, but I nodded. The thought that Curtis was depending on me felt good, but it also made me a little nervous.

13.

I MOVED UPSTAIRS for a few weeks and slept in the spare bedroom, but that had its own drawbacks. While I appreciated having my own space and a door I could lock during the night, it also meant sharing a thin wall and narrow hallway with my parents.

Dad woke at the crack of dawn, blasted NPR, and did a twenty-minute calisthenics routine that included grunts, groans, and other bodily sounds. Mom's prep for her early shift at the hospital somehow involved opening and slamming every closet, cabinet, and dresser drawer in the room multiple times. At night I listened to them bicker while their television blasted the local news, followed by Letterman's opening monologue.

And since the spare bedroom was directly above the room I shared with Caleb, he discovered a way to keep me awake, too. He began tapping the ceiling below me with a broom handle to resume our bedtime conversations.

"Leo." I could hear him through the floor. "Leo," he repeated. "Leo, who put butter on Monica's nose?"

While it was creepy hearing his voice coming out of the woodwork beneath me, and I knew I shouldn't be encouraging him, I'd still answer his questions.

"Leo, what car God drive?"

I suppose I could have tried earplugs, but his voice sounded sad and sorry, like he missed me. But I was still wary of sleeping next to him in a dark room.

Then Caleb had his first seizure.

Epilepsy added a whole new dimension to Caleb's problems. His seizures were like crazy lightning storms in his head that made his neurons zip and zap dangerously and caused his body to convulse like a flopping fish.

I'd just walked into the house after a brutal workout, a nine-miler followed by strides and abdominal work. The bike ride home nearly did me in. I made a quick cheese sandwich to hold me off until dinner and had just collapsed on the couch to watch some *Jeopardy!* when I heard thumps and clatter coming from the bathroom. I figured Caleb was probably going ballistic about something, like maybe we had run out of Comet cleanser, but then the sound softened and began to follow a rhythm and tempo unlike his usual tantrums.

I got up off the couch and treaded the hallway carefully to the bathroom. Caleb was lying on the floor thrashing and writhing. His eyes were rolled back in the sockets, eyelids fluttering, and he was making this terrible wheezing sound like he couldn't breathe. Both arms were stiff and extended, and his head lifted and thudded against the tile floor.

"Caleb!" I yelled, but even as the words came out I realized he clearly wasn't conscious. I knelt beside him, held his head, and continued calling his name. I didn't have a clue what was going on, or what I was supposed to do. His lips and face began to turn a strange bluish gray and I started shaking, thinking he might die any second. Just as I was about to bolt for the phone, the thrashing and wheezing began to subside. Finally, he let out this strange moan, and his breathing relaxed and softened.

Caleb lay still on his back for a moment, looked at me, and blinked in confusion. Then he just closed his eyes and drifted into a deep sleep. I bent closer to him and pressed my ear to his face and listened. A warm wind brushed against my cheek, and I knew he was breathing.

I sat beside him for a few minutes, then gently roused him. He opened his eyes again, reached for my hand, and squeezed it. He gazed for a long moment with this expression on his face like he wanted to tell me something, but then he slipped back into deep sleep.

I grabbed a towel from the rack, folded it, and placed it under his head, then ran to the phone. Mom was virtually impossible to contact when she was on shift at the hospital, so I called Dad.

When Dad arrived twenty minutes later, Caleb was still asleep on the bathroom floor. "What exactly happened?" my father asked, holding Caleb's head in his lap. Caleb stirred lightly but didn't wake.

I told Dad about the thrashing, the wheezing, his face turning blue. Caleb tried to get up but then struggled and lay back down. In all my life, I'd never seen my brother so frail and weak.

Dad bent down and gently shook him. "Are you all right, Caleb?"

He was groggy. "All right," he repeated. "What happen?" His

glazed eyes looked around in confusion at the bathroom, at my father, and then at me.

Dad looked pretty shaken. "I'm going to call your mother," he told me. "Don't let him try to stand up."

When Dad left the bathroom, Caleb closed his eyes and began thrashing and wheezing again. I shouted for Dad, and he cradled Caleb's head in his lap again until the episode ended. He then placed my hands under Caleb's head in the same way. "I'm calling an ambulance," he told me, and dashed down the hall.

I kept my eyes fixed on the ambulance's red flashing lights in front of us and wondered whether my brother was still alive inside. "What happened to him?" I asked.

My father was quiet. "I have no idea, Leo," he finally said. "My best guess is that your brother just had a few seizures."

Mom met us in the emergency room. She made me recount the entire story a couple of times, then the three of us just sat in the waiting room in silence, except for the drone of the evening news playing on a television set suspended from the ceiling.

Mom perched her purse on her lap and wrung her hands gently. I couldn't tell if her lips were trembling or if she was mumbling prayers. Dad paced and pretended to study some old black-and-white photographs on the wall of the hospital during its construction. His eyes were glazed, his mouth slightly open, and he rubbed his chin.

I picked up a few magazines and flipped through the pages and tried to read, but I couldn't concentrate. So I got up and wandered over to the reception desk, where there was a large aquarium. I don't know why, but watching fish just swim around in a tank and listening to the bubbles always calmed me. I studied the movements and patterns of the mollies and tetras as they slipped and darted past one another, and wondered why fish never collide with one another. At the bottom there was a little catfish perched on a white stone.

It made me think about the time a few summers ago when Caleb and I went fishing at my grandparents' farm. It was early evening, and we were drifting on the still pond water in silence. I remember wondering what it would be like to talk to Caleb if our situation were different. I wanted him to be like an ordinary older brother who would tell me stupid jokes and give me advice about stuff. Instead I was baiting his hook with a grasshopper, teaching him how to handle a fishing pole, and listening to him talk about fans on Greyhound buses.

"Keep an eye on that bobber," I told him. "If it moves, yank your line," I said, mimicking the motion with my hands.

"Keep eye on bobber," he repeated. "Right!"

I baited another grasshopper on my hook and tossed my line into the water. We waited and waited, and just when I was getting ready to quit, my red-and-white bobber began to wiggle and dance. It disappeared below the surface and my pole curled and I thought it was going to snap. The line pulled tight in one direction and I yanked hard in the opposite. It took forever to reel the fish in, but eventually I got it out of the water and hauled it over the side of the boat.

It was a catfish, the biggest fish I'd ever caught. Together

Caleb and I watched that fish flip and fight on the boat's metal floor, neither of us saying a word. When the fish finally stopped moving, I slowly moved my hand toward it, but I knew full well I wasn't going to touch it. Then it started flipping and tossing itself again, and I panicked. It lay there between Caleb and me, its gills slowly flapping, exposing flaming-red tissue.

All of a sudden Caleb bent toward it and pinned it with his right hand to the floor of the boat. Then, for the first time I could ever remember, he looked at me with this expression in his eyes that told me I shouldn't be afraid. With his hand holding that fish down, I pulled the hook from that catfish's mouth, then reached for the bucket and scooped a little water from the pond. Caleb lifted the fish and gently slipped it into the pail. The catfish thrashed for several more seconds, thumping its tail fin against the metal, and then surrendered.

Caleb and I eventually paddled to shore, removed our fishing gear from the boat, and headed back to the house. I carried the poles and Caleb carried the bucket, and he laughed out loud the whole way home.

"Leo, who put butter on Monica's nose?" he asked me.

"Caleb did."

"Who put cat in mailbox?"

"You did."

"Who drew train tracks on dining room floor?"

"You did."

"Caleb get in big trouble! Right!"

We were side by side but in two different worlds.

The one thing Caleb had known for sure was that I was

too scared to put my hand on that fish. He might not understand a lot, but he'd understood that.

By the time I wandered back to Mom and Dad's corner of the waiting room, I could tell by her crossed arms and his clasped hands that they were in the middle of a spat.

"I can't believe we're even discussing this, Elise," Dad whispered. "We don't know the facts yet. Let's just wait and hear what the doctors have to say."

"I'm a nurse, Niles! I think I have a pretty good idea of what's going on."

Dad finally acknowledged my presence with a nod before turning to Mom. "I never said you didn't know what's going on, Elise. I'm just asking you to keep an open mind."

Mom bit her lip.

I took advantage of the break in the action. "What are we talking about here?"

Dad glanced at Mom and raised his eyebrows, his offer for her to initiate the discussion, but she shrugged and shook her head. "Nothing really, Leo," Dad finally said. "Your mother is just worried about what this might mean for your brother."

"Like what?" I asked.

"We're trying not to get too far ahead of ourselves at the moment," Dad said as he reached for Mom's hand. "Maybe we should save this conversation for later."

Mom snatched her hand back and pulled away. She wasn't going to let this go. She took a moment to compose herself, looked me in the eye, and spoke slowly. "All I was trying to explain to your father is that it's very possible it might not be safe for Caleb to do some of the things he's done in the past."

"For example?"

"Well, swimming, for one."

"Yeah, right," I said, with a nervous laugh. "Have you thought about how you're going to explain that to the human fish?"

Dad scoffed as well. "Yeah, good luck on that. Do I need to refresh your memory, Elise, about what happened the last time the pool closed?"

Mom raised her arms in exasperation. "So now it's two against one!"

"Elise," Dad pleaded, "let's wait for the facts and let's try to stay positive."

Mom closed her eyes and nodded.

The doctor finally appeared and told us Caleb was stable at the moment. The episodes probably had been seizures, and they were going to keep him at the hospital to run some tests.

Mom drove me home while Dad stayed with Caleb at the hospital. "I thought he was going to die," I half whispered to Mom in the car.

"Your brother is going to be all right, Leo," she told me. I really wanted to believe her, but when I glanced up at her she was staring through the windshield shaking her head slowly, her eyes wet and glazed.

"Leo, I used to fight with Caleb, too," she said, suddenly shifting the topic.

"What are you talking about, Mom?" I had a pretty strong

hunch what she meant, but this didn't seem like the right time or place.

"I'm worried about you, too."

"You don't have to worry about me," I assured her, thinking about Caleb back in the hospital.

"I'd fight with him when he was a little boy when he didn't want to put on his clothes," she continued. "I'd fight him when he'd have a temper tantrum if a thunderstorm closed the pool. I'd fight him in the grocery store when he was hell-bent on opening every box of breakfast cereal to get the prizes inside."

"Oh, I remember, Mom," I answered, wondering where this conversation was heading. "I remember the time you ran into a neighbor at the grocery store and started talking. Caleb slipped away from us and emptied ten boxes of Lucky Charms to get the Matchbox cars inside."

"It was twelve boxes, Leo." She laughed softly. "The manager of that store was a saint for not making us pay."

"And for letting him keep the prizes," I reminded her.

"Leo, for all your brother's successes, most of the time I feel like an absolute failure. People hear the word *autism* and they think of these amazing children who sometimes go off to Ivy League colleges. He's got a lot more issues he's contending with besides autism."

I felt guilty for taking advantage of her guilt, but I allowed myself to vent. "Mom, just when I thought things were getting easier with him, it's getting harder. Way harder."

Then Mom just started crying. "All I want to say to you, Leo, is that I wish I were still the one he was fighting with—me rather than you."

She needed a hug, but we were strapped into our seat belts, so I simply reached over and put my hand on her shoulder. "Mom, if it has to be one of us, I'd rather it be me. I think I'm stronger than you, and I'm faster, too."

Her sobs turned into those awful sniffle-snort sounds that waver between crying and laughter.

"I know he can't help it, Mom, and I know that you and Dad don't know what to do," I told her. "But it does suck."

"I just don't know why he does it." She sighed. "I used to think it was to get a reaction, or because he wanted something."

"All I know is that he's angry, Mom."

"At what?" she yelled. "Caleb has come so far. He has accomplished so much. He has so much. What's he so angry at?"

"Christ, Mom!" I looked at her and offered a smile. "I don't know. I'd give anything to know what trips his wires."

"He's going to be okay," she assured me.

———

They ran tests on Caleb the next day. He stayed in the hospital again the next night, and finally he came home the following day.

I didn't sleep too well those two nights Caleb was in the hospital, because I kept wondering if he'd had any more of those seizures. Seeing his body thrash and his face turn that strange shade of blue was the scariest thing I'd seen in my life.

So I moved back downstairs with him.

"Medicine make me sleepy," he told me when he finally came home.

Caleb was strong as an ox, though, and he rebounded quickly. In a few days he was the same old Caleb. Caleb's seizures had freaked me out, but he didn't seem to have a clue that he'd come within a breath of dying.

14.

GORSKY GAVE US STRICT INSTRUCTIONS to take it easy, because our first race of the season was the next day. So we took a break from the superblock and headed out the back exit of school for an easy five-miler. Passing the swimming pool, Curtis spotted five nylon flags hanging from the latches of the open windows, flapping lazily in the warm breeze.

"What are those things?" I asked.

Curtis snatched one from the window, unfurled it, and examined it more closely. He buried his nose in it and inhaled deeply. "This, my friend, is a female swimsuit." He held it up against his body. "Practical," he whispered, and winked, "yet alluring."

Rosenthal took a moment to consider his assessment. "I have to agree," he finally decided.

Curtis removed his T-shirt and struggled to step into the swimsuit. "How the hell do girls get these things on?"

We watched him wiggle himself into the bottom portion of the suit and then manage to pull a strap over each shoulder. Satisfied, he tucked what was still visible of his running shorts beneath the swimsuit's lining. "How do I look?" he asked. He was dead serious.

I took my pointer finger and swirled it in a circle. He didn't understand. "Turn around," I said.

He twirled his body, an exaggerated spin, and we pretended to evaluate his modeling potential. That's when a custodian burst through the back door of the building, lugging two large garbage cans toward the dumpsters. He furrowed his brow but pretty much just kept walking and shaking his head. I rewarded Curtis with polite applause.

Curtis plucked another swimsuit from the window and tossed it at Stuper. "Put it on," he ordered. "We're running in these today."

"Are you kidding me?" Stuper asked.

"They're formfitting, and I think you'll find them quite comfortable," he informed him matter-of-factly. "In your case, Stuper, I think you'll appreciate that they provide virtually no chafing."

Stuper examined his legs, which were still a little pink and rashy from the poison ivy, then nodded and stepped into the bathing suit.

"Rosey, I think you'll fill this one out nicely," he said, tossing him a red suit with green and black swirls. Unlike Stuper, Rosenthal slipped into the swimsuit willingly.

"That leaves you, Coughlin, with this one," he said, holding up a simple black tank suit. "It's a timeless classic, and the high-cut sides will elongate your legs," he joked.

"You seem to know a lot about women's swimwear," Burpee commented, clearly unsettled but putting on a suit.

"I study my mother's catalogues," Curtis explained. "They make excellent bathroom reading."

"I'm really not sure about this, Curtis," I said, looking to the others for some support.

"Consider it a character-building exercise, Coughlin," he said with conviction.

"Yeah," Stuper agreed. "Now quit wasting our time and put the suit on."

I took off my shirt and squeezed into the swimsuit. Lately I'd fallen into this pattern of following Curtis's orders. Most of the time his advice was keeping me on track and helping me adjust, but I didn't know where this was going. We jogged to the other end of the parking lot, tossed our shirts into the bushes, and began our afternoon run.

The first few cars that passed us slowed a bit as they went by, but the drivers didn't offer much of a reaction—just mild curiosity.

"See? If you act natural, it's not such a big deal," Curtis assured me. "Gentlemen, we might very well be setting the next fashion trend in men's running."

"I doubt it," I said. "This is ridiculous, not to mention humiliating."

"Nonsense, Coughlin," he said, laughing. "Chest out, men! Run with confidence!"

That was when we heard several long honks from behind us. I looked over my shoulder and spotted a white pickup hauling landscaping equipment. It pulled up beside us, the guys inside whistling and yelling crap about our "fine asses" until they realized we were guys too. "What the hell?" one yelled before the truck sped away.

Stuper waved and blew a kiss. Apparently that was going a little too far. The truck pulled over onto the shoulder, and the two burly dudes climbed out of the cab and started charging toward us.

"Split!" Curtis yelled. "Stuper, Burpee, and Rosey, go right! Coughlin and I go left!"

Curtis and I made a quick detour through a few backyards before popping out on a side street where the coast was clear. I was tempted to pull off the swimsuit and just run shirtless, but Curtis would have none of it. Every time a car honked from behind, he provided a little wiggle of his hips and flashed a thumbs-up to the driver. The reactions varied from amusement to confusion, embarrassment, anger, and outright harassment. When we headed down another road and hit less traffic, the swimsuits hardly seemed worth the trouble and discomfort. We were just a mile and a half from school, our mission thankfully almost over, when Curtis decided to change the route.

"Follow me," he ordered.

"Where are we going?"

"It's a shortcut," he assured me.

We ran another quarter mile down the road to a traffic light, where Curtis veered right onto the entry ramp of Highway 40. We merged onto the shoulder of the interstate just in time for early-rush-hour traffic. I hesitated, but when I contemplated running back to school alone—forgetting that all I needed to do was remove the swimsuit—I panicked. I followed Curtis, and soon enough I was running on the shoulder of the highway in a girl's Speedo.

Even worse, he'd lied. The highway sign said our exit was a

little over a mile away. Fortunately, cars were still moving at a pretty good clip.

"Isn't this illegal?" I yelled anxiously as I caught up to him.

"Only if we get caught," he said, laughing. "We'll be back at school in ten minutes, tops. What are the chances of running into a cop?"

Cars buzzed by at sixty miles an hour, and all I could hear was the drone of their engines. There was an occasional loud horn blast from an eighteen-wheeler, its driver probably confusing two young male runners with slight figures for the opposite gender, but mostly we attracted little attention.

Then a couple of hundred yards up ahead I spotted a silver car pulling onto the shoulder. A man opened the door, stepped out the driver's side into oncoming traffic, and quickly ran over to the passenger side. While the car looked familiar, it took me a moment to recognize the head of hair on the man standing beside the freeway.

I stopped dead in my tracks. "Oh, crap."

"What?" Curtis finally realized I'd halted, and turned toward me. "What's the problem? We're almost there, Coughlin. I promise."

"That's my father," I said, nodding up the highway.

Curtis turned toward my father just as Dad pointed his finger directly at me, signaling me to come and face the consequences. Curtis stood studying my father from the distance. "Did your father do something with his hair?"

I jogged slowly toward Dad while Curtis ran beside me, proudly snapping the shoulder straps of his swimsuit against his bare chest. "These are the great father-son moments, Leo, that you and your father will talk about years later. You'll be able to tell your children all about it," he assured me. "And it's all thanks to me."

"I'll be forever grateful," I muttered, already feeling a flush of shame rolling beet red across my face.

My father just stared at us when we finally reached him. Thankfully, the passenger side of his car blocked us from the view of oncoming traffic.

Dad looked us over. "Well," he finally said, "what do we have here?"

We didn't answer.

"Well, young man," he said to Curtis, "you certainly look different from the last time we met."

I looked at Curtis and prayed he could read the situation, but to no avail. "You certainly look different as well, Mr. Coughlin."

I buried my head in my hands.

"What are you doing here?" I asked. It was all I could muster.

Dad shook his head in disbelief, and I noticed his new hair didn't move at the powerful blast of wind from a passing truck. "What the hell, 'What am I doing here?' The question, young man," he yelled angrily, "*is what in the hell are you doing here?*"

"I'm running," I offered sheepishly, looking at the gravel beneath my feet.

He lifted his arms in disbelief. "Christ! I can see you're running," he continued yelling. "What's with the swimsuits?"

"Those were my idea, sir," Curtis interrupted. "I take complete and total responsibility for our attire."

"I'm not talking to you," Dad snapped. "*You!*" He pointed at me. "Get in the car!"

I opened the passenger door, climbed in, and put on my seat belt. Curtis reached for the back door.

"Not so fast, pal," Dad said. "I think you can find your own way back to school in that little number you're wearing."

Dad walked around the front of the car, and when there was a quick break in the traffic he dashed to his door. As he accelerated down the shoulder, I saw in my side-view mirror Curtis standing alone in his swimsuit on the side of the highway. When we merged into the driving lane, his image disappeared.

"You mind telling me what's going on?" Dad asked.

By the time I gave him the whole story, we were sitting at the stoplight a block from school. I thought the story was pretty funny, but Dad was pissed.

"Let me ask you something. If this guy Curtis told you to take a flying leap off the Eads Bridge, would you do it?"

"That's stupid, Dad. Curtis is a good friend."

"Some friend," he muttered.

It had to be the longest stoplight in the world.

Dad drove to the far side of the high school parking lot, the farthest point from the main building and, more important, from the locker rooms. He looked over at me once more and scowled. "Now, get out of the car. I'll see you at home for dinner in a little while."

The girls' field hockey team was breaking from practice, and football players were passing by the car as they headed toward the locker rooms.

"Really? You've got to be kidding. You're going to drop me off right here?"

"That's correct, my boy," he affirmed. With a dismissive flick of his wrist, he ordered me out of the car. "I figure a little humiliation might help you think twice before you pull a stunt like this again."

"C'mon," I begged.

"Out."

I made my best attempt to slip out of the car without being seen. Just when I thought the situation couldn't get any worse, I spotted Mary sitting on a bench outside the gym, waiting for a late bus. She gave me a strange look, but she also waved.

A police car then rolled into the lot and drove directly toward me. Curtis was in the backseat. The officer rolled down his window and winked. "I think I found your friend," he said.

The cop and Curtis exchanged a few words, then Curtis climbed out of the back, still in his swimsuit. The officer tipped his hat at us as he drove away.

"Relax, Leo," Curtis told me. "I told the cop the whole story. He actually thought it was pretty funny but strongly discouraged us from doing it again."

We removed the swimsuits in the parking lot and gathered our shirts from the bushes. On the way to the locker room we made a detour to the swimming pool and put the swimsuits back on the window latches exactly as we'd found them.

After we changed I walked alone to my bike and saw a small plastic bag attached to my handlebar, fluttering in the breeze. There was a little yellow flower poking from the opening. Inside was a folded piece of paper. It was an ink sketch of two runners in bathing suits—a simple silhouette, a few swashes of water-color painted for depth. The paper was still damp.

Beneath the drawing:

You look cute in your swimsuit. 314-901-1512.
Mary

I liked her handwriting. It wasn't that wide loopy writing like a lot of girls', but small and pointy, the kind that's hard to read.

15.

THE FIRST RACE OF THE SEASON was the University City Invitational. Curtis and I nabbed the back seats of the bus and he gave me a rundown of what to expect in the race.

"This is a tricky course," he emphasized. "If you don't get out quick, you're going to find yourself up shit's creek without a paddle."

"Suddenly I feel nervous," I mumbled to Curtis.

"You're also going to want to piss ten times between now and when that gun goes off," Rosenthal said, looking over his shoulder. He and Stuper were in the seat in front of us and eavesdropping on our conversation.

"Rasmussen sometimes pisses thirty times before a race," Stuper announced loudly. "And Burpee can verify."

"He once pissed forty-seven times," Burpee confirmed.

"I'm writing a paper on it for biology," Rasmussen announced.

"And what have you discovered thus far in your research?" Curtis asked.

"I've only come up with my title so far," Rasmussen admitted. "I'm calling my work 'The Rasmussen Phenomenon: The Trickle-Down Effect.'"

I turned to Burpee. "Speaking of urine, what kind of name is Burpee, anyway?"

"It's Welsh," he informed me. "I have not one but two bodily functions in one last name," he said proudly. "What more could a guy want in life?"

"That his future life partner feels the same way," Stuper said, laughing.

When we pulled into the parking lot, Curtis refocused the conversation. "We'll have plenty of time to jog the course and squelch the butterflies," Curtis assured me. "You've got to have a plan for this race, or you'll get killed."

"I feel like I'm going to puke. I'm serious."

He laughed. "Just do me a favor and make sure and direct it toward Stuper if you're going to hurl."

The parking lot was full of school buses unloading runners in sweats who were lugging gym bags toward an open field bordered by forest and a golf course. Our team set up camp beneath a tall, shady oak tree between the Clayton and De Smet teams. After we dropped our stuff, Curtis and I met up with Stuper and Burpee to preview the course. "We'll start on the opposite side of this field," Curtis explained as we headed off in a slow jog. "It's wide open, so runners get a brief chance to sort and position themselves, and then the course angles toward that tree line we're running toward now. We'll follow it over a series of hills for about a mile before we head into the forest down a very narrow trail. That's where things get interesting," he told me. "Just jog slowly, shake off the bus ride, and try to settle your nerves."

Inside the forest, the path was no wider than two feet across in most sections, and bordered by trees that forced us to run single file. "Once you get in here, it's going to be virtually impossible to pass anyone. It's about eight hundred meters of single-track running before it opens up again, so if you get out slow, you're pretty much screwed."

"And after this?" I asked.

"You'll find out." We jogged in silence down the narrow forest trail. There were a few places where the trail was maybe wide enough for two abreast, but Curtis was right—it would be difficult to slip past anyone. The trail eventually opened into the large field where the start and finish were located.

"That's it?"

Curtis laughed. "Not a chance. You run past the starting line and circle the edge of that field." He pointed to an expanse of baseball diamonds opposite where we started. "Then we repeat the loop. When you come out of the trail the second time, you make a beeline for the finish straight ahead. It's over before you know it."

We jogged the rest of the course in silence, did some light stretching with the rest of the team, and, with ten minutes before the gun went off, put on our spikes and did a few long strides across the field near the start. There were at least a hundred runners competing from schools all across the city.

Gorsky met us as we made our way to the starting alleys. "How are you doing, Leo?" he asked.

"I feel sick to my stomach."

He laughed. "Nervous is good, son. You should be nervous. If you weren't, I'd worry about you."

My body felt tight. I grabbed my foot, pulled my knee back toward my butt, and tried to stretch my quads.

"Today you're just learning what a race is all about, son. What you do today will help you understand what you need to do next time." Gorsky patted me on the shoulder. "Once that gun goes off, Leo, all those butterflies will go away. Try to relax and have some fun."

Curtis was already on the starting line. He waved me over. "Stay with me," he said, swatting me lightly on the back. "I know you can do this," he encouraged me. "Just stay right behind me, and you'll be fine."

The race official lined us up in alleys by school, a hundred runners tightly packed behind a white chalk line. At the pistol blast, the pack exploded off the line. We were a mass of elbows and knees churning at high speed. Runners held their line for the first hundred meters before the mass began to untangle.

I spotted Curtis ten meters beyond me. He had made an aggressive move toward the front of the pack as he promised, so I threaded my way through a mob of red and white singlets to pull beside him. His face was relaxed, his eyes focused toward a distant target. Sensing my presence, he paused his arm midswing and signaled a thumbs-up.

The pack now began to funnel into a line like a swarm of bees, in clusters of threes and fours. When we hit the dirt path skirting the forest, I saw about twenty-five runners ahead of us, a medley of yellows, greens, maroons, whites, and golds. My eyes stayed fixed on Curtis. He extended his right hand slightly and motioned me to move up as he accelerated. We passed fifteen runners in the next three hundred meters as we headed toward the narrow trailhead.

Curtis entered first, and I let a gap of a few meters open up between us so I could see my footing. There were five guys ahead of Curtis tunneling single file through the trail. The pace slowed, the tempo steadied, and I began to settle into myself and find a rhythm to my stride and breathing. The warm, dry September air was still, and it packed my lungs. It was quiet now: only breathing, the snap of twigs, and the crunch of leaves and stone beneath our spikes. I focused on the path and Curtis's shoulders in front of me and reminded myself to relax and drop mine.

We exited the trail, circled the open meadow, and began the second loop. There were about ten guys ahead of us now, including three way up front. In the open I pulled beside Curtis, and he motioned me to follow him as he accelerated. The first runner we passed was struggling, gasping for air, and made no effort to respond. We passed three more as we made our way toward the tree line and twelve hundred meters of rolling fairway. Cresting the first hill, we snagged three more who had begun to fade. I glimpsed the three leaders beginning their descent down the final hill. I was running stride for stride with Curtis, our breathing strong and steady. Then he suddenly yelled, "Go!"

I looked at him.

"Go!" he yelled again. "Go now or you're screwed." He swatted my back and I took off.

I passed a lone runner on the uphill and spotted the three

leaders funneling into the trailhead, the final segment of the race. Inside the forest, the bright afternoon light disappeared again, the trail narrowed, and it was quiet. My breathing amplified. The pounding of my heart felt steady and strong, and I leaned forward to glide over the trail, remembering to touch thumbs to index fingers and pump my arms. I spotted two runners just forty meters ahead. I'd made up a lot of ground, so I willed myself to run faster, to catch them before the trail ended.

A bright light appeared, the end of the forest path, and the runners disappeared from view. Seconds later I was out of the forest, with just three hundred meters of open field to the finish. The guy in first had distanced himself, but I had a shot at taking the other two. My chest felt like it was going to blast open, but I could see the finish. I passed one, but the other guy had another gear left in him and I wasn't able to close the gap. I crossed the line in third place.

I stumbled through the chute and turned back toward the finish line. I saw Curtis come out of the forest in pursuit of two guys twenty meters in front of him. His form was steady, composed. He caught them easily and crossed the finish line in fifth. I met him as he walked out of the finishing chute. He pointed to me and raised his hands in question, and I held up three fingers.

"I think I could have actually won the damn race if I'd taken off a little earlier," I told him.

"No doubt," he agreed. "But not a bad first race, Leo. Not bad at all." The guy was barely out of breath, and I suddenly realized he gave me that race. No one had ever done something like that for me before in my life, and I wondered what his ulterior motive was. I wasn't quite sure if, or how, I was supposed to thank him.

We put on our sweats and jogged the course once more to cool down, running the first few minutes in silence. Curtis finally spoke. "Didn't I tell you it would be over before you know it?"

"You did," I said.

We jogged a few more minutes. "It hurts like hell when you're doing it," Curtis said. "But when it's over there's no greater feeling than right now."

I thought about it for a moment. "Yeah, I think you're right."

We repeated the forest trail one more time, a perfect loop to the day. "You held back today," I said to him.

Curtis laughed. "A keen observation, young padawan. It's my senior year, Leo. I'm treating this season like a chess match."

"What do you mean?"

"You'll see, my friend."

Our feet tapped the packed soil, and the fall leaves crunched beneath our steps. "You're a runner, Leo," he told me. Then he accelerated up the trail and flashed me a thumbs-up, just like he had in the race. It was the best I'd felt in a long time.

16.

THE PHONE RANG at seven on the dot.

I was sitting at the kitchen table trying to grind out a history essay for Mr. Ohlendorf while Caleb busied himself with sweeping the kitchen floor for the third time. I handed Caleb the phone and listened as he skipped the customary greeting. "WHO IS IT?"

Besides sharing a bedroom with my brother, I also shared a cell phone. It was part of the deal when my parents finally caved and got one for me, and it wasn't a problem because Caleb only had one friend who called him. And he called each night at the same time.

James and Caleb had gone to school together since age ten, and James was more socially adept. He bagged groceries at the Shnucks store a couple of afternoons a week, and from what I could gather, James was one of the few kids in the class who Caleb seemed to get along with.

The two of them basically had the same phone conversation each night. It was the opposite of a typical phone call, the kind where one person calls the other in order to tell them something or ask for something. When James phoned Caleb, my brother answered the phone and immediately directed their conversation with a series of questions, typically the same ones every time.

Their conversations were brief, lasting three to five minutes tops, and then Caleb just hung up the phone abruptly without a good-bye.

"What favorite breakfast cereal?"

A momentary pause followed.

"What car father drive?"

"What car mother drive?"

"What have dinner tonight?"

"Who make Mr. Baims the principal very angry today?"

That question was typically followed by a slightly longer pause.

"Do you like Cap'n Crunch cereal?"

"What year born?"

"Do you have kitty-cat?

"Have bunny rabbit?"

"Who put butter on Monica's nose in the girls' bathroom?"

"Where buy groceries?"

Caleb's phone conversation was going on longer than usual. The questions he asked were all familiar to me, ones I'd heard him ask James countless times, not necessarily to fact-check but to maintain his compulsive habit and ritual.

But there were more questions going on during this phone call, and longer pauses after each question.

"Like Dr Pepper?"

"Ride Greyhound bus?"

"What hospital born at?"

Caleb suddenly put the phone receiver in my hand, grabbed his broom, and began sweeping the floor again. I held the phone a moment, then heard a girl's voice.

"Hello? Hello?"

I recognized her voice. "Mary?"

"Leo, is that you?" she asked.

"Yeah, it's me." It took me a moment to figure she'd gotten my number from Curtis.

"Who was I just speaking to?" she asked. "Was that your brother?"

"Yes. That was Caleb. Didn't I mention he was a little . . . on the spectrum?"

She laughed. "He might be, but weren't you the one wearing a girl's swimsuit the last time I saw you?"

"Maybe we can change the topic? Uh, maybe talk about breakfast cereals?"

"Well, that was one of the more interesting conversations I've had on the phone, or anywhere, for that matter." She laughed again. "Why does he ask all those questions?"

"God knows." I sighed. "He'll ask a person all these questions about themself, then he catalogs it, and he never forgets it. And then when he talks to them again, he repeats it all back to them, or repeats the questions. It's kind of like a detective doing fact-checking. Then he'll ask some more arbitrary questions, and that info goes into the memory bank too. He never forgets anything. Trust me."

"That's fascinating," she said.

"It's a challenge at times," I told her.

"Why?"

"Um . . ." I had to think a moment because I'd never really had to put it in words. "Maybe because he always asks the same questions. Maybe because his questions are bizarre and unpredictable. Maybe because he asks random strangers inappropriate questions, and I'm the one who has to deal with the situation. Does that make sense?"

"Yeah, I guess that makes sense." She laughed softly, then was silent for a moment. "So that's why your family moved here?" she finally asked.

"Partly, I guess," I told her. "He put up with a lot of crap from the kids in the neighborhood."

"What did they do to him?"

"Made fun of him. Sometimes made him do stupid stuff for laughs. There were some real dipshits in that neighborhood," I told her. "We don't have to talk about this anymore."

"Okay," she said, and it was silent again. "Leo, did you get my note that I put on your bike?"

"I . . . I kind of thought it was a joke."

"A joke?"

"Well, it wasn't exactly one of my finer moments. In fact, I kind of wish I could wipe it from my memory bank," I said. "And, if I could, I'd wipe it from yours as well."

"So why, exactly, were you wearing a girl's swimsuit?" she asked.

I was grateful at that moment that she was on the other end of the phone line and couldn't see that my face was flushed red, but I told her the whole story, every detail, including running into my father. It wasn't a proud moment, and I was actually kind of ashamed, but she laughed the entire time. By the end I was laughing, too. Then we hit the dreaded silence again. It wasn't like I'd run out of things to say. It was more like I just didn't know what I was supposed to say. This was new territory for me. Thank God she was the one who finally spoke.

"You're funny, Leo," she said.

"I guess it's funny now, but it wasn't funny then. Trust me."

"I'd like to meet your brother sometime," she told me.

Suddenly I no longer wanted to talk. "Now is not the greatest time," I finally told her. "He's been a little off lately."

"How?"

"I'd rather not get into it," I said.

"Okay," she said. "But can I ask you a question?"

"Sure."

"How will I know if your brother really memorized all that information about me if I never get a chance to meet him?"

The girl was certainly making it easy for me. All I had to do was pull the trigger and ask her out, but that involved letting her into my world. I didn't like my world.

Keeping Curtis out of my world was simple. All we did was focus on running. Mary was curious and asking me lots of questions. She wanted to know me.

"Sorry, Mary, but I've got to get going. My mom needs help with something," I finally lied. "I'll see you tomorrow," I said, and the line got quiet.

"All right," she said. "I guess I'll see you tomorrow," she said, and hung up.

"Damn it," I mumbled to myself.

Caleb stopped sweeping for a moment, leaned the broom against the counter, and crossed his arms. "WHO MARY!"

"Mary is my friend," I told him. "I met her at school."

"Mary like granola," he told me. "Right!"

"I wasn't aware of that, Caleb."

"Mary like Dr Pepper!" he yelled.

"Mary like Dr Pepper," I repeated. "I think Mary also might like me, but I was too chickenshit to ask her out."

Caleb laughed. "CHICKENSHIT! RIGHT!"

I trudged down the steps to our bedroom and felt like thwacking myself in the head a couple of times, just like Caleb did when he was pissed. Mary had clearly put the ball right over the plate, but I hadn't had the nerve to swing.

17.

I RAN INTO MARY A FEW TIMES at school the next week. Our class schedules, coupled with the school hallways' crazy traffic patterns, provided few opportunities for our paths to cross. And even when chance did provide that rare moment to flirt, I basically came across like a bumbling fool. The truth was I basically froze up whenever I saw her. I got this woozy feeling and my cheeks started sweating.

On Wednesday afternoon I checked out of Ohlendorf's class in the middle of a lecture to use the bathroom. I spotted Mary at the end of the hallway chatting with a few friends. When I gave her a wave, she seized the opportunity and pretty much cornered me.

"What's going on?" she asked.

"I'm just taking a little break from a deep lecture on the ideological and military differences between the States and the Soviet Union during the Cold War."

"Ohlendorf?"

I nodded.

She smiled and sighed. "I suffered through him freshman year," she recalled. "Does he still only make eye contact with the far right corner of the ceiling?"

"Yeah. I'm starting to wonder if the guy has two lazy eyes."

"Whatever it is, it's unsettling," she said. She then tapped the top of my shoe with hers. "Curtis mentioned that you guys have some big race here on Friday. My friends and I are going to come watch it."

"Cool," I said. With those words a sudden tidal wave of nausea washed through me and lasted all the way until the gun blasted to start Friday's race.

Ladue was hosting its thirtieth annual invitational, with twenty-three schools from around the area competing. After the University City Invitational I'd gotten two more races under my belt—small meets with only a few schools. I'd won one and placed third in the other. Curtis continued to restrain himself and seemed content to push me to my maximum and boost my confidence. I didn't understand his motives, but it was working for me.

As Curtis and I began our warm-up, he gave me a quick summary of the competition. "You will have the privilege of competing against Mr. Nathan Fromm today, as well as the legendary Amos Newcombe."

"Why should I feel privileged?" I asked.

"They're two of the finest runners in the state," he told me. "By far, they're the favorites today. You'll see."

I was a little more confident since my last few races. "What's going to happen if I try to go with them?"

"Don't even try, Leo. Not yet." He pointed them out to me as we jogged the first loop of the course. Fromm looked relaxed and confident. He was laughing with a couple of his teammates as they surveyed the course. Newcombe was a little more serious. He was alone behind the bleachers, in full sweats and doing a series of strange leg-lifting drills that looked like a cheerleading routine.

I pressed Curtis. "When are you finally planning to show up and actually race, Curtis?"

He laughed. "I'll continue to keep my cards close, Leo. My goal is to stay under the radar as long as I can."

Our home course was basically a one-mile loop around the boundary of the campus, repeated three times with a few subtle variations. The course included a downhill on each loop and long stretches of tree line along the farthermost part of the campus. It wasn't the most exciting course, because with the exception of the single hill it was basically flat as a pancake. But it was fast.

As Curtis and I passed the tennis courts and school parking lot, I saw Dad getting out of his car.

"Oh, crap," I muttered. "My father is here." Dad spotted us and waved, and we trotted over to greet him. I was nervous enough. The last thing I needed was to screw up in front of him.

Dad was in good spirits. "How are you boys doing?"

"Hey, Dad. What are you doing here?"

My dad watched packs of runners jog by us, finishing their warm-up. "What the hell do you think I'm doing here?" he said, laughing. "I came to see what this running business is all about." He turned and looked at Curtis. "Hello, Curtis. I almost didn't recognize you without your bathing suit."

"Why hello, Mr. Coughlin." Curtis's eyes darted back and forth across Dad's new hairline a few seconds, but he managed to exercise self-control and not engage. "Thanks for coming to the race."

"Wouldn't miss it for the world. Where do I get a seat for this event?" Dad asked.

"Most people don't sit, Dad," I explained. I pointed to the top of the course's only hill. "If you go up there, you should be able to see us about six times during the race."

He checked his watch. "When does this thing get going?"

"We'll start in about twenty minutes," I told him. "I've got to go warm up, Dad."

"All right, then," he said, walking toward the hill. "I'm looking forward to this, Leo." As I was jogging away, he called out, "Mom was supposed to be here, but she had to make a trip down to her parents' to help your grandmother with something. She told me to wish you luck!"

When Curtis and I began jogging again, I spotted Mary sitting on the hill with a few of her friends. She waved to us. Curtis acknowledged her, but I just buried my head. "What's that all about?" he asked me.

"I don't understand why all these people are here."

"Christ, Leo, we should feel honored that these people are here. Cross-country isn't exactly a spectator sport. Lighten up," he told me. He pointed back at Mary and smiled. "Put on a show for the girl."

As we headed to the line for the start, I was shaking. My stomach felt empty and my legs light and weak. When the gun fired, I blasted off the line toward the opening in the tree line where we'd make our first turn. By the time we reached the hill, I was ten meters in front of the pack. It wasn't exactly my plan, but it was now the situation.

I could hear my father screaming above the cheers, "That's my Leo!" I'd never heard him so animated. His scream gave me another jolt of adrenaline. By the time I reached the downhill, Fromm and Newcombe had pulled beside me. They were barely breathing.

Fromm looked over at me with a shit-eating grin. "Do you know what you're doing, kid?"

We were flying, and I felt great. We rounded the front of the school, followed the tree line toward the tennis courts, and threaded our way through the narrow dirt trail inside a small wood separating the baseball and soccer fields. As we exited the trail and headed up the only hill, I saw Mary and heard my father screaming again. I extended my lead by five meters as we made our way toward the tree line bordering the soccer fields and the end of the first loop.

Heading into the second loop, Fromm made a move and began pressing the pace. Newcombe went with him, and I tucked behind. I decided I'd try and hang with them until the final loop, then see if I could just barely hold on.

We passed the crowd again and I heard Dad hollering at the top of his lungs as we attacked the downhill. My legs and arms were turning like flywheels just trying to maintain my balance. I had no problem hanging with Fromm and Newcombe on the hill, but when we hit the flat, I felt like they'd turned up the momentum another notch. By the time we hit that dirt trail again, my breathing was labored, my shoulders felt tight, and my legs were heavy. I felt like I was dying.

I ran beside Fromm and Newcombe as we hit the tree line once more, in full view of the spectators, but as we began the third and final loop, I started to fade, and they opened up a thirty-meter gap on me in what felt like a flash. I managed to pull myself together as I passed the crowd, and my father's voice once more gave me a brief boost. I was hoping that the long downhill might provide an opportunity for me to recover, but by the time I'd made my descent I was done. My legs refused to lift and I was gasping for air. One runner passed by me, then another, and then Curtis, who gave me a tap on my shoulder. "Hang in there, buddy," he encouraged me. "Just focus on finishing."

I wanted to quit right then and there.

A steady stream of runners soon flew by me, including a few guys from the team.

"Something is definitely wrong if I'm passing you," Rosenthal said, patting me lightly on my shoulder as he charged by me.

At least forty more runners overtook me, including Stuper and Burpee, who offered similar words of encouragement. The final loop was an eternity of pain and suffering, and I eventually stumbled through the finish chute in fifty-sixth place. I staggered away from the crowd bent over, hands on knees, before collapsing beneath a tree.

Curtis urged me to sit up and get some air into my lungs. "I can't breathe," I gasped.

"You're going to be fine," he assured me.

Just when I thought it couldn't get any worse, I saw Mary rushing toward us, carrying a bottle of water. Thankfully, Curtis held up his hand and gently brought her to a halt. I closed my eyes and wished the earth would open up and swallow me. I looked pitiful.

"Is he all right?" she asked.

"I think he's just experiencing a little oxygen debt," he told her. "He's going to feel like crap for a few minutes, but it will go away."

"Is there anything I can do to help?"

"Just give him a little space, Mary," he urged her. "He's going to be fine."

I opened my eyes partly and gave her a pathetic thumbs-up. She understood and backed away.

Dad found me a few minutes later. "How are you doing, Leo?" He looked concerned.

I was still having a hard time breathing, and struggled with my words. He jogged over to the scoring table and returned with a white paper bag. "Breathe into this," he encouraged me. "I think you're hyperventilating."

I crumpled the bag and tossed it. "I'm fine, Dad," I told him. My breathing steadied, and I began to relax. "I just had a really crappy race, that's all."

"I'll drive you home," he offered.

"I've got to cool down and stick around for the awards ceremony," I told him. "I thought you had to get back to work."

"That's okay," he said. "I'll hang out. Just let me know when you're ready to go."

I eventually got up and had just plodded a few steps into my cooldown when I heard Gorsky's gruff voice. "Leo! Come over here."

I jogged over to him. "You don't have to say it," I told him. "I know I blew it."

"Leo, how many races have you run in your life?"

"If you want to include today's catastrophe, the grand total is four."

Gorsky laughed, gripped me by the shoulders, lifted my chin, and made me look him in the eyes. "You gained some very valuable race experience today, son," he said to me. "You learn something new with each race. You learn what you need to do next in your training, and you learn what you need to do in your next race." Gorsky was quiet for a moment, giving me the opportunity to think about his words. "So what did you learn today?"

"I learned that I need to get a hell of a lot stronger," I told him. "And I learned I shouldn't be a jackass and take off like a bat out of hell when the gun goes off."

He laughed. "Your words, not mine," he said. "It will come, Leo, I promise you, but it's going to take a little time. As much as you want to forget about this race, think about what you can learn from it to make yourself a better runner."

I nodded.

"I like what you did today, Leo. You showed some guts," he continued. "You just need to learn how to harness that energy."

He gave me a little shove. "Remember, son, our training was not intended to prepare us for today. We are preparing for the more important meets at the end of the season. Now get a good cooldown with Curtis. And ask that clown when he plans on finally showing up to race."

The drive home with Dad was mostly silent, but as we turned into the driveway he spoke. "How are you doing?"

"What do you mean, how am I doing? That was perhaps the most humiliating experience of my entire life," I told him.

Dad pulled into the garage and turned off the ignition, and we sat in silence for a long moment, just the ticks of the engine cooling down. Then Dad finally spoke. "You went for it, Leo," he said to me. "I know it didn't work out the way you wanted it to, but you went for it." He opened his door and looked over at me. "And when you were out there in the lead, I thought it was one of the most amazing things I've ever seen in my life, son. I was very proud of you." He closed the door and left me alone inside the car with his words.

———

I opened my gym bag, pulled out my sweaty singlet, and tossed it into the laundry basket. Inside, on top of my spikes, I saw the note, an ink-and-watercolor drawing of a lone runner against a bright-orange setting sun.

It's your turn.
- M

Outside the kitchen window I saw Caleb in the front yard making grass piles. He was bouncing around on his toes. He was in a good mood at the moment, but I wasn't sure which direction he was heading.

Counting the day's race, I'd embarrassed myself twice in front of this girl. I looked at her note once more, and I figured it was time to try and get over myself. So I picked up the phone and called her.

18.

I PLOPPED DOWN ON THE SOFA and watched *House* with Dad until Mary arrived.

"So is this a date?" he asked.

"Not sure," I mumbled.

"Is she the blonde who was hovering around you guys after the race?"

"Yeah," I answered, keeping my eyes glued to the tube and trying to avoid the awkward topic with my father. "How did you know?"

He took a sip from his glass of wine and raised a toast to me. "Not bad, Leo."

"Kind of creepy, Dad."

Mom drove down to the country earlier in the day to my grandparents' farm. According to Dad, Grandma was having some odd side effects from her high-blood-pressure medications. Dad was taking full advantage of Mom's absence by parking himself in front of the television for the night and knocking down a bottle of red wine.

The doorbell rang just as I was beginning to question whether I should have followed through with calling her. Suddenly I got that woozy feeling, kind of like I felt before a race.

Caleb was certainly going to be unavoidable, so I threw

caution to the wind. I stayed put on the couch and let Caleb answer the door. It would need to happen sooner or later. I prayed that the situation would play itself out harmlessly, and Mary and I would soon be on our way.

Our den was close to the front hallway, so when Caleb opened the door to greet her, I could hear his interrogation crystal clear. I imagined him blocking the entry with arms crossed like a prison guard.

"WHAT NAME!" he barked.

I knew Caleb's routine, but it still made me cringe. I didn't hear her response, but there was a brief pause before Caleb spoke again. "Mary like granola," he stated. The inquisition was now under way, but he had already calmed.

"Mary drive blue Volkswagen Golf," he said.

"Yes, I—" Mary answered.

"Mary mother drive black Honda Accord," he interrupted.

"That's true. She also—" she began.

"Mary born August 14."

"Mary like Dr Pepper."

Eventually I heard her footsteps. Caleb had decided to let her in the house, but not before providing her with one additional piece of juicy information.

"Mary," he suddenly said in a raised whisper, "last night, who poke Leo's eyes out in the middle of night?"

"I'm here!" I announced loudly, hoping to squelch Caleb's confessions. Caleb had a habit of divulging his deepest, darkest sins to acquaintances and strangers. The woman who cut his hair at Supercuts, the cashier at the supermarket, the pharmacist at Walgreens, the people he might see and chat with for a few minutes once a week. Caleb would say hello, ask them how they were doing, then lean in close and whisper his guilt. When they'd recoil, that's when I would have to step in and do damage control.

Mary was wearing jeans and a Shins T-shirt with a red-and-black checkerboard flannel shirt layered on top. Our eyes met, and she killed me once more with her smile.

Caleb abandoned us in the hallway and returned to the kitchen sink to wash dishes.

"I assume that's Caleb."

I turned to Caleb. "Caleb, why don't you introduce yourself to Mary?"

He slammed a few plates into the dishwasher and yelled, "CALEB! CALEB COUGHLIN! RIGHT! NICE TO MEET YOU! RIGHT!"

I turned to Mary and nodded. "So now you've met my brother."

"His memory is impressive," she said, smiling some more.

"You faced the inquisition and you survived," I said. "That's a pretty impressive debut, I might add."

"And have I earned the privilege of meeting your parents as well?" she whispered.

Dad shouted from the den over the television set. "Caleb! Could you bring me the bottle of wine?"

I grabbed my coat from my chair and made a move to the front door. "Let's save that for another time," I said to her, and I guided her out the door and toward her car. I glanced over my shoulder at the kitchen window and saw Caleb jumping up and down in front of the sink, a fist pushed into his mouth. Something obviously had set him off and I was going to be in for it tonight if I wasn't on my toes.

Mary flipped on the stereo as we pulled out of the driveway and Pink Floyd's *Dark Side of the Moon* filled the space. I started to relax. I had asked her if she wanted to see a movie when we'd talked on the phone, but only under the condition that she decide what we'd see, and that we didn't talk about my epic failure that afternoon.

"So where to?"

"Have you seen *Corpse Bride?*" she asked.

"Nope." I'd seen the sneak preview, and a brief glimpse of the bug-eyed characters was enough for me. I was more in the mood to watch something with gunfire, explosions, and high-speed chases, but I kept my preferences to myself.

"You haven't?" she asked incredulously. "It's amazing! 'A tale of wit, charm, and strife,'" she recited from the trailer. "I'm taking you."

"Really? But you've already seen it," I reminded her, hoping she might consider an alternative.

"Three times," she said enthusiastically. "Tim Burton is brilliant, and I want to talk to you about it. Besides, I'll have no problem watching Johnny Depp again."

"I thought it was a cartoon."

"For your information, it's an *animated film*," she said, laughing. "Not a cartoon."

I was tempted to suggest *Jarhead* or *Flight Plan*, but I figured

I'd better keep my mouth shut. It occurred to me that the movie was just an excuse to sit next to her. "*Corpse Bride* sounds awesome," I lied. "As long as you're not one of those people who talk through movies and tell everything that's going to happen before it really does. My mom's all over that."

"No worries. If you open your mouth during the movie, I'll probably smack you."

"Thanks for the warning."

We headed across town to the Esquire, this cineplex that plays artsy retro stuff. October's new moon and the early-evening darkness cast a thick blanket over the day. Through the thin cracks of the car's open windows, the cool night air amplified the music. As we sat at the stoplight at Hanley and Clayton, the streetlights illuminated our faces and she shifted the conversation. "He doesn't look like I thought he would."

"Who?"

"Caleb," she answered, her eyes focused on the taillights of the SUV in front of us.

"I'm not sure I know what you mean," I told her. "What were you expecting?"

"I didn't mean anything by it," she said defensively. "You and your brother have the same eyes."

"Really?"

"Yeah," she said. "But your brother's eyes are even bluer. He's a really good-looking guy, Leo. If you were just looking at him, you'd think he was normal."

"Wait a minute," I began to question her. "Who's to say what's normal?"

"I didn't mean it that way, Leo. Seriously, he looks like he could be the quarterback of our football team."

I thought about Caleb calling and running plays from scrimmage. "I would pay anything to see that," I said, and laughed.

"By the way, what was up with that question about poking your eyes out?"

"God knows," I lied. "Sometimes he says things that make absolutely no sense," I explained, and quickly shifted the topic. "What about you? Any brothers or sisters?"

"I have an older brother at Northwestern," she told me. "He's the star child. I'm the average one."

"You're not average, Mary. I may not know much, but I know that." That made her smile.

"I want to go to Riz-Dee," she told me. She glanced over at me and clearly recognized that I had no idea what she was talking about. "The Rhode Island School of Design," she explained. "I want to be an artist, maybe work on costumes and sets for movies someday."

I nodded. "That sounds cool."

"My parents don't seem to think so. They'd prefer I do something more conventional."

That Friday night the Esquire was packed. We circled the lot several times and were about to bail when the parking gods made a spot miraculously appear right in front of the theater. The ticket line stretched from the lobby, out the door, and partly around the building.

"We might miss the previews," Mary warned me as we awkwardly power walked beside each other, "but we're still good."

"I'm all right with that," I told her, still hoping *Corpse Bride* might sell out. "But I do find it helpful to know how a story begins."

"No worries," she assured me. "I'll get you up to speed if we miss anything."

While the ticket line inched along, I watched Mary study the movie posters displayed behind the framed glass, analyzing each one with a careful eye. Her hair lay easy on her shoulders, a little messed and out of place. I wondered how in God's name I'd scored a date with this girl. When she turned her eyes toward me, I didn't want her to catch me ogling, so I looked away. That was when I spotted Mom standing inside the theater lobby with some dark-haired guy about Dad's age in a black leather coat. They were in the same line as us, laughing and holding hands. I stared for a moment. Mom had this huge smile on her face and was giggling. I couldn't remember the last time I'd seen her so happy.

This sick, queasy feeling suddenly washed over me and I began to panic. "What do you say we get out of here? There's no way we're going to make it in time," I said, trying my best to sound both calm and convincing.

Mary looked at me with this confused expression. "Really? It's only going to be a few more minutes. I'm sure the previews haven't even started yet."

When Mom leaned in closer to the guy and whispered something into his ear, my stomach felt like it was about to heave. "I have to get out of here right now," I said abruptly.

Mary looked at me in an unsure way as I shifted back and

forth, ducking and lowering my head behind her like I was suffering from paranoia. Realizing I was clearly rattled about something, she gave in. "All right," she said, turning toward the parking lot, "I guess we can see it some other time."

We sat for a few minutes inside her car in awkward silence. She studied me a moment while I tried desperately to pull myself together. "Are you feeling all right?" she finally asked. "Do you want me to take you home?"

I thought of Caleb biting his fist, and Dad in front of the tube with his bottle of red wine.

"No," I mumbled. "I don't want to go home just yet."

I looked back over my shoulder, into the lobby again. My mother and the man had disappeared, and I wondered for a moment if I really had seen her. Then I wondered how long Mom had been sneaking around like this. "I'm sorry, Mary. I just needed to get out of there," I told her, hoping she'd let it go.

She looked over her shoulder in the same direction, seeking an explanation. "Where do you want to go?"

"Anywhere you want."

She started the car and drove a couple of miles down Clayton, then took a right onto a road that disappeared into forest, her headlights capturing only the short span of pavement in front of us. I was usually ready to hurl on roads like this, but Mary was driving slowly, and I could focus on tracing the yellow lines in front of us that divided the road, just like Mom taught me when I was little so I wouldn't get sick.

"Where are we going?"

"You said you didn't want to go home." She turned left off

the road down an even narrower one that eventually dead-ended at the entrance to a park. A tired-looking chain hung across the entrance with a sign clearly stating CLOSED AT SUNSET.

"Ever been here?" she asked as she parked on the shoulder.

"I have no idea where we are."

"My father used to bring me here all the time when I was a little kid," she told me. "It's been a long time."

"When did your parents split?"

"Eleven years ago this December, the day after Christmas. My brother and I got an amazing haul of presents. Best day ever. Then Mom and Dad started yelling after Christmas dinner, and"—she snapped her fingers—"Dad moved out the next day."

"A merry Christmas," I said, "but not a very happy New Year?"

"That's one way to put it."

We stepped over the chain, cut across a small path, and walked into a large, grassy field turned deep purple by the moonlight. "There's a playground just over there," she said, pointing. We walked a few more strides, and there it was, a maze of dark metal emerging from a bed of sand. There was a swing set, a single seesaw, and a sad set of monkey bars that looked like it belonged in a prison yard. In terms of playgrounds, it was pretty lame.

Mary sat on a swing. I took the one beside her. We pushed off together and swung gently in synch.

"I guess I owe you an explanation," I offered.

"Maybe," she said.

We swung for a moment. "When we were standing in line, I'm pretty sure I saw my mother with another man."

"Really?" She started giggling. "That's awesome."

"I don't know if I'd use the word 'awesome' to describe it."

"I'm sorry. I shouldn't be laughing."

"I just know it's going to be hard to look her in the eye next time I see her."

"So your father has no idea?" she asked.

"She told him she was heading down to the country to help my grandmother with some health issues."

We swung together for a few more minutes in silence.

"My father had an affair with his secretary," Mary finally said. "How original is that?"

"And he told your mom on Christmas day? That blows."

"Not exactly. Dad gave Mom this necklace with a little card and note. Mom loved the necklace, but she didn't care for the note that came with it."

"Because?"

"The note was addressed to the other woman."

"Awkward."

"Turns out Dad bought gifts in pairs, but this time he got a little sloppy. My mother told me she figured it had been going on for a long time. It's probably the best thing that ever happened to me."

"Why is that?"

"Well, let me ask you a question, Leo," she said. "Is your home a happy place?"

I didn't answer, just continued swinging in silence. I started to think about a conversation I'd had with Mom as we headed home from my grandparents' two summers ago. She and Dad weren't getting along at the time, so Mom had driven us down to her parents' for a few weeks so they could take a break from each other. When I asked Mom if she and Dad were going to get a divorce, she told me not to worry about a thing, that as long as she and my father had Caleb and me, they would stay together. I thought about Caleb, and I thought about Mom and Dad, and I wondered if only one of them could take care of him.

"Let's change the subject," I suggested.

Mary hopped off the swing. "No problem," she said, facing me. "Let me show you the best part of this place."

She took me to a steep concrete slide built into a hill that bordered the playground. We grabbed a couple of pieces of old cardboard we found on the ground, dashed up the steps, sat down, and pushed off. We flew.

When we walked back to Mary's car, our shoulders touched and she reached for my hand. It got a little awkward when we reached the car. Neither one of us wanted to separate toward opposite doors. So I made the first move, which was actually not moving. She turned to me and we looked at each other for a moment, and when she tilted her chin up at me I knew what I needed to do. I slowly leaned toward her and closed my eyes, then felt our lips touch. I felt her hands gently moving up to my biceps. In terms of a first kiss, I didn't see fireworks or feel my skin tingle or anything. I just couldn't believe how sweet her skin smelled and how soft her lips felt. I'd take it any day over watching *Corpse Bride*.

We drove home, listening to some more Pink Floyd, my new favorite band, holding hands and not saying a word. I figured she'd want to have a conversation, but Mary was silent. My mind was racing with all kinds of images and memories, some good, some bad. Maybe her mind was racing as well. I always thought the expression "Silence is golden" meant keeping your mouth shut when you didn't have anything good to say. Now I wasn't so sure. Maybe I had finally stumbled upon somebody who was on my wavelength.

When Mary pulled up in front of my house, I could see Caleb in the kitchen window, sweeping the floor for probably the tenth time that night. He then started shaking the broom with one hand and biting his other. I knew it was going to be a rough night, and I made a mental note to put my running shoes by the back door.

"Maybe next time we can actually go to a movie?" she asked.

"Yeah, that would be nice." I laughed, but then the image of my mother with that guy popped back in my head and triggered another wave of nausea. We kissed once more. I knew I probably should have kissed her longer, but family problems kind of wrecked the mood.

19.

MOM WAS MAKING PANCAKES for Caleb and my father when I wandered into the kitchen late the next morning.

"So how's your mother?" Dad asked her, his nose buried in the paper.

Mom busied herself at the stove. "About as well as you'd expect for a woman her age," she mumbled. "I think we got her med situation sorted." She turned from the stove and greeted me. "Congratulations, honey. Your father was just telling me all about your race."

"If he was telling you about the race, I'm not sure why you're congratulating me," I said.

Mom looked over at Dad. "My mother said to give you all her best."

Dad didn't look up from his paper. "Somehow I find that hard to believe," he mumbled.

"On more than one level," I added.

"Pardon?" Mom asked, glancing at me with an unsure expression.

Thankfully, Curtis came to the rescue. He'd texted me the night before and told me we were going running. His car pulled into the driveway promptly at ten thirty. I grabbed my stuff and was in his car within a minute.

"Where are we going?" I asked.

Curtis turned right onto the highway entrance ramp, heading south toward the Mississippi River. "You will soon see, my friend."

As we cruised down the highway toward the mystery location, he ordered me to put some decent music in the CD player, then drilled me about my whereabouts the previous night.

"So, what's up with you and Mary?" he asked after I told him I went out with her.

"Nothing," I told him.

"She's obviously into you." Curtis turned to me and raised an eyebrow. "Seriously, what girl shows up at a cross-country race? Our sport only attracts the most devoted fans, except for guilt-ridden parents."

"That's just it. What in the hell does a girl like her see in me?"

He nodded. "I've been wondering the same thing myself."

"Seriously?"

"Christ, lighten up, Coughlin. You're not perfect, but you do have a few redeeming qualities."

"Like what?" I asked.

He thought for a moment. "Well, for one thing, you're. . ." He pounded the steering wheel and burst out laughing. "I can't believe I'm having this conversation!" He looked wistfully out the window. "I wish some girl would show up sometime and watch me run."

"Yeah, look how much it helped me."

"Leo, my friend, the female species has no interest in our talents as runners. Trust me," he said definitively. "Shall we end this conversation?"

"Please," I begged. Still, it left me wondering what Mary saw in me.

Curtis took the last exit before the river and followed the signs for Macklin Park. "Why Macklin Park?"

Curtis parked the car, turned off the ignition, and opened his door. "Because Macklin Park is the location of our district meet in four weeks. And this is where both of us are going to qualify for the state championship," he suddenly informed me.

"We?" I asked. "Curtis, our team doesn't stand a chance in hell of qualifying for the state meet. We'll be lucky if we don't come in last at conference."

"Point taken," he said, "regarding the team. But allow me to educate you on one of the more beautiful aspects of this fine sport. Even if you run on a team as pathetic as ours," he explained, "you can still qualify for the state meet as an individual."

"How?"

"Let's begin our merry jaunt and I'll enlighten you."

Curtis took me to the starting line of the course and we began to jog. "At the district meet, as long as you place in the top ten, you automatically qualify for the state meet no matter how crappy your team performs."

"Top ten? Do I need to remind you where I placed yesterday?"

He responded instantly. "You've already proved you have the talent, Leo. Your last race was a minor blowup. We've got four weeks and five races to prepare," he explained. "I've got it all figured out. We'll both place in the top ten," he told me. "And you know what?"

"Do tell."

"This course is designed for you. You're going to win the district meet. If the two of us can execute the race plan I've masterfully crafted based upon our collective talents and my shrewd tactics, we'll both advance to state."

We jogged the course, and Curtis explained his strategy. The way Curtis figured it, if we went out hard enough, and he could lure the competition to go with him, he'd eventually wear them down. He had enough confidence in his own strength that he'd be able to hang on to easily place in the top ten.

"How does that help me?"

"Well, if you don't pull a bonehead move like you did yesterday," he said, "and you're patient, you should be able to pick off, one by one, the guys I've wasted," he told me. "This is a flat course, Leo. And you have speed."

"I don't know," I said.

"Believe me," he said casually, "I know every guy who will be in this race, and if you let me take it out hard and let me beat the crap out of their legs over the first two-and-a-half miles, you can take them down. And I'll easily have enough in the tank to finish in the top ten."

"I don't get it. What's in it for you?" I asked.

"I'm going to need you to return the favor," he said mysteriously.

As we continued running I processed his plan. "So how much of this hinges on me winning the race?" I asked.

He was quiet for a moment. "I guess it really doesn't," he finally admitted. "But it would be cool if you did."

Curtis pointed out the significant landmarks and subtleties of the Macklin Park course while we ran. I let his idea sink in. When we completed the loop, he asked me, "Are you in?"

I nodded. "We came all this way down here, Curtis. We might as well run the loop again."

"All right," he said. "This is my last chance at state, Leo. I've thought this all out. I need you there at state to help me."

"So we get to state," I said. "Then what?"

"It's a beast of a course. Monster hills," he said, smiling. "If we get there, I'll kick your ass. Yours and everyone else's."

We ran the loop again, mostly in silence, a mock rehearsal of the challenge ahead. I wasn't exactly sure why Curtis was investing his energy in me, or why he believed I could pull this race off. But I liked the idea of winning a race, and I liked the idea of returning a favor.

We stopped at Imo's on the way back and devoured a couple of sausage-and-onion pizzas and watched a few innings of baseball. The Cardinals tapped the Reds for three runs in the first inning. It was the second-to-last game of the regular season, but the Cards had already clinched a playoff spot, so we lost interest after a few innings.

I smelled pretty ripe by the time Curtis dropped me off, and I was going to make a beeline from the car to the shower, but Mom was standing in the doorway, creating a roadblock.

"Can we talk?" she asked in her tone that meant it wasn't so much a question as it was a command. She stepped outside on the porch and sat down.

"I'm kind of tired from my run, Mom," I answered, trying

to avoid the confrontation. "And if you haven't noticed, I need a shower. I stink."

"Sit down," she said, patting the space beside her.

I obeyed. The sun was just above the trees, and a slight wind rattled the leaves and chilled me.

"Where are Dad and Caleb?" I asked.

"Your father took him to the pool."

I sat down beside her and stared at the porch floor in silence for a moment before being startled by the loud sounds of shaking branches. We spotted two gray squirrels chasing Al, the white squirrel, up the large oak tree at the edge of our yard. Al leaped from branch to branch creating commotion and chaos before finally eluding the gray squirrels.

"Those squirrels sure do give Al a hard time," she said.

"I think it's the other way around, Mom. I think Al is a little-shit disturber."

"Maybe so." She laughed.

"They'll never catch him." I said, smiling.

The sun turned a deep crimson as it began its descent below the treetops. Now it was downright cold and I was shivering. "Leo, look at me," she whispered. "I saw you at the Esquire last night," she confessed. "And the look in your eyes and your little comment this morning told me you saw me as well."

"What are you talking about, Mom?" I answered, doing my best to appear clueless, but Mom wasn't buying my act.

"His name is Carl," she told me. "He works at the hospital with me. In fact, your father met him a couple of months ago at a party."

"So Dad knows you hang out with this guy?"

"Not exactly," she answered, wincing. "It's a little more complicated than that."

"Is that why you told him you went to see Grandma?"

"We're just friends, I promise you."

"Friends that hold hands?" I pressed. "Isn't that an affair?"

"Friends can hold hands," she protested.

"In places like France *friends* hold hands," I protested. "In America *friends* who hold hands are *more* than friends."

"That's not true," she said. "But just so you know, your father has his confidante too."

I'd never heard that word before, but I had a pretty good idea what she meant.

"It's that woman named—"

"Too much information, Mom!" I said, cupping my hands over my ears.

She was beginning to make it sound like this was all normal adult behavior. I didn't know what to say at that moment, because suddenly I wasn't angry at all. I was now on overload.

"Life is so complicated, Leo," Mom sighed. "Your father and I should never have gotten married."

I didn't know how to respond to Mom's depressing statement. I wanted desperately for this bleak conversation to end, but Mom felt the need to elaborate. "We met when I was in nursing school. Your father was working at the Steinberg Skating Rink during college, and I would figure skate in the mornings, when the ice was free between early-morning hockey practices. He let me skate in the middle of the rink an extra few minutes while he drove the Zamboni," she told me, looking out into the yard. "He must have driven a thousand circles around me before he finally asked me out."

For the second time that day, a car pulled into our driveway and rescued me from an uncomfortable situation. This time it was Dad and Caleb returning from the pool.

"It's a long story, Leo," Mom said sadly as she stood up. "Just don't rush to be a grown-up like I did. I guess that's what I'm trying to say."

We walked inside the house, and Mom insisted on a hug. "Do you mind not mentioning this conversation to your father, Leo?"

"My lips are sealed," I promised as I headed downstairs for a much-deserved shower.

Mary made things even more muddled and confusing when I told her about my conversation with Mom. "I think your mother might be having an emotional affair," she suggested to me over the phone that night. "I've read about them in some of my mother's self-help magazines."

"What the hell is an emotional affair?"

"It's like being friends, but being *more* than *just* friends. Does that make sense?"

"Eww!" I fought hard to block the images forming in my mind. "Like 'friends with benefits' friends?"

"No, it's not like that," she said, giggling. "It's like having some huge crush on someone but not really acting on it. I don't think you have to worry. It's not like it's one of those affairs where people are running around sneaking into sleazy hotel rooms. I think it's more like an escape."

Maybe Mary was right, but thinking about all this crap made my stomach turn. Maybe it was just an escape for Mom, but I still couldn't wrap my head around the whole concept. "Technically, it's still cheating, isn't it?" I asked.

There was a long pause before she answered. "That's the big question," she finally said.

20.

I GOT ON MY BIKE Monday morning actually eager to get to school. Running gave me something to look forward to at the end of the day, but knowing that I might see Mary for five minutes between classes gave me something else to look forward to every eighty minutes.

The first true signs of autumn were in the sky. The green leaves of the trees were starting to curl inward, faint yellow veins beginning to appear. Soon our house would be blanketed in red and gold. As I headed down the driveway, I spotted Al scurrying around the yard, taking advantage of a brief opportunity to gather a few fallen acorns before Caleb confiscated them.

Despite my regular run-ins with Caleb, I liked the new house. I liked that the neighbors were mostly older people with children long gone. They were a lot nicer to Caleb than our old neighbors had been, and he was even picking up odd jobs from some of them, like Mr. Hunker. Caleb raked his lawn once a week, and Hunker paid him with a ten-dollar bill that Dad promptly converted to ones. The neat stack of bills Caleb kept in his dresser was growing taller by the week.

All this open space meant it was less likely Caleb would do something inappropriate, like walk into a neighbor's house uninvited, or plant a cat inside a mailbox. I didn't have to worry about kids getting their kicks by making Caleb do something stupid. He could skip and talk to himself in the driveway without calling attention to himself. The only thing I had to worry about here was my own business with Caleb. All things considered, I'd take that over the old neighborhood any day.

Gorsky was inhaling an entire roast chicken when Curtis and I barged into his office during his lunch break. With a drumstick in one hand and his newspaper in his other, he barely looked up to acknowledge us. "Gentlemen, what do you need?" he grumbled.

Curtis grabbed a marker and began diagramming the course and race strategy on the board. He rambled off names, locations, descriptions of terrain, turns, splits, and surge points. Curtis went over the plan for the district race, and Gorsky simply listened, nodding occasionally with interest. When Curtis finished, Gorsky took another bite from the chicken leg, gnawed on it slowly, and mulled the idea over in his head.

"I'm intrigued, Kaufman," he finally said. "By the way, how's the body holding up for you at the moment? You a hundred percent?"

"Never felt better," Curtis assured him.

"Then is there another reason you've been running like a wuss all season?"

"I'm staying under the radar," he told him.

"Duly accomplished, Kaufman. I think you've got your fellow competitors fully convinced you're a has-been. Or that you're too chickenshit to go for it."

Curtis laughed. "I know what I'm doing. You're the one who always told me, 'Run within yourself.' Besides, you and I know the only race that counts is state."

Gorsky nodded and laughed.

"You know that I can dominate on that course, old man," Curtis assured him. "You said it yourself last year."

Gorsky took a sip of coffee from his thermos and studied the grand scribble Curtis had mapped on the whiteboard. "That state course is certainly designed for a runner like you, Kaufman," he finally agreed. "At least the Kaufman I think I know."

"Damn right it is, but I'm going to need some help."

Gorsky glanced casually at me, then focused his attention on ripping the remaining leg from the chicken. "And you think you can pull this off, Leo?"

"Well, according to him I can," I said, nodding toward Curtis.

"It's simple, Coach," Curtis assured him. "I press the pace and waste them. Coughlin just locks in, runs solid, and plucks them off one by one at the end with his speed."

"Your plan might be simple, but if we're going to pull this off, we're going to need to step it up," Gorsky said as he glanced at his watch. "Now why don't you two go and get yourselves back to class and try to learn something. This ol' geezer needs to make some adjustments to your workouts."

Except for Monday's meeting with Gorsky, I spent my lunch periods with Mary. We'd grab something edible from the cafeteria and head out behind the school to the baseball fields, sprawl out on the grass, and set up a little picnic. We spent most of our time just making small talk, bitching about homework, or assessing some teacher's fashion sense or nervous tics. It was the best part of the day. By Wednesday, I had progressed to lying on my back, head in her lap, just soaking up sun and loving life.

That's when she nudged me.

"Hey, Leo. Check it out." She pointed across the field, toward the back of the gym. I sat up, rubbed my eyes, and saw eight guys from the football team lifting a red Ford Escort. Two guys stood on each side of the car, their hands gripping the bumpers and frame. They were shuffling the car toward the handball courts.

"What the hell?"

She started laughing. "It happens every year. A group of guys wedge a teacher's car inside one of the handball courts." She pointed out four other guys connected to the scene stationed at different points around the building. "Those guys are on lookout."

The guys still had a good fifty yards to carry the car and they moved slowly. "Whose car is it?"

"I think it's Stickler's," she told me. "He's such an ass. The guy derives a perverse pleasure from making kids feel stupid. This should have happened long ago."

We were both laughing as one of the guys holding the front bumper stumbled and almost caused the other guys to drop the car. Then I felt Mary's finger tickling my neckline just below my collar.

"What's that, Leo?" She began to pull at the collar of my shirt.

"What's what?"

"Is that a bruise?" she asked.

I pulled her hand away. "It's nothing," I told her. I wasn't about to tell her about Caleb coming after me the other night.

She laughed. "I don't remember giving you a hickey."

"It's not a hickey," I told her.

"I know that, Leo." She began to press me. "Seriously, what happened to you?"

I put my hand over my neck and did my best to wrinkle my brow and pretend to be puzzled as well. "I don't know, and I don't remember. It probably happened when I was doing lawn work last weekend. Probably bumped it on something."

"Let me take a look at it." She reached for my collar again, and I brushed her arm away.

"It's not a big deal," I assured her.

"It's a bruise, Leo. I would think you would remember it."

The bell rang and lunch was over. Mary stood up and stared at me a moment. "I have to get to class. Call me tonight."

She left me sitting there in the field, thinking about the damn bruise on my neck. The truth was I didn't want to remember it. I felt this flood of shame rush through me as I thought about my older brother straddling me in the middle of the night and beating the crap out of me. It made me want to crawl into a corner. Only running made the shame go away.

I stood up slowly and found my way to class. Those guys now had Stickler's car fully wedged inside the handball court. The way they had it positioned, he was going to have one hell of a time getting it out.

I didn't call Mary that night, or the next night either. At

school I didn't try to avoid her, but I didn't go out of my way to see her, which was pretty easy given we didn't take any classes together. When our paths crossed, I pretended everything was cool and that I was just busy with stuff. She asked me about what was up over the weekend, and I made up some lousy excuse about having to get together with some relatives.

I directed all my energy into running. After our meeting with Gorsky, the intensity and focus of our workouts began to shift and heighten. I began to see why Curtis thought the guy was brilliant. Into almost every workout, Gorsky incorporated elements structured like potential race scenarios. In some I was set off with a head start over a hilly terrain and Curtis had to pursue me, catch me at a predetermined point, stay with me, and then accelerate in the final stretch. In other workouts I pursued him over flat terrain, then pounced on him in the final stretch. Gorsky pushed us. We did more hills and strides at the completion of each workout. We ran on legs not fully recovered. There was no more tapering for any races before the district meet, because the races between now and then were the workouts.

We were tired, but we felt our bodies become stronger. We remained competitive, but we also held back and kept something in our tanks. We looked forward to unleashing ourselves when the moment really counted.

21.

A THICK MORNING FOG CREPT over the bluffs from the Missouri River and blanketed Macklin. As our bus pulled into the park, we passed a steady stream of runners moving through the gray mist like ghosts. Bundled in sweats, they jogged slowly, shaking off the stiffness of sleep, cold weather, and long bus rides.

I couldn't believe it when I spotted Dad's car already parked next to a playground. He was behind the wheel, sipping from a cup of coffee and reading the paper, and Mom was sitting at a picnic table nearby, texting on her phone. Caleb was on the swing set laughing his ass off about something, going so high, the chains went slack at the height of each arc.

"Isn't that your brother?" Curtis asked.

"Yep."

"Man, he sure is testing the limits of physics."

"Yes, he is, and he'll go even higher."

The bus finally came to a halt in the parking lot, and Gorsky stood for his customary pep talk, but this morning he kept it brief. "Young men, need I remind you that this is the district state qualifying meet? In other words, it's do or die!" he announced, his voice booming, and waking Rosenthal and Stuper from their deep sleep. They shook their heads and looked out the bus windows, disoriented.

"Stuper!" Gorsky yelled, trying to rouse him. "Is this going to be your last race of the season?"

Stuper yawned and scratched his head, contemplating Gorsky's question. "More than likely," he finally decided.

Gorsky slammed his clipboard down on the bus seat. "Wrong answer!" He surveyed the team, shook his head, and let out a sad sigh. "Unfortunately, for some of you this might be your last race of the year. And for some of you," he said, glancing at Stuper, "this probably *is* the last cross-country race of your entire life."

I looked around the bus at my teammates. Rosenthal and Burpee had some serious bed head going down, Rasmussen's chin was beginning to droop as he dozed off again, and the rest of the guys on the team looked dazed and groggy.

Gorsky rambled on about tenacity, intestinal fortitude, and some other stuff I was too nervous to take in, before making his final point. "All I'm trying to say, gentlemen, is give this race an honest effort, so when you leave here today you can say to yourself that you gave it your best. You've got about an hour before you step on that starting line. Use that time to set a goal for yourself: a time, a place, a guy from another school you've never beaten. Challenge yourself, and leave here today knowing that you took a risk, tested your limits, and gave everything you had out there," he concluded, pointing toward the course. He took a moment and scanned the bus, looking each of us in the eye. "That's all I have to say."

The guys on the team slogged down the aisle off the bus like they were headed toward their execution, and Gorsky shook hands with each of them and grumbled a few words of encouragement. As I approached him he tapped me on the shoulder and motioned for Curtis and me to take a seat and wait until the bus emptied.

He looked first at Curtis. "Kaufman, is this going to be the last race of your high school career?"

"Are you joking, old man?" Curtis laughed. "Hell no."

"Just checking," Gorsky said, patting him on the shoulder. "But do you have a strategy in mind if this little game plan of yours doesn't work?"

"Not going to happen, Coach," Curtis scoffed. "And the last thing I need right now is you planting seeds of doubt in Coughlin."

Gorsky then looked at me. "How about you, Coughlin? You good to go?"

"I hope so," I said.

"Hope?" Gorsky asked. "It's going to take a lot more than hope, Leo," he said, laughing. "It's going to require guts, talent, and brains," he said. "You can do this, son, but you're going to need to use your head as much as your body."

Gorsky turned to Curtis. "Kaufman, you're going to have to run smart as well. If you're going to take over this race early, you'd better know your threshold. You cross it, and you might not have anything left for the finish."

"I've got it," Curtis said.

Gorsky gathered his clipboard, zipped up his jacket, and

looked over his shoulder at us as he stepped from the bus. "Gentlemen, it's as cold as a well-digger's ass out here," he told us. "Get yourselves a good warm-up in and I'll meet you at the starting line."

"Ready?" Curtis asked me.

"Yeah," I lied. "I'm ready. By the way, any theories on why a well-digger's ass would be cold?"

"No idea."

Twenty schools were participating in the district race, with the top four teams advancing to the state meet. We'd competed against most already this season in duals and invitationals, so I was familiar with the majority of the field. As Curtis and I jogged the course, threading our way through competing teams warming up in tight packs, he pointed out some of the major competition.

"Lucky for us, Fromm and Newcombe aren't in our district. We'll worry about them next week. Our biggest concerns are Palermo from Northwest, Snell from Lafayette, Webster from Lindbergh, and Fox from Kirkwood. They're the guys most likely to place in the top ten and not be from an advancing team either," he said with certainty. "The way I figure it, the other guys placing will be from the top four teams."

"Just remind me what to do again and keep it simple," I said.

"I know these guys well," Curtis said. "Palermo, Webster, and Fox will blast their way to the front and form the lead pack as soon as the gun goes off. I'll go with them, press the pace, and mess with their heads," he explained. "You just get out steady and lock in."

I nodded. He made it sound simple, but my gut told me it was going to be a little more challenging than that.

"I'll be with them for the first mile, until that ascent to the bluff," he continued. "I'm going to push the pace there, and I guarantee they'll go with me." He pointed at a redheaded guy in orange warm-ups running ahead of us. "That's Snell. You hang with him. He's patient and likely to make his move late in the race."

"What makes you so sure?" I asked.

"Just stick with him, and he'll eventually try to make a break for it. I'm betting that will be a little after the two-mile mark. Then it'll be time for you to execute."

"How?"

"Just draft off him. Let Snell go by us gradually and just hang a few meters behind. The other guys will try and stick, but they'll be dead by then. When Snell takes the lead at that point, I guarantee he'll be looking over his shoulder thinking he's got this race" he said, laughing, "so do your best to grimace like you're in serious pain."

"That shouldn't be a problem."

"He doesn't know who you are, Leo. Besides your fifty-sixth-place performance a month back, you've done nothing notable in the races. Nobody is going to take you seriously."

"You didn't have to remind me about that."

"Are you kidding, Coughlin? That race was the best thing that could have happened to you this season. None of these guys are thinking about you. And today we're going to take advantage of that."

I let his words sink in.

"Wait until the final three hundred meters, then go strong for a two-hundred-meter surge," he told me. "That should do it. Then settle in and maintain. It will be just you and Snell at that point. Stay with him and wait until the final thirty meters to kick."

"That's it?"

"That should do it," he said with certainty.

"All right, then."

By race time the sun had burned off the fog and the air had warmed slightly and was easier to breathe. Gorsky met us at the starting line and arranged the team in our narrow alley, placing Curtis and me next to each other. Our team squeezed in, and we shook and jumped in place to keep loose and calm our nerves. Gorsky tapped Curtis and me on our shoulders. "Get out quick," he told us. "I believe that you can do this, but that's not what matters. You must believe it yourselves. Be bold."

Curtis delivered a soft tap to my heart with his fist and nodded. I turned and got myself positioned on the line as the starter gave final instructions. Then it was silent.

I looked straight out to where we'd soon be running and spotted Mom and Dad sitting on the hood of the car, side by side. Dad pumped his fist high, a gesture of good luck and strength. Behind him I saw Caleb continuing to test the limits of the swing set. He appeared at the crest of each swing, and still he pumped his legs to go even higher.

Then the gun exploded, and we were off.

Curtis did exactly what he said he was going to do: he

blasted aggressively from the line into the lead. Palermo, Fox, and Webster were in a sizable group that took Curtis's bait, running at a blazing pace. Just as Curtis predicted, Snell was more sensible, remained calm, and drafted a good distance off the lead. I caught up to him and we settled into a reasonable pace. Clearly this guy had confidence in his own strategy and abilities and was content with trailing the pack.

The first mile was forest trail that circled back to the starting line and finish area. I hung with Snell, and we threaded our way through several runners who went out too quick but weren't serious contenders. We came through the first mile in just under five minutes, which meant Curtis and the lead pack were flying. As we broke into the first clearing, I spotted him leading a group of eight runners. Snell and I were still a good eighty meters back.

We passed the parking lot playground, where Caleb was still pumping his legs and buckling the chains at the height of his swing. Dad was standing on the hood of the car, but Mom was now atop the picnic table. Dad yelled, "You're tenth, Leo! Run!"

The second mile headed into another forest trail and led east toward a bluff that overlooked the river. As far as courses went, Macklin was the most beautiful one I'd ever run. The cool morning air, the colorful fall leaves, and the smell of damp earth and stone being crushed beneath my feet provided a rush, and I began to cruise.

As we approached the pivotal hill where Curtis planned to break the race open, I remained patient and maintained a five-meter deficit on Snell. He pushed the pace a bit up the hill, but it was easy to stay with him. I wanted to take off more than anything, but I stuck to the plan and waited.

Snell and I passed three guys on the ascent, and when we crested the hill I saw the lead pack. Curtis was still in front. I knew I was in the top ten, but the crucial portion of the race had yet to begin. Snell and I had closed the gap considerably and were now only thirty meters back. He pressed the pace once more, and we started closing in fast on the leaders.

When we passed Curtis, I allowed a momentary gap between Snell and me. "How are you doing?" I asked him.

"I'll be fine," he said. "It's your turn."

I accelerated and pulled up behind Snell as we gained ground on Fox, Palermo, and Webster. Snell definitely knew what he was doing. He was cruising at this point, clearly relying on patience and his strength to eventually capture the lead. In fact, I sensed he was running too comfortably, so I knew I had to modify the plan. When we pulled beside the lead pack, I surged. It was earlier than Curtis anticipated, but I felt I had enough in me to deliver a quick burst of speed that was intended to be the nail in the coffin and enough to mentally bury them.

Just as Curtis predicted, the three tried to counter with their own surge, but they started dying. Fox glanced over his shoulder a couple of times, and the look in his eyes told me he was hurting. I allowed him, Palermo, and Webster to battle it out with one another for another hundred meters, and then I kicked it up another gear and passed them for good.

It was just me and Snell now. I followed Curtis's instructions and let Snell pull beside me. I gasped like I was suffering, but I felt awesome.

There were three hundred meters to go, and now I wondered if I'd gone too early and it was going to come back and bite me. I allowed Snell to open up a five-meter lead, and he casually looked over his shoulder a few times. I tried to pretend I was nothing more than an annoying pest, like Curtis had instructed, but I didn't need to exaggerate my pain, because I was truly beginning to feel it. My shoulders were tightening and my legs were getting heavy. Snell believed he had a comfortable cushion at this point, and all he had to do was unleash his final kick. I couldn't allow him any more of a lead, and I needed to prepare myself to pounce.

The trail veered left and opened up, a slight downhill and final stretch of flat, grassy field that led toward the fifty-meter roped-off funnel and the finish line.

Snell began his kick as we hit the downhill. I responded and began to gain ground. Not knowing whether this guy had an extra gear, I followed Curtis's advice and waited until we were inside the funnel and thirty meters from the finish.

The crowd was screaming, and he didn't hear me coming. When he finally sensed I was on him, he glanced back and tried to accelerate once more. I had him. I pulled up beside him and unleashed my final kick. As I flew by him, he let out a gasp. Seconds later, I broke the tape.

I made my way through the chute, then dropped my hands to my knees for support. I felt a tap on my back and turned to find Snell with his hand extended. He was too exhausted to speak. He closed his fist and tapped his heart two times and gave me a thumbs-up. I shook his hand, exited the chute, and jogged back to where I could see the rest of the runners come in. Fox, Webster, and Palermo were approaching the chute, and Curtis was just a few meters behind them. Of the four, Curtis looked the strongest.

Dad grabbed me from behind and tried to congratulate me, but I shook him off and watched Curtis come in. With twenty meters left, he clenched his teeth, pumped his arms, and elevated his knee lift and cruised past the three other runners to finish in third place. I circled back and met him as he exited the chute.

"What place?" he asked, his arms on my shoulders, panting in exhaustion.

"It was a close one," I told him, smiling. "Got him at the finish."

"I told you so, Leo" was all he said.

There was something utterly magical about executing a race exactly as we rehearsed it. Gorsky met us a few minutes later, lugging our gym bags, and he began barking orders. "Gentlemen, keep your celebration brief. Change into your sweats quickly, keep warm, and get in a proper cooldown."

He tossed our bags at us and finally burst out in a huge smile. "Kaufman, that was perhaps the most courageous race I've ever seen from any athlete I've ever coached," he said. "And Leo, that wasn't too shabby either. You won that race as much with your brains as you did with your body. Well done."

We removed our spikes, bundled ourselves in our sweats, and jogged back in time to cheer the rest of the guys to the finish.

I could still feel the dry burn in my lungs from the race, but my legs felt light and strong. "You do remember what I told you was going to happen if we got to state?" Curtis asked.

"How could I forget?" I told him. "You're going to kick my ass."

"Yours and everyone else's," he reminded me with a sly smile.

———

"Wasn't that something, Elise?" Dad asked as he began to recount the race at lunch. He had his sandwich in one hand and was waving a forkful of potato salad with his other. "He comes out of that forest and chases down that kid from Lafayette and then passes him right at the finish. Spectacular!" he yelled, pounding the table with his fist.

"Could you please not talk with your mouth full?" Mom pleaded. "And could you wipe that potato salad off your chin?"

Dad took another bite from his sandwich and smiled at me. "Honestly, that had to be one of the most exciting things I've ever seen in my life."

Mom turned and smiled at me. "It was really amazing to watch, Leo. I'm very proud of you."

"It still really hasn't quite sunk in yet," I told them, trying to play it down.

"You know," Mom began, "my uncle George was a great runner when he was your age. My mother used to talk about him winning races all the time. I'll see if Grandma has any of his medals."

"Your uncle George?" Dad blurted, his mouth still full of sandwich. "Your uncle George who had a heart attack when he was fifty? That man was obese. The last time I saw him, he could barely walk across the room. No way he could ever run even ten steps." Dad emphasized the final words of his sentence by stabbing his fork in the air, this time in Mom's direction.

Mom got up and began doing the dishes. "He didn't become obese until he became a chef, you fool," she told my father. "Leo certainly didn't inherit his talent from your side of the family, if that's what you're suggesting."

"And why's that?" Dad was yelling now.

"As far as I know the only thing your mother and father were good at was—"

"Let's not start this game!" Dad yelled, holding his hands up to signal a truce.

Mom turned and glared at him. "No. I don't want to start this game. Let's just call ourselves even."

I got up, placed my dish in the sink, and headed downstairs to my room. I could still hear them arguing, but I couldn't understand what they were yelling about. I wondered if *they* even knew what they were arguing about anymore.

22.

"YOU'RE FIFTEEN MINUTES LATE, Coughlin!" Curtis shouted when he opened the door.

"Got anything to eat?" I asked. "I'm starving."

He dismissed me. "Follow me!"

Curtis's parents were history professors at Washington University and on sabbatical for the semester. He explained to me that basically meant his parents got to go on a lot of vacations.

I trailed him down a long hallway into his parents' bedroom, where he led me toward an enormous walk-in closet and pointed at a large collection of suits hanging on the far wall. "Take your pick," he said. It was more of a command than an invitation.

I scanned the collection and selected a peach suit with bold brown stitching running along the seams of both the coat and the matching pants.

"Excellent choice, Leo. The color combo is both thought provoking and revolting. I particularly like the slacks."

"What are these?" I asked. "And please don't use the word *slacks*. It's creepy."

"These, my friend, are my father's leisure suits, a fine collection he obtained from his father and was wise enough to keep in the family," Curtis explained.

"They're hideous," I said.

"Exactly," Curtis agreed. "And one day I will inherit them, despite my mother's fierce objections. Now put one on."

"You've got to be kidding," I said.

"Coughlin, I take Halloween seriously," he said with conviction, removing a pink jacket with purple lapels, the pants a reversal of the same colors. He held the suit up and considered his image in the mirror. "I think I'll wear this provocative number," he said.

Curtis dropped his pants and put on his father's suit. "What are you waiting for?" he snapped. "The party is already well under way." He tossed me a garish orange shirt and tie.

I shrugged and put on the suit. "We look ridiculous."

"Precisely," he agreed. He was standing in front of the full-length mirror, squaring his tie knot.

We were headed to an open party at some football player's house whose parents were also out of town for the weekend. Apparently it was going to be a huge bash, with rumors of kids showing up from some of the Catholic schools in the area. I was still on a high from the district race that morning and in the mood to celebrate, but Curtis was stone-faced, like we were going to a job interview.

"Now for a few finishing touches," Curtis said.

He selected a pair of white shoes and lobbed them to me. "See if these bad boys fit," he said. They were shiny white slip-ons, and unfortunately they fit like a glove and were actually kind of comfortable.

We moved next into his parents' bathroom, where Curtis applied a thick layer of hair cream to our scalps. He spent several minutes styling my hair so it looked like a bad comb-over. He combed his own hair straight back. He worked with an intensity and attention to detail that bordered on disturbing. After adding the final touches to his hair with his father's comb, he spoke to our reflections in the mirror. "Shall we be on our way?"

"I guess." I looked into the mirror and reminded myself that once again Curtis had managed to coerce me into something stupid that I'd probably regret.

The party was not far from Curtis's house, so we walked, hopping fences and cutting through a few backyards. A surly Rottweiler on evening patrol pursued us through the last yard and nearly took a bite out of Curtis's leg before we scrambled over the fence to safety.

"Clean living until after state," he told me as we entered the party.

I saluted him. "Aye-aye, sir."

"That means no booze, Coughlin."

"As you said, we shall treat our bodies as holy temples, Curtis, until our mission is completed next Saturday," I assured him.

"I'm serious," he said.

"You've made that very clear."

I followed Curtis as we threaded our way through a crowded backyard past clusters and cliques I recognized from school. We found Rasmussen, Stuper, Rosenthal, and a couple of other guys from the team gathered in a clump near a birdbath filled with ice and beer in the corner of the yard. Rasmussen and Stuper were wearing long white underwear tops and bottoms, swim goggles, curly black tails, and white capes. Rasmussen had a giant X spray painted on his cape, and Stuper's had a Y.

"Guess what we are?" Stuper asked proudly.

"I'm going to take a wild guess that you're sperm cells," Curtis answered.

"Correct!" Rasmussen laughed. "You're the first person to figure it out."

"I think the X and the Y make it abundantly obvious. Do I need to remind you I took AP Biology?" Curtis answered.

Burpee was in a Batman costume. Rosenthal had a potato dangling out of his fly from something that resembled a coat hanger.

"I'm a dicktater," he explained. "What are you guys supposed to be?"

I didn't have an answer, and Curtis was distracted. Some guy in a pretty good Yoda getup had arrived and was making a quick move toward a group of popular girls from school. Yoda paused and entertained them for a few minutes. He then removed his mask, whispered a few words to Missy Hamlin, took her hand, and led her away.

"Unbelievable," Curtis said. "Why can't I do that?"

"I think she's already had a few," Rasmussen said. "Just wait until Glusker gets here."

"Why's that?" I asked.

"Until last week she was Glusker's girlfriend," Rasmussen explained. He was the only guy on the team remotely connected to the social scene, so we hung on his words. "She dumped him, but he's not over it yet. At least that's the word on the street."

The hounds were out in force at this party, guys from the all-boys Catholic schools in the area sniffing the grounds for available girls. I spotted Mary and a few of her artsy friends amid a cluster of guys from Jesuit who'd got wind of the party. She was wearing a black cape and had powdered her face so it glowed like white marble. I'm pretty sure she was supposed to be a vampire. With her lips painted ruby red and her green eyes framed in eyeliner, I was mesmerized. The guys she and her friends were hanging with looked harmless enough, but one guy filled her cup from the keg and was now cozying up to her. She cast me a quick glance, then shifted her hip toward the dude in a way that made my gut turn.

"What are you going to do about that, Coughlin?"

"What am I going to do about what?" I answered, pretending to be unfazed.

Curtis chomped on some ice and spat it in the direction of the budding romance unfolding before our eyes. "Don't be an idiot, Coughlin. Have some balls and go save the poor girl from that creep," he said. "Show some honor, for Christ's sake."

The dude was now leaning against a tree, his body shifted toward her. He said something to Mary and she laughed.

"She doesn't look like she's suffering, Curtis."

"Are you shitting me? That's all an act, Leo. The girl is dying for you to rescue her."

"I didn't know you were an expert on romance," I told him.

"Grow some, Leo," Curtis mumbled as he walked away. "I'm going to see if I can find someplace to take a leak. I'd make a move if I were you, unless you're content with people thinking you and I are a couple."

"Screw you" was all I could muster for a comeback.

"Leo, that's fine by me," he said over his shoulder. "I'm not on that team, but I'm an enlightened individual. I've got no problem if you are."

I gave him the one-finger salute but lingered with Stuper, Burpee, Rasmussen, and a few other losers at the sanctuary of the birdbath.

I figured Curtis was probably right about Mary. I needed to step up and take action, but when I turned to make my move, Mary had already beat me to it. She was standing just three feet away, hand on her waist, glaring at me.

She gave my costume the once-over, then sipped from her cup. The expression on her face was somewhere between curiosity and mild disgust. "Do I know you?" she asked.

My hair was heavily oiled and slicked over, and my body covered snugly in polyester. "This is Curtis's creation," I mumbled. "Courtesy of his father."

"Is Curtis now dressing you too?" she asked snidely.

"Very funny," I said.

Mary held out her hand and felt the fabric of my coat. "You'd better be careful," she told me. "You get anywhere near a flame and you'll catch fire. If I had a match on me, I'd be tempted." She looked at me for a long moment, a slight frown on her face, those amazing green eyes fixed on mine. "Can I ask you something, Leo?"

"Sure." I knew what was coming.

"Is there a reason you haven't called me?"

I stared at the ground and said nothing, but she wasn't about to let me off the hook.

She took another sip of liquid courage and then let me have it. "You want to hear something pathetic?" she asked.

"Sure." I wasn't exactly looking forward to it, but at least she was talking to me.

"I sat at home every night this week waiting for my phone to ring," she told me. Her eyes started getting all watery, and I was panicked thinking she was about to lose it and make a scene. "I've tried to figure out what I did to piss you off. I thought you were a nice guy, but now I'm starting to think you're a prick." She let that word hang for a couple of seconds. "What's even more pathetic is, the other day my friend Laura and I drove back and forth past your house. I was hoping that you would step outside so that we could pretend we were just passing by."

Now I was starting to feel like shit. I really liked her. I had to do something if I was going to salvage any chance in hell of making it with this girl. "I'm not a prick. I promise you that. I like you. I really suck at girl stuff, in case you haven't noticed. This is new territory."

"Are you shitting me, Leo?"

I shrugged my shoulders.

It was silent for a moment. Mary chucked what was left in her cup toward my feet. "Damn it," she whispered. "I can't believe I just told you all that crap."

I hesitated, then rested my hand on her shoulder. "You really drove back and forth past my house looking for me?"

"Yeah," she said. "I mean, what kind of person does that?"

"According to the law, I think that might make you a stalker." I regretted saying the words as soon as they left my mouth.

She punched my arm, and for a second I worried she was going to storm away. But she started to laugh. "We must have driven past your house fifty times," she said through laughter and tears. "By the way, what in the hell is your brother doing making all those little piles of grass in your yard?"

I seized the moment. I put my arms around her and whispered into her ear, "You must not tell anyone. Our family belongs to a pagan cult that worships the moles that reside in the underworld. Our winter-solstice ceremony is fast approaching. Caleb has been commissioned by the high priest to create the burial mounds where we will make sacrifices."

When she laughed again, I knew I had finally broken the ice. "How is Caleb?" she finally asked.

I ran my fingers through my hair like I always did when I was at a loss for words, then let out a long sigh. I'd forgotten that my hair was an oil slick. "Caleb can be a real pain in the ass," I told her.

Mary let those words sit for a long moment before she spoke. "Do you want to get out of here for a while, Leo?"

I looked into her eyes, and that was it. "Sure."

We walked away from the party and into the darkness of the adjoining backyards, passing a few couples making out behind trees. I wasn't going to tell her about Caleb trying to beat the crap out of me on a random basis, but I wanted to talk. I just didn't know what I wanted to say.

Mary spoke first. "Honestly, Leo. What's going on with you?" she asked.

I didn't really have an answer, but all of a sudden I had this crazy childhood memory. "Do you remember how you learned to ride a bike?" I asked her.

"I think my father just decided to remove the training wheels and I spent a little time with him holding me up in the driveway. I might have fallen a few times, but then I got the hang of it," she told me.

The thing I liked about this girl was, I knew I could ask her a random question and she'd answer me, letting our conversation wander wherever it might. We walked for a few seconds in silence before she took my hand. "How did you learn to ride a bike?"

"My father was actually trying to teach Caleb how to do it. I think he was maybe six, and Dad thought he was getting too old for training wheels. Not that it mattered, because Caleb didn't really give a shit. He would ride around the old neighborhood back and forth, just talking to himself, laughing, lost in his own world. But my father didn't want him to stick out from the other kids, and he was determined to get rid of those training wheels.

"So one day Dad threw the bike into the trunk of the car and drove us to this park that had this long grass hill, not steep or anything, just a grass hill that would cushion a fall. Dad took the training wheels off, but Caleb wouldn't have anything to do with it. My father put him on the bike and pushed him along, but Caleb wasn't interested. Even when my father let go of the bike, Caleb would just coast a little until the bike fell over."

I guess we weren't really walking so much as slowly wandering. She leaned in closer to me and put her head on my shoulder, but I kept talking, trying to make sense of the sudden memory.

"My father finally got frustrated and gave up. I remember Caleb just walked over and sat down under a tree and started twirling his stick. So I picked up Caleb's bike, got on it, and coasted down the hill all by myself. I'd only been on a bike with training wheels for a few weeks, but now I was riding a two-wheeler. My father couldn't believe it. He pushed the bike up the hill, placed me back on it, and ran alongside me, cheering me on. We did this a couple of times together. It must have bothered Caleb, because he finally stood up and walked over to me. 'My bike!' he yelled. I got off the bike and gave it to him, and then he rode it down the hill perfectly, like he'd done it his entire life. He did it a couple more times, and then he just said to Dad and me, 'Go home.'"

"What made you think of that story?" she asked.

"The hell if I know," I told her, but right then I figured it out. "I sometimes wonder if it pissed him off that I learned to ride a bike before him."

"Maybe he just needed to see someone else do it," she said. "Maybe you helped him."

"There were other kids in the neighborhood who were riding bikes," I said. "I think it was something else."

"What?"

"Maybe he felt like he was supposed to be a step ahead of me but he didn't really understand it at the time."

"So?"

"How would you feel if your younger brother could do everything better than you?"

"Do you think Caleb even thinks about that?"

"I never really thought about it until now, but I think he finally gets it. I think he's started putting the pieces together and realizes I can do a shitload more than he can, and that I always could."

"Why are you thinking about this?"

"I'm not sure," I said. "Lately, Caleb and I haven't been getting along too well."

"What's going on?"

I didn't feel like going there. "It's not a big deal, Mary. We don't need to talk about it anymore."

"We can talk, Leo," she said.

"No. I'm good," I told her.

I feared she was going to press the issue, but instead she took my hand and squeezed it softly. We headed back to the party, shoulder to shoulder, a guy in a leisure suit with a thick layer of hair cream nestled up to a chic vampire. I loved how this girl could read my energy. Before we returned to the light of the party, she turned and put her arms around me. "Now's the time you should probably suggest we try this again . . . if you have any guts."

"I've been hearing a lot about some movie called *Corpse Bride*," I said. "Word on the street is Tim Burton is 'brilliant.'"

"No, thanks," she said, laughing. "That movie is now bad karma. This time you choose what we'll see."

I looked into her eyes. "Sure. I'll ask my mother if she's seen anything good lately."

Upon our return, we found Curtis entertaining the masses. He had retrieved the discarded Yoda mask owned by the dude who was somewhere else on the premises, engaged with Missy Hamlin. Someone had put on the *Saturday Night Fever* soundtrack at full volume, and Curtis was performing an impressive rendition of Travolta's dance routine. Curtis in his leisure suit, helped along by Yoda's sage, stoic face and some tight choreography, was now the focal point of the party.

"Find your rhythm! Find your rhythm!" Rosenthal yelled, sounding remarkably similar to Gorsky.

I was laughing my ass off until Mary pointed out Blake Crawford saying something to Glusker. Crawford was another of Glusker's goons, and whatever he said to him ignited something. Glusker came barreling across the lawn and blindsided Curtis, rolling him onto his back and pummeling his head with his fists. What made it surreal was that Glusker was unleashing his savage fury upon Yoda, whose expression remained fixed, calm, and pensive.

It took Rosenthal, Burpee, and me to haul Glusker off Curtis and explain the misunderstanding. When we finally got the mask off Curtis's head, his nose was gushing. "Well, that didn't exactly go as planned," he moaned. Curtis pressed his father's coat to his nose to halt the flow. Glusker, embarrassed but still loaded for revenge, mumbled some bogus apology and stormed off to find the true competition.

When the crowd realized Curtis was going to live, they dispersed, and it was just Curtis, me, and Mary alone. He lifted his arm slowly and pointed toward Glusker trudging through the crowd with his crew. "Like his master before him, be destroyed he must," Curtis said in Yoda voice.

"Seriously, dude. Are you all right?" I asked him.

Curtis stood up slowly, examining his father's shirt and coat, which were covered in blood.

"I think I'd better get him out of here," I mumbled to Mary.

"Agreed. Better go take care of his nose. Next weekend?" she asked.

"I'll be at the state meet."

"Weekend after?"

"You bet."

———

Curtis and I walked back to his house mostly in silence. "I don't think the blood is going to come off those clothes," I said.

"My friend, as always I'm already one step ahead of you," he said. When we arrived at his house, he walked directly to his backyard and toward the Weber grill at the edge of the patio.

"What are we going to do?" I asked.

"Something that should have been done long ago," he said. Curtis lifted the grill lid, removed the cooking racks, and took off his clothes. "Trust me. My mother will thank me for this," he assured me.

He tossed the leisure suit, shirt, and tie into the grill. I removed my clothing as well and tossed them on top of the pile. Curtis took a large bottle of lighter fluid and doused the clothing. He opened a Tupperware container, grabbed a box of matches, struck one, and tossed it onto the clothes. A fireball exploded from the grill.

Mary was correct—the suits were highly flammable. We stood there in our underwear and socks, and I entertained him with my description of Glusker going ballistic on Yoda in a leisure suit. It was a cold October night, but the grill warmed us.

Wearing a leisure suit had certainly backfired on Curtis, but the party had gotten me back on track with Mary.

23.

GORSKY CUT OUR MILEAGE in half the final week to rest our muscles for the final race. We didn't know what to do with all our excess energy, so by Friday morning's departure we were bouncing off the walls. I was plenty nervous, but Curtis was an absolute train wreck.

We met Gorsky outside at his van and climbed in with our bags.

"Got everything?" Gorsky asked.

We nodded.

He turned to Curtis. "Spikes?"

Curtis blasted from his seat like someone had hit the ejection button. He sprinted back toward the locker room. For once I wasn't the more nervous one.

Gorsky turned to me. "So how are you feeling, Leo?"

"Awesome," I told him. "What could be better than a day off of school?" It was even better to be getting out of my house for a night, but I wasn't going to mention that. He knew me only as a runner, and that was good enough.

"You ready to run fast?" he asked.

"Curtis says the course is a beast."

He laughed. "He's right about that. It's a true cross-country course. The winner won't necessarily be the fastest guy, but he'll definitely be the strongest."

"Think Curtis has a shot?"

"Of course he's got a shot. But he'll need to run a smart race like you did last week." Curtis burst from the building and jogged toward the car. "Speak of the devil."

"Onward!" Curtis yelled.

As soon as we hit the interstate, Curtis pulled out this old crumply photocopy of last year's program with a map of the course and gave me the lay of the land. "It's going to be an ass-kicker from the start," he explained. "As soon as the gun goes off, we climb a long, steep incline, and then it's basically a roller-coaster ride. This course is going to beat the crap out of most guys' legs by the end of the first mile if they go out too fast."

We looked at the list of previous state champions and their times. For a 5,000-meter course the times were relatively modest. "Not very impressive times," I said.

"It's all relative, Leo. It's not a fast course," he agreed. "But it's my course."

The drive to the capital took a little over two hours. Gorsky wouldn't let us touch his CD player. Instead he introduced us to some guy named Herbie Hancock, and the smooth, mellow sounds actually settled Curtis. He walked me through my role as the sacrificial lamb in his quest to become state champion, just as he'd been for me in the district race. He reviewed the course topography in precise detail, drawing lines and arrows to mark the inclines and descents. His strategies and explanations weren't really necessary, but I allowed him to ramble. My job was quite simple. When that gun went off, I was to take off like a bat out of hell and let everyone chase me, just like they chased him at district.

———

The Ramada Inn looked like a tank of tropical fish. The parking lot was filled with school buses and vans from all over the state, and cramming the lobby were runners in sweat suits of all colors looking one another over, some measuring themselves against tomorrow's competition. Curtis once more came unglued. "Don't look anybody in the eye, Leo," he mumbled as we made our way to the front desk.

I was feeling loose for once and enjoying the reversal of roles. "Jesus, Curtis, can you relax?" I asked him. "You're acting like we're about to rob the place."

"Everybody is just trying to get into each other's heads at this point. I can smell the nervous energy."

I inhaled deeply. "I think most of it's coming from you."

"Shut up, Leo."

We took our bags to our room, changed into our running clothes, and headed over for a final preview of the Oak Hills Golf Center, where the race was being held. Gorsky parked his van and told us to meet back up with him in ninety minutes. I looked around at the cast of hundreds in their school colors, jogging, striding, and doing sprints, and finally got sucked into the collective nervous energy. I broke into our customary warm-up jog to take the edge off.

"Easy, Leo," Curtis said. "Let 'em run. We've already put in plenty of miles to get here. We're going to walk today."

"You're the boss."

"Stay relaxed," he told me. "I'm going to need you to focus now." We walked over to the starting line, a long white line of chalk dust across the fairway. Curtis stood behind the left side of the line and pointed toward the first portion of the course, a level fairway that extended about seventy-five meters before curving into a steep ascent.

"This is a par-five hole. It's the longest hole on the course. That hill up ahead is almost four hundred meters before it crests, and it gets steeper as you ascend. Four hundred meters," he repeated. "That's a monster. It's how the race begins, and it's how this beast ends." He pointed at a funnel of red and white flags leading toward a tent on the far right side at the top. "That's the finish line up there."

He then directed my attention to a small sign and a line of yellow flags opposite the tent. "When the gun goes off tomorrow, it's going to be chaos. There will be plenty of fools chasing early glory. By the time you reach that sign up there, I want you to be in the top five," he said. "And if anybody is trying to open up on you, go with them."

I thought it was a pretty hefty challenge, but I played it cool and said nothing.

"That's going to take a little bit of work on your part, but if you're careful and alert and don't fall down in the first seventy-five meters, you'll be fine." We walked down the fairway toward the first hill. "Just be careful," he told me. "And be aggressive."

As we walked the course, the map we'd reviewed in Gorsky's van came to life. Curtis was certainly right about one thing:

there wasn't much flat ground. He reminded me to allow my body to roll with the terrain and let gravity do the work.

I would let my body fall down the hills with quick, light steps and have momentum carry me upward until I naturally felt the moment my muscles needed to respond and propel me upward. If I didn't, he said, this course would beat the living crap out of me.

"Keep your arms pumping, Leo. Short, quick strides when it's steep, lengthen when the hills begin to open up," he reminded me. "Running is nothing but leaning forward, eyes and nose over your shoelaces, just letting gravity do the work. *Racing* is nothing but running full tilt, leaning a little farther forward, and moving your legs fast enough that you don't frickin' fall down. It's a balance between running with reckless abandon and staying in control. If you find that balance, you feel like you're flying."

"I got this, Curtis. Just win the damn race."

Still walking the course, Curtis began pointing out the guys I had to manage. "Keep an eye on that dude," he said, pointing to a tall, lanky runner in a black sweat suit. He mentioned names and pointed out a few more notables, but I was no longer listening. I'd already decided I was simply going to take the lead when the gun went off and hang on for as long as I could.

That night Gorsky took us to Bones, this little place a few blocks from the old Missouri State Penitentiary. "All that nonsense you hear about carbo-loading before a race is bunk," he told us as he marched ahead of us. "You're running three measly miles—not a marathon. Now's not the time to fool with your body. Eat what you normally eat."

"Sounds good to me," I agreed.

"He just wants to have a steak," Curtis mumbled.

The place didn't have much in terms of pasta or pizza, but Curtis caved and ordered their burgers and fries, which Gorsky promised were legendary. We settled into a booth, and Gorsky and Curtis got into a lively debate about whether America should get out of Iraq, while I zoned out to a *Seinfeld* rerun playing on this rickety old television dangling from the ceiling in the corner. It was a quick dinner, as Curtis mandated that lights be out by nine.

I was wide awake as I lay in bed that night. I couldn't figure out if it was because I was actually nervous about the race or because I generally don't like hotels or if it was something else. The hotel room smelled funny, and it always creeped me out being in a bed that's been slept in by God knows how many strangers. So I slipped out the door to the hallway balcony overlooking the hotel's empty kidney-shaped swimming pool.

Staring at the pool, of course, made me think about Caleb. I was happy to be away from him for the night. He was really starting to scare the crap out of me, and that pissed me off. Then I felt guilty for feeling that way, because I knew he couldn't help it. Just a year ago things were fine between us, but now I was beginning to wonder if he wanted to kill me. I tried rewinding the year, searching for the turning point, a pattern, the trigger that flipped some switch inside him, but came up empty. I was left with just my gut feeling that he was getting more and more frustrated and angry that his younger brother was leaving him in the dust.

It was past midnight and I figured I'd better go back to bed and try to fall asleep. But my mind wouldn't shut down. I wondered if I was destined to never get a good night's rest. As I lay awake listening to Curtis snore, I thought about how I might become a better brother.

24.

GORSKY KNEW CURTIS WAS AMPED, so he kept the pep talk simple. He just gripped him by the shoulders, looked him in the eye, and said, "Kaufman, you know what you need to do. Just stick to your plan and go get the damn job done."

Curtis nodded and climbed out of the van with his bag and I followed, but Gorsky tapped me on the shoulder. "Leo, wait a moment." I waited until Curtis was out. "Leo, you know you've got a shot at this too today. You can win this thing as much as he can," he told me.

"Coach," I started.

"Leo," he said. "You ran the race of your life last week. All I'm saying is, if he doesn't have it in him, don't be afraid to think that this day could be yours."

———

The individual qualifiers were positioned to the west side of the starting line, separate from the qualifying teams. As we did our final strides, I spotted Dad, Mom, and Caleb coming toward me. Caleb was carrying a short stick in one hand and twirling it furiously. Dad read the tension in my eyes, gave me a thumbs-up, and guided Mom and Caleb up the hill away from the start. He knew by now that I liked to be left alone on race day.

Curtis stepped beside me as the race marshal announced last-minute instructions. I realized it was now my turn to calm him.

"Are you ready?" I asked.

He tried to laugh. "That's my line."

The marshal sounded the bullhorn and made the final call, and we lined ourselves up behind the white line. It was cold and still, and in the final seconds there was a pure silence that allowed me to center myself. I looked straight up the long hill where Curtis said I needed to be leading in only a minute's time.

We were given just one command: "Runners to your mark." The pistol blast pierced the silence, and we were off.

Curtis gave me a strong nudge from the back as I sprang from the line. I propelled forward quickly and angled my way toward the center of the course and the continuous white line marking the race route. I breathed deeply, and the air seemed to seep right into my lungs and legs. I felt light but strong, and after the first two hundred meters I was already positioned in the top five. The sound of the spikes of two hundred runners pounding the hard turf, our collective breathing, and the spectators' cheers all gave me a burst of adrenaline. I stayed focused, eyes intent on the crest of that hill, my chest and arms strong. I relaxed my shoulders, tilted my torso forward, and pumped my arms toward the target.

Running beside two runners I didn't recognize, I suddenly panicked that maybe I was going too fast, amid a few fools who had no business leading. Then Fox, Fromm, Newcombe, and Palermo settled in beside me, and I knew I was in the right company. At the crest of the hill, Fox took the lead and I went with him. Now it was nothing but three rolling hills leading to a narrow bridge and a trail skirting golf fairways bordered by forest.

The pace was furious, and I couldn't afford to look back to see where Curtis was; I had to wait until the course turned. The thunder of footsteps diminished after the first eight hundred meters as the throng of runners thinned out.

Fox opened up a few meters on me, but his pace felt fast, so I let him do the work. I knew even he couldn't maintain this pace forever. I decided I would wait until we reached the first-mile mark at the lake before I took over.

Webster, Newcombe, and three other runners pulled up beside me as we descended the hill, and Fox, sensing a growing pack creeping up from behind, couldn't help himself. He tried to push the pace even faster. It was early in the race, so I stayed patient. I opened my stride on the downhill, breathed deeply, and said a quick prayer that I would have enough strength for when it was time to do the real work.

We crossed a cart bridge at the bottom of the hill, our spikes making the wood planks thud and echo in the still morning air. The white chalk line stretched in front of us in the direction of the lake, where two lines of flags formed an enclosed alley skirting the banks. Spectators were sparse at this position on the course, but a small crowd of the devoted had gathered a hundred meters ahead at the first-mile mark, eager to catch our splits. The lead pack had grown to about seven guys, and I wondered if it was time for me to make the move.

Where the course curled around the lake, I caught a glimpse of the runners behind us. Curtis was a good fifty meters back. I glanced at the clock when we passed the mile mark: it read 4:46, by far the fastest split I'd run this season. It was suicidal, considering the terrain we'd covered, but I wondered whether it was good enough, since I was still surrounded by seven runners.

Fox continued to lead as we circled the lake and made our way toward the tree line on the eastern portion of the course. The trail bent south there and made a two-hundred-meter steady climb, then turned west onto a long fairway and into yet another series of rolling hills.

When Fox hit the tree line and began the first uphill, he tried to increase his gap. I shot away from the pursuing pack and joined him, fearing he was about to make a break and possibly slip away. As we climbed the hill, I sensed we were breaking from the pack.

Before the descent I glanced over my shoulder and saw Curtis beginning to close in. He was just thirty meters back, exactly where he needed to be. So I continued to trail Fox over this series of hills until the two-mile mark, where the race truly began.

The initial adrenaline rush was now long gone. I breathed heavily, the searing beginning to creep into my lungs, but my legs still felt strong. This was the most challenging part of any race: I had to focus, concentrate, and remind myself that each stride was taking me one step closer to the finish.

On this brief stretch of the course, the runners were alone. Fox accelerated once more and opened up his lead by about five meters, but I remained locked in and maintained the gap. We passed the two-mile mark in 9:40. A quick calculation: we'd covered the second mile in just over 4:50, eight seconds slower than our first mile, but well ahead of course-record time. Fox was still rolling, still looking strong.

The terrain relented at this point and flattened for the next five hundred meters before we'd be descending a steep ravine with an equally sharp ascent. The course would then level briefly and circle back toward the starting line and the final deadly climb toward the finish.

I spotted Curtis over my shoulder, now twenty meters back. He appeared strong and poised to make his move, and I knew it was time for me to execute. I surged hard and attacked, but as soon as I overtook Fox, four guys closed on us out of nowhere so we were now running in a tight bunch. I had to make the next two hundred meters painful, because we were all about to get a breather when we hit the descent.

Just five hundred meters earlier I'd felt awesome, but now the race was starting to take its toll. My breathing became labored and my shoulders grew heavy, but I could tell the others were struggling as well.

A runner in purple and gold pulled beside me and I surged once more, imagining the crest of that ravine as my finish line, and the completion of the mission I needed to accomplish. If I could force the pace to that point, I would be able to use the descent for one final push. The five guys with me were content to let me lead the pack, most likely reckoning that any pace faster would be too costly, given the energy that would be necessary for that final ascent. I was too tired to look over my shoulder for Curtis. I trusted that he would be true to his word and close the gap.

We made a sharp turn before descending. I spotted my father waving and yelling, but I no longer heard anything except for my own breathing. I leaned forward as I made the descent and ran down that hill as fast as I could, my arms paddling at my sides like windmills and causing me to nearly lose my balance twice. My reckless abandon somehow allowed me to hold my lead, and momentum carried me halfway up the steep incline aptly nicknamed "Manbreaker," its pitch so steep that I had to reach down with one hand to steady myself and keep from collapsing. When I looked over my shoulder, my surge had put fifteen meters on the pack, and now there were four guys in a panic trying to pursue me before the final five hundred meters. Curtis was one of them.

I made it to the top of Manbreaker in the lead, but after ten strides my shoulders seized and the blood in my legs began to turn to slush. Three guys went by me in a tight pack, and I felt like I was moving backward in slow motion. Then I felt a strong tap on my shoulder, and Curtis flew by me, sitting just five meters behind the pack. He looked strong and relaxed, but I didn't have an ounce of energy left in me to even offer a word of encouragement. If I knew him, he would press the pace at the base of the hill as much as necessary to weaken them, and he'd be wise enough to save something in the tank for the final kick.

I was dying. Another runner passed me, then Fox, and then another. The next two hundred meters were an eternity, but I continued to simply focus on breathing, take one stride after another, and try to maintain some semblance of form. A few more streamed by me, but I began to regain a bit of strength.

At the base of the final hill, I saw Curtis now with the leaders, with just two hundred meters to the finish.

The spectators lining both sides of the final stretch were screaming, and the cheers gave me one final shot of adrenaline. I was out of contention, but I began kicking, mostly because I wanted to see the outcome of the race. Curtis and one other runner now separated themselves from the third with under seventy meters left. Then Curtis unleashed that final gear and opened up a ten-meter gap in what seemed like a second. I saw him clearly now up the hill. With twenty meters to the finish line, he was pumping his fists outward with both arms in celebration.

My last two hundred meters were not pretty, but I managed to pass a few guys on that beastly hill and cross the finish line in tenth place—good enough for a medal.

Curtis met me with a rib-crushing bear hug as I staggered from the finish chute. "I owe you, Coughlin" was all he told me.

"You owe me nothing," I gasped.

"You keep logging the miles and get more base under your belt, you're going to lead this race start to finish," he promised me.

Our postrace celebration was a slow jog, a repeat of the race loop. We went over it together step-by-step from start to finish, both of us boasting about executing our mission exactly as planned. While the moment was past, neither of us would ever forget it.

25.

MOM DROVE SEPARATELY AND HAD TO cut out before the awards to make her shift at the hospital. Dad insisted on driving me home from the meet.

"Tell me something, Leo," Dad asked me. "Where did that performance from Curtis come from?"

"Dad, Curtis is a damn good runner," I told him.

"Yeah, but you kicked his butt just last week," he said to me. "Do you think maybe you went out a little too fast?"

"Today went off exactly as planned," I assured him.

"I'm not sure I get it, Leo."

"Let's just say Curtis gave me my moment of glory last week, and today I returned the favor."

"Whatever you say. I may not know much about this sport, but I'm very proud of you. I can't wait until next year." Dad was looking through the windshield with a little smile on his face. Caleb was quiet in the backseat, still twirling that stick. I sensed he was working himself into a very foul mood.

Dad said he knew about this great burger joint called Lester's at the next highway exit, and he wanted us to celebrate. Everything was going fine until Caleb found out Lester's was out of fish-and-chips. Then all hell broke loose.

"MENU SAY FISH-AND-CHIPS!" he screamed.

"They ran out, Caleb," Dad whispered. "If I could make fish-and-chips appear out of my ass, I would."

"FISH-AND-CHIPS!" Caleb screamed.

"We'd better beat it," Dad said. He grabbed Caleb by the wrist, and we scrambled out of that restaurant before he was able to make more of a scene. The rest of the way home, Caleb was kicking the back of my seat, pounding the windows, and screaming bloody murder about fish-and-chips. Dad flipped on the radio, clenched the steering wheel, and tried to tune out. When Caleb delivered a donkey kick that jolted my seat toward the dashboard, I just focused on the white lines of the highway in front of me and pretended I was somewhere else, too.

"Damn it, Caleb," Dad finally said. "What do you frickin' want me to do?"

"FISH-AND-CHIPS, DAMN IT!" Caleb screamed. "Long John Silver's fish-and-chips restaurant!"

"Frickin'-A!" Dad yelled.

I thought for a moment. "Well, the way I look at it, Dad, you can either drive him to the Long John Silver's, or you can drive him to Children's."

Dad smacked the steering wheel before finally caving to the absurdity of our situation. "Jesus," he swore, laughing quietly, "it's never a dull moment."

It was a zoo inside our car until Dad pulled into the parking lot of Long John Silver's, our old standby whenever Caleb needed a guaranteed fix of fish-and-chips. Dad brought Caleb here almost every other week because of some television commercial Caleb became fixated on seven years ago. The place was always empty, and I feared the day it would eventually go out of business.

"Order food by self!" Caleb said.

"You got it," Dad agreed. "I wouldn't have it any other way." He pulled out his wallet and handed Caleb a ten-dollar bill.

Then Dad turned toward me. "Let's wait out here a moment," he said. "I could use a breather."

When Caleb was young, Dad had taught him how to order from a menu. It was painful. Caleb ordered by giving not only the name of the entrée but the entire description as well, plus his own special requests. It sometimes took him up to five minutes to place a simple order.

Caleb marched purposefully toward the two women behind the counter, who were conversing. They stopped talking when they saw Caleb and stood at attention. They knew him well. The lunch-hour trickle was over, and the restaurant was empty except for an older couple seated at a two-top near the front window.

Dad timed our entrance just as Caleb was placing his order. "LONG JOHN SILVER'S TWO-PIECE COD MEAL!" Caleb demanded. "Choice of Sweet and Zesty Asian or Creamy Garlic salad dressing. Want Creamy Garlic. Sides green beans and corn cobbette. Two hush puppies. RIGHT!"

Despite all his challenges with communication, Caleb had no problem expressing his needs in restaurant situations. The women behind the counter treated the situation like a stickup. One grabbed the microphone and slowly repeated Caleb's order verbatim. The announcement reverberated throughout the entire dining room: "Long John Silver's Two-Piece Cod Meal! Choice of Sweet and Zesty Asian or Creamy Garlic. The customer would like Creamy Garlic. Sides green beans and corn cobbette. The customer has requested two hush puppies. Right!"

He had Long John Silver's completely under his command.

"Large Diet Coke. TWO ICE CUBES!" he demanded.

She relayed his precise drink order into the microphone: "Large Diet Coke. The customer would like two ice cubes."

The woman at the beverage dispenser went out of her way to show Caleb that she was fulfilling his demands. Aware that she was under his watchful eyes, she clutched a pair of tongs and slowly placed the ice cubes individually into the paper cup. Caleb paid his bill with the money Dad had given him, counted his change, and took his receipt to an empty table and waited for his order.

It was our turn to order. "Hope you're in the mood for fish-and-chips," Dad said.

As we made our way to Caleb's table, Dad patted me on the shoulder. "Just remember, Leo. Life is always going to throw you curveballs."

26.

MARY WAS CRAZY-BUSY PAINTING sets for an upcoming production of *The Crucible* at school, so she hadn't made it to the race that morning. Not that she was crushed she couldn't be there. Driving more than two hours each way to see someone run a fifteen-minute race, perhaps catching a glimpse of them for maybe twenty or thirty seconds, wasn't exactly enticing. I got that.

Instead I met up with her that night and drove her across town to this place I loved called Charley's Drive-In. It's this cool little dive Dad sometimes took Caleb and me to that he knew from his college days.

Charley's was way out on Manchester in Brentwood, and the place was usually packed with people wolfing down cheeseburgers and onion rings off paper plates, but that night the place was almost empty. Charley's was tiny, just a long counter with several swirl stools that wrapped around a grill, fryers, and a soda fountain. The cook was none other than Charley himself. We ordered a couple of cheeseburgers, a basket of fries, and two icy mugs of his special homemade root beer. It tasted like heaven.

I gave Mary a detailed recap of the race, but I knew she didn't really understand or give a rip about the tactics Curtis and I pulled off that morning. So I shifted the conversation in her direction and learned a few things about drama and set design that were probably about as compelling to me as my race tactics were to her.

Charley had this old-fashioned jukebox, and the guy changed the playlist religiously each month. It was music you'd never heard before, and it was always great stuff. I slipped a bunch of quarters into the machine, and we pressed random numbers and letters. Soon the sounds of Tommy James and the Shondells crooning "Crimson and Clover" provided the right mood. I wanted to hang there forever.

We settled back down into our stools and lingered over our root beers and a few remaining fries for another hour, listening to old tunes and talking about movies we liked, songs we loved, and teachers who confused us. Then Charley told us he was getting ready to close up.

As we headed out the door, I directed Mary's attention to this old, grizzly guy with no teeth who'd been sitting alone across from us. He was gnawing on a plate of cheese fries and sipping black coffee and making a mess of himself. We sat in the car and watched him for another minute really going at those cheese fries, the sauce now smeared across both cheeks and dripping from his fingers.

"I wonder what his life story is," I said to her, thinking we might create some juicy life story for the poor guy on the journey home. But instead Mary decided to get all serious on me.

"Why don't you tell me a little more about your life story, Leo," she said.

That confused me. "What do you need to know?"

"Like, I want to know more about you."

I put the car in drive and made a move toward the radio dial, but she hit the off button. Now I was trapped by silence. "I hate to break it to you," I said, laughing, "but it's been a pretty uneventful life up to this point."

"Cut the crap, Leo."

May the traffic gods be with me, I thought, because I didn't know where this conversation was going.

"I want to know if you're okay," she said.

"What's up, Mary?" I asked. "We just had this amazing time at Charley's, and I had this great race this morning, and now you think there's something wrong with me?"

"I'm not talking about right now, Leo. Sometimes you shut down, you check out for a few days, or you're just not there. Is something up?"

"I'm a man of few words."

"That's bullshit. In case you need reminding, your mother is running around having some kind of an affair. I'm not exactly sure what your Dad's deal is, but I imagine he's not clueless and knows something is up. And as much as I love your brother, that can't be easy."

"It's all cool, Mary. It is what it is."

"That's so clichéd, Leo. And what's up with you always having some scratch on your face or a bruise on your neck, arm, or some other place I haven't seen yet?"

"Is that a pass?" I joked.

"Does your father hit you?"

"Christ, Mary! No! What's up with you tonight? I know you're into theater, but maybe you've been hanging around the drama crowd a little too much."

She stared hard at me for a moment. "I think you're full of shit." She slapped the radio dial, and the Red Hot Chili Peppers flooded the car. "Enjoy your damn music!" she shouted.

By the time I pulled into her driveway, the ice had begun to melt. I put my arm around her and kissed her on the forehead.

"I'm sorry," I told her. "Maybe I do sometimes shut down." Then I kissed her cheek. "Sometimes my family brings me down," I admitted. "But I'm okay," I promised her. Then I found her lips and we kissed a little longer.

Before she got out of the car, she looked at me for a long moment, but she didn't push the matter any further. "I care about you," was all she said.

I figured I dodged that bullet, but when I got home Caleb hadn't quite worked the fish-and-chip tantrum out of his system, or whatever the hell was bothering him this time.

Within minutes I was running the empty streets in the darkness of night. But it felt great. The sear in my lungs from wasting myself in the race that morning was still there, but my legs felt light and strong, and the runner's high seeped through me and I began floating above myself. Again I felt like I was soaring. I took inventory of the day, its highs and lows, and despite Caleb's outbursts and the little clash with Mary, I decided it was a pretty damn good day.

Five miles later I slipped back through the door and into

the bathroom, where I stripped and wiped down with a wet towel.

Before heading back to the bedroom, I took a good look at myself in the mirror and examined my face and torso, and I didn't see a single scratch or bruise. I was all right.

I crawled into bed, Caleb and I went through the forgiveness routine, and the room became silent, but just as I closed my eyes, he spoke.

"Why Leo run?" he asked.

"Leo runs because it makes him feel damn good," I mumbled. "Maybe you should run too."

Part Two

27.

THE FIRST TIME I SAW HIM running was on a cold December afternoon. The sky was gray, with a mist in the air that could turn to snow any second. I was on my way to pick up his meds at Walgreens when I saw his familiar figure and his loping stride on the shoulder of Clayton Road. His form looked painful. He ran with an awkward skip, his knee lift exaggerated and uneven, his hands clenched in tight fists.

But it was definitely Caleb, and he was miles from home.

He'd started running the week after the state cross-country meet. One afternoon he simply asked me, "How far Leo run?"

I told him, and he asked, "Where Leo run?"

I told him, and then he put on his shoes and charged out the door. He began to disappear for long periods of time when he got home from school, often not returning until after dark, and at dinner he'd rattle off the directions and street names of the routes he ran. He had become a long-distance runner too. He wasn't stupid. He was aware of the attention I was getting from my parents, especially Dad.

I passed him in the car and thought briefly that I should keep going, but I decided to pull over and got out to greet him. "You're a long way from home, buddy," I said to him. He stopped running.

"LONG-DISTANCE RUNNER!" he yelled.

I laughed. "You're a long-distance runner all right," I told him. "Why don't I give you a ride?"

"NO!" he screamed. "Long-distance runner!" he repeated. He started running again.

I gave him a two-honk salute as I pulled back on the road. In the rearview mirror, I watched his clumsy stride. It had to hurt like hell to run like that.

Forty-five minutes later I saw Caleb again on the return. I slowed as I went by him, and he looked over at me, then refocused his gaze straight ahead. I didn't even bother to ask him if he wanted a ride.

When I got home I told Mom and Dad where I saw him.

"I think it's great he started running," Dad said.

"Yeah," I agreed. "But Christ, he's a long way from home."

"You don't need to worry about that," Dad told me. "Your brother has a very high pain tolerance."

"Tell me about it," I mumbled. I looked outside. It was dark now, and it had begun to snow.

28.

BY JANUARY I WAS HANGING OUT at Mary's place two or three nights a week. My parents liked Mary, and I think it made them feel better that it also gave Caleb and me a break from each other so we weren't getting into it as often. As long as I got my homework done and maintained mostly As, Mom and Dad pretty much let me come and go as I pleased.

Mary and her mother loved to cook, and between their homemade pizza and awesome Mexican, I was staying well fed. All I had to do was put together a decent playlist on the computer and wash the dishes.

After dinner Mary and I would park ourselves in front of the television. On Saturday nights we tapped into a local cable station that featured what they guaranteed were the worst movies ever produced. We watched '60s classics like *They Saved Hitler's Brain* and *Santa Claus Conquers the Martians*. Before each movie this flamboyant host named Montrel Sinclair, dressed in a peach suit and purple feather boa, introduced the featured film with an in-depth explanation noting the faulty plotline structures and artistic flaws that viewers should pay attention to. Mary and I would sit back and critique it for ourselves. She had a keen eye for the set and costume-design complications, while I paid attention to plot and dialogue problems.

For the most part Mary and I were acting like old people, the kind who never get off their porches to do anything. That was, until Mary's mother began dating some new guy. Then we started getting to know each other in new ways.

———

When Curtis started dogging me about starting up our training again, part of me was craving the structure and discipline of a daily workout. The other part of me dreaded going back out on the roads with him and running at full throttle.

He cornered me on a Monday morning at my locker after Ohlendorf's class. I was starving, and I wanted nothing more than to head to the cafeteria. "Your time is up, Leo Coughlin."

"My time is up?"

"You've had your month's rest," he explained. "It's time for you to commence winter training."

"Come again?"

"For track," he explained. "You're going to be the next state champion in the 1600, Coughlin," he informed me. "The metric mile. Track and field's premier event. We start tomorrow."

"The last time I checked my calendar, track didn't begin until March," I reminded him.

"You're getting soft." He laughed. "Bring your running shit tomorrow," he said over his shoulder as he headed off to his next class. He jumped up and down a few times in the hallway and shook out his arms like a prizefighter. "I'm getting a little restless, Coughlin. It's time to start up again."

After school the next day, when Mary asked me if I would help her make homemade tortellini, which she explained was basically little curly pasta pillows stuffed with cheese, my stomach began growling. I seriously considered ditching Curtis, but guilt got the better of me. I knew my gut was getting soft and it was time to get my body back in shape.

When I met him in the locker room, he tossed me a Gatorade and directed me to take a seat on the bench. I laced up my shoes and prepared myself for another one of his lectures.

"You have raw talent, but you still lack the base necessary to ascend to the next level. On the other hand, I've got some raw talent, but I basically won state with my brute strength and cunning. You need to work on your base this winter, then come spring we'll sharpen your speed and you'll dominate," he told me. "This is the hard part, my young protégé. Just grinding it out and logging miles."

"Sounds like heaven."

Curtis pulled out his car keys. "Let's take a break from our customary superblock, Leo. I propose we launch our winter training season by running someplace inspiring."

Within fifteen minutes we were out of suburbia, heading west toward Chesterfield and the Missouri River. Winter had arrived, and the light had already shifted to the blue and orange of late afternoon. Curtis reached into his backpack beside him and pulled out a plastic folder. He tossed it onto my lap.

"What's this?"

Curtis was looking blissfully through the windshield as if the barren Missouri landscape before us was the most beautiful sight in the world. "Open it up," he said.

Inside was a collection of letters from collegiate cross-country coaches, expressing interest in Curtis joining their programs next year.

"Wow, these guys are actually offering you scholarships?" I asked.

"No offers on the table yet," he said casually. "Just some expressions of interest. I really don't have much to my credit besides that state championship."

"Christ, Curtis. Isn't that enough?"

"For all they know, it was just a fluke. Gorsky is going to help me out and make some calls. Besides, all we're talking about is a partial scholarship, maybe. Cross-country and track don't exactly bring in the cash for a university like football and basketball do. We're talking about covering the costs of room and board at most."

"Still, do any of them interest you?" I asked.

"Sure as hell would be cool to run for Mark Wetmore in Colorado, let that mile-high altitude make me some more red blood cells, which might be all I need to take this finely tuned machine beside you to a whole new level."

I leafed through the letters once more, recognizing the names and logos of some prestigious colleges and universities, and felt envious. "This is pretty cool, Curtis. I'm happy for you."

"We shall see, Leo. We shall see. I show these offers to you not to be a braggart. If you pursue this fine sport with the same intensity as the runner beside thee, I have no doubt you'll be courted with even greater rewards."

I stared down the highway, thinking about Curtis heading away to college and not being around next year. I was happy for him but also bummed out. As much as he was a freak sometimes with the way he spoke and acted, he'd also kind of become like a big brother to me.

"What made you start running, anyway?" I asked him.

"I run to keep my demons at bay, Leo." He sighed.

"Demons?"

"Nothing serious. I used to have a few anger-management issues when I was younger. I might have gotten a little frustrated if school didn't move at a fast enough pace. If I wasn't in the mood for doing something pointless or inane, I might have gotten a little defiant. Sometimes I tossed a few chairs across the classroom. I threw an occasional punch if I lost my patience with another kid because he was bugging the hell out of me. Just the usual shit they don't tolerate in school."

"So when did you start running?"

"I finally had a counselor in middle school who suggested I go for a run every morning before school."

"And?"

"Let's just say that running took the edge off. Plus I realized I was pretty good at it. I was never too good at anything that had to do with throwing or kicking a ball, but I could run. By the time I was in eighth grade, I was the fastest runner in the school." He glanced over, squinted his left eye, and wagged his index finger at me. "Still am the fastest, as a matter of fact, Leo. Don't forget that."

"No more anger issues?"

"Nope. Running made me a changed man. How about you, Leo? Tell me about your demons."

"I don't have any demons," I lied.

"C'mon, Coughlin. Everyone has demons."

"No demons in my life yet," I assured him. "I guess when they show up, I'll be able to kick your ass."

"We'll see about that."

Curtis turned onto a dirt road and parked at a trailhead.

"Where are we?" I asked.

"We're near the boundary of one of our county's most unique golf courses, my friend—the Landings at Spirit Golf Club," he explained in a snooty tone. "I'm going to let you in on a little secret: for eight months of the year, this is a closely guarded piece of real estate, but for the next few months we have the opportunity to take advantage of these plush fairways for some prime training."

"That sounds like trespassing," I told him.

"Correct."

We parked the car and began our run. The ground was firm, and the dead grass and bare trees against winter's gray sky provided a fantastic backdrop for the next hour. "We'll do a little half-hour jog, then do tee to greens—running at an aggressive pace from one tee box down the fairway to the green, then a short recovery jog to the next tee box," he explained. "Think of it as a round of golf without clubs. As far as I'm concerned, this is the only good use for a golf course."

It didn't take long for us to pick up the pace and push each other. By the eighth hole we were hauling ass. The grass felt awesome under my feet, and the winter air felt clean and crisp inside my lungs. We were going flat out down the last fairway when a four-point buck darted from the forest just fifty meters in front of us.

"Check that out," Curtis said. "That's why I come here."

The buck was in midstride when it suddenly stopped and fell to its side. The shaft and quill of an arrow were plunged deeply inside its heart.

Two men in camouflage came hooting and howling from the woods in celebration. They were big guys with round guts and long hair, unshaven, with bows slung over their shoulders and toting a couple of Budweisers.

Curtis and I halted. I looked at the fallen buck, its torso still rising and falling slowly, its legs still clawing at the earth as it clung to life. One of the guys pulled a pistol from his pack, ready to finish off the job.

"What the hell!" Curtis yelled, his voice echoing in the cold air.

The men finally realized they were not alone on the golf course. One tossed his empty can onto the grass, reached into his backpack for another beer, and popped it open with a loud hiss.

"This isn't your business, boy," he told Curtis calmly. "So why don't you and your little faggot friend just run along."

"You can't just frickin' kill a deer here on this golf course!" Curtis screamed.

The two men just looked at each other and laughed. One reached into his pocket and removed a card from his wallet.

"This here license sure seems to say that I can." He took another sip of his beer.

"Let me see that," Curtis said, walking toward them. I stayed still. These guys were starting to make me nervous.

The other guy pulled an arrow from his quill and casually ran his fingers along the shaft. "Run along now, boy."

"I doubt that crappy piece of paper allows you to pop a deer on this property," Curtis said.

"I do believe you've made my friend upset," the other said. "Now before things get ugly, I suggest you turn around and run on back where you came from, and forget about anything you might've seen here today. We're just a couple of honest men trying to put some food on the table for our families."

The guy with the arrow in his hand pointed it at us. "Go on," he said. "You all be good little boys and go on home."

Curtis slowly turned toward me. "Let's go," he mumbled. When we were far enough away to feel safe, he couldn't help himself. He turned and yelled, "Assholes!"

Three seconds later an arrow whistled into the three meters separating us. We took off running, hearing rolls of laughter behind us as a final stab of humiliation.

We reached the safety of the forest bordering the golf course and turned back to look. One man had hold of the deer's front legs, the other guy held its hind ones, and they were dragging the deer across the fairway toward the forest. Their empty beer cans lay crushed on the grass.

I didn't say anything to Curtis until we were back in the car heading home. "That sure was a great place to run," I said, trying to make light of the situation. "Maybe we can come back here tomorrow and run with bows and arrows and capture our dinner," I suggested.

Curtis pounded the steering wheel. "Assholes," he repeated.

As we rounded the bend, we saw an old pickup parked on the shoulder. Curtis pulled over. He got out of the car, opened the trunk, and pulled out a tire iron. I closed my eyes and shook my head. I heard glass shatter once and, a few seconds later, again. I heard his feet crunch gravel and the tire iron clank into the trunk. Curtis was whistling a happy tune when he climbed back into the car.

"I thought running was supposed to help you with your anger management," I half joked.

"That wasn't anger, Leo," he calmly stated. "That was justice."

"So that's winter training?" I asked.

"Look at it this way," he said. "It can only get better."

Five miles from the school, we spotted a lone figure loping along on the side of the highway. Caleb.

"Who runs on the shoulder of a highway?" Curtis asked.

"I think we did the same thing once. Only we were wearing swimsuits."

"Point taken," he admitted before glancing out the window and realizing who the runner was.

"Holy shit," he said. "Is that Caleb?"

I nodded.

"Should I pull over?"

I shook my head.

"He's pretty damn far from your house," he reminded me.

I nodded.

"Are you sure?"

I nodded.

"Whatever," he said. "Running must be in your family's blood."

I watched Caleb's image disappear in the rearview mirror, and I hoped that running might start to help him keep his demons at bay.

29.

WINTER TRAINING BASICALLY SUCKED.

Winter training included running twice a day, four times a week. It meant waking up well before the sun appeared and logging five miles in arctic air.

Winter training included afternoon eight-milers with Curtis, our faces covered by bandanas frosted over with ice from subzero crosswinds that pelted our bodies from every direction.

Winter training included hitting the weight room three times a week to strengthen the upper body and core.

Winter training included sometimes running streets and sidewalks shin deep in soft snow after another winter storm.

Winter training included running in temperatures so frigid that even after a warm shower I didn't see portions of my anatomy that had recently become very important to me for six hours. When I considered Mary in the equation, I wondered if it was all worth it.

And winter training included still having to bust out the back door in the middle of the night when Caleb came at me.

———

On Saturday night Dad slipped me a twenty-dollar bill and

asked me to put some gas in the tank on the way home from Mary's.

"You can have the car tonight if you fill the tank," Dad said. He was already into his third glass of red wine, collapsed into the center of the couch watching college hoops.

"No problem."

"So what's on your agenda this evening?" he asked.

"Just hanging with Curtis and Mary."

Dad took a sip of wine and shook his head. "Leo, in case you didn't know, we call guys like Curtis a third wheel," he informed me. "It's not a good look—for either of you."

I was about to make a smartass retort, but Dad had made a valid point. So I called Curtis and bailed on him, despite his insistence that Mary and I needed a proper chaperone.

Caleb followed me out to the garage as I was leaving. He was all riled up about something.

"WHY LEO GET TWENTY DOLLARS?"

"It's for gas," I explained as I opened the car door.

I wasn't sure if it was the money Dad slipped me, if it was that I could drive and he couldn't, or even if it had something to do with me hanging out with Mary all the time that made Caleb pissed. It was probably a combination.

"MR. BAIMS TAKE YOU TO PRINCIPAL OFFICE!" he screamed.

Oh, crap, I thought. I began to panic whenever I heard Caleb say that name. Mr. Baims was his principal, and I'd never met the guy before in my life. All I knew was that once Caleb started screaming his name, it was time to bolt.

"Caleb, Dad paid you ten dollars for shoveling the driveway yesterday," I tried reminding him. "You've got more money than I do! I've seen that stack of cash in your dresser."

"MR. BAIMS NOT LIKE YOU!"

"Me or you?" I asked him.

"MAKE MR. BAIMS VERY ANGRY!"

"I don't know what the hell you're talking about, Caleb!" I yelled.

He slapped the garage wall with an open hand and started biting his fingers. I jumped in the car and slammed the door just as he began thumping the windshield.

When I returned later that night, he was still enraged. By the time we went to bed, I was ready for him. He came at me quick and had my shoulders pinned with his knees and both hands around my neck in seconds. I thrashed and kicked. He went for my eyes with one hand, pushing two fingers deep into my left socket. I shut my eyes tightly to resist the pressure and managed to free my right hand. I grabbed the baseball bat tucked beside my mattress and smacked his shoulder blades sharply three times before he rolled off me. I flipped on the nightstand light and watched him jump up and down in the center of the room, one fist shoved inside his mouth, teeth bared and clenched on two knuckles. His other hand waved wildly. I walked over toward the closet, baseball bat still in tow, and grabbed my shoes and sweats.

"God not punish you?" I heard him say. I turned and saw him standing in the light of the doorway. He was beginning to calm down. "God not punish you?"

I looked at him for a moment. "Hell, I don't know, Caleb. Maybe God will punish you!" I told him as I laced up my shoes. I figured I'd let him think about that threat for a while, and I stepped out the door into the dark and quiet of night.

It was snowing—large, heavy flakes that fell slowly. A thin layer dusted the yards I ran across, and my footsteps made the snow crunch and creak. The neighborhood was asleep. An occasional porch lamp illuminated my path, and the moonlight reflected on snow cast a grayish-purple glow. I ran onto Brattlebrook, a side street, and made my way toward a short, steep hill I knew.

I sprinted up it once, an explosive burst lasting just fifteen seconds. Then I turned around and jogged slowly back down the hill, watching my shadow shrink and grow on the pavement beneath the streetlight. At the bottom, I turned around and sprinted up the hill again, then turned and jogged back down, watching my shadow move through the falling snowflakes.

I ran until I felt my anger toward Caleb wane. I ran until I felt the fear and frustration of living within the same walls as him begin to fade. I ran until I felt my guilt about having those feelings recede deep inside me. I ran that hill a hundred times, and then I ran home, dried myself with a towel in our bathroom, slipped quietly back into the room, and crawled under the covers of my bed. "God not punish you," I whispered to him, knowing that he couldn't help it.

Caleb was sound asleep now. It didn't matter any longer whether we shared a bedroom or not. I realized Caleb would come at me anytime now, anywhere inside our house, and I just needed to be ready when it happened.

30.

VALENTINE'S DAY FELL ON A TUESDAY, and I basically blew that one with Mary by caving to Curtis and hammering twelve miles in arctic winds. Somehow Mary seemed to get that I needed to run.

On Friday she left me a folded piece of paper inside my locker. It was a watercolor of a boy and a girl inside a diner, the jukebox in the background telling me it was Charley's. In black ink she'd written a note inside a light, fluffy cloud.

I'll pick you up at 6:30.
-M

We were heading to the Saint Louis Art Museum, one of Mary's favorite places in the city. The museum was open late on Fridays, and, even better, it was free. When she tapped the horn that night, I grabbed my parka and practically sprinted to her car. It wasn't like I was one of those people who love museums or was really into art. I mostly liked following Mary around, then finding something bizarre to look at and spacing out on it for a few minutes.

On Clayton Road, Mary recognized Caleb's unmistakable stride as he ran in the same direction along the narrow shoulder.

"Hey, that's Caleb," she said as we passed him. She tapped her foot on the brake and began to move her hand toward the blinker.

"Don't," I said to her.

She glanced over at me with a confused expression. "What's your problem?" she asked. "Let's take him with us."

"Some other time," I told her. Caleb and I had gotten into it again a couple of times already this week, and the last thing I wanted was to spend more time with him.

She pulled into a side street so that she could turn around. "Just let me drive him home to change clothes. It will only take a few minutes."

"He doesn't give a rip about looking at art, Mary. Really."

She wasn't letting it go. "How do you know, Leo? I've seen his paint-by-numbers. I'd like to see what interests him." We were stopped on the side street, and she took my hand. "Besides, it was my idea to go in the first place, so I get to decide who I invite. C'mon, Leo. Be a good brother and let him come along."

"Damn it!" I pulled my hand away from hers and slapped the dashboard. "Would you just drop it, Mary? Christ! In case you haven't picked up on it, I really don't want him to come. I could use a break from him."

Her face was flushed red like I had slapped her or something. I didn't offer an explanation. "It would probably just piss him off," I finally told her, trying to calm myself down.

"Why would it piss him off?"

"He's running and you'd be disrupting his routine," I said, making what I thought was a reasonable excuse. "Would you please just back off?" I finally pleaded, my voice rising in tone.

Mary waited a moment. "I'm sorry."

I felt like shit. I reached over, put my arm around her, and kissed her forehead. "No, I'm sorry," I told her. "It's really not a big deal. Like I said, I just need a little space from him. That's all." I kissed her one more time before retreating to my side of the car.

"I'm sorry," she repeated. "I guess I really wasn't listening, Leo. I didn't think it would upset you so much to bring him along."

We passed Caleb again on Clayton Road as we continued to the museum.

"I think it's cool that your brother runs, like you," she said.

"To tell you the truth, Mary, I'm a little sick of his running."

"Your brother envies you, Leo. He runs because he looks up to you."

I watched his image disappear in the side-view mirror as the road curved.

"My brother hates me, Mary. I don't think you get it," I mumbled.

We made the rest of the trip in silence.

The museum was nearly empty when we arrived, which surprised me. We were supposed to go see some David Hammons exhibition called *Phat Free* about black history, racism, and street culture. Instead, Mary took me to an exhibition of a collection of art by Max Beckmann. Mostly we wandered a network of hallways displaying Beckmann's paintings, which were sequenced by dates and the different stages of his career. The exhibit ended inside a large gallery with an enormous mural on its far wall. It was a portrait of acrobats from another time and place in their various poses. The colors were bold and stark, the lines thick and definite. The figures were sad, pensive, and forlorn. Mary stopped and studied the painting.

"What do you think?"

"I don't know what to think," I mumbled, upset over our fight about Caleb.

We continued in opposite directions around the gallery, and I saw paintings of a large woman in a carnival mask, a trapeze artist, and a man and woman looking at their reflections in a dressing-room mirror. Not one figure was smiling. It was depressing.

Mary sat down on a bench in the middle of the gallery, her back to me, studying the somber trapeze artist with the enormous eyes. I sat beside her and leaned into her shoulder. We were the only ones in the gallery. "What do you think he's thinking about?" I asked.

She paused. "That's up to each of us to decide."

I turned my attention to a portrait of a man with his face buried in his hands, with a woman next to him, her arms outstretched. I felt Mary's fingers wrap around my hand.

"Leo," she said after a silent moment. "Tell me what's wrong."

"What do you mean?" I said to her. "I'm fine, Mary."

"Something's not right. And it hasn't been for a long time. I want to know," she told me. I could hear the frustration in her voice.

I kept my eyes on the man with his face buried in his hands. Then I finally unloaded. I told her everything Caleb had done to me over the course of the last year. When I finished, we resumed our silence, still looking at the paintings. Then the loudspeaker crackled: the museum was closing.

"Does Curtis know about any of this?" she asked as we drove home.

"He doesn't need to know about this," I told her.

"Why?" she asked.

"This thing will eventually fix itself," I tried to assure her. "My parents are still hoping it's a phase. I guess I am too. Besides, you know Curtis," I reminded her. "He wouldn't hesitate to confront my parents, and I don't think he gets that it's super-complicated."

"Really?"

"They don't know what to do," I told her. "I know my parents feel crappy enough about this, and I think they'd feel even worse if other people knew about our situation."

Mary was quiet. When she pulled into my driveway, we sat in the car a few minutes, watching Caleb at the kitchen sink washing dishes. He was talking to himself and laughing. He appeared calm.

"It's a lot to carry on your shoulders, Leo," she told me.

I thought about Caleb and about my father hauling him back to Children's. "It's going to get better. It just needs a little time," I assured her before I headed into the house.

While I felt a little lighter for finally getting everything off my chest, I also felt ashamed. The last thing I wanted was Mary thinking of me as damaged goods.

31.

I KNEW THE NIGHT BEFORE when I set the alarm for six a.m. that it was only wishful thinking. Caleb had been jacked up all week and couldn't wait.

So when I was awakened by the bright light and clatter of dresser drawers opening and shutting, I began having second thoughts about my great idea. The closet door was sliding and slamming against the insides of our bedroom wall, and I was beyond groggy, but I didn't even bother making a fuss. I looked at my alarm clock: five in the morning, and outside our window it was still pitch-black. I reminded myself that at least it wasn't a tantrum I was dealing with.

"Christ, Caleb. We can still sleep another hour," I reminded him.

"WHAT TIME RACE START!"

"What time race start?" I asked him back. I went into parrot mode, despite having told him the race details at least twenty times last night.

"SEVEN THIRTY RIGHT! Race start seven thirty. Don't be late. Right!

"HOW FAR RACE!"

"How far race?" I asked.

"13.1 MILES. HALF MARATHON. LONG DIS-TANCE!"

By mid-January Caleb had been logging close to ten miles a day, sometimes more. He'd head out the door after school and disappear for a couple of hours, and at the dinner table he'd retrace his routes with me, cataloging the street names and directions in meticulous detail. So I figured I'd maybe try and be a better brother and invite him to run a road race with Curtis and me.

I slipped my legs out from under the sheets and sat up and huddled beneath the warmth of my blankets, rubbed my eyes, and yawned. Caleb was now in pacing mode, stomping back and forth across the room, twirling his stick in front of his face. He was fully decked out in his new black warm-ups Dad had bought him.

"Not be late. Right! Race start seven thirty. Right! DON'T. BE. LATE!"

There was no choice now, so I hauled my sorry ass out of bed and made a move toward my closet and the warmth of my sweats. I knew he was excited as all hell about his first race, and I wasn't about to let him down. "Let me put on my clothes and grab a cup of coffee, Caleb, and we'll be on our way," I promised.

As we headed out the door, I discovered that Dad had left me two twenties on the counter with the car keys. He never did that.

Curtis and I had started running road races on the weekends— hard tempo runs to build strength, and a welcome change of scene from our regular routes. While it sucked getting up in the wee hours on weekend mornings, it was also kind of cool to be blasting down empty city streets in packs with like-minded lunatics.

This morning was the Frostbite 10K and Half Marathon, an annual duo of winter races that looped through downtown, followed the river, and finished in front of city hall. Curtis and I had signed up for the 10K. When I invited Caleb to join us, Dad told me to put Caleb in the half marathon. "He runs nearly that distance every day," Dad said. "Besides, it's probably better if the two of you are in separate races."

"It's a half marathon," I argued. "That's a hell of a long way to run for a first race."

"Your brother can run forever," he assured me. "He could run through a concrete wall if he wanted to."

"What if he gets lost?"

He dismissed that notion too. "Your brother's sense of direction is better than yours, Leo. I think he knows every street in this city. Just get him on that starting line and he'll find his way back."

———

By the time we arrived at the race, the weather had turned to crap. A cold sleet pelted us like tiny knives as we dashed from the car to the registration tables to pick up our numbers. Just as I predicted, Caleb and I were among the first there, so we nabbed our race bibs and dashed back to the car to stay warm and dry until race time.

"How far run?" he asked again.

I hit my resend button: "How far Caleb run?"

I knew it was nervous energy, so I indulged him with the repetition and familiar script. I didn't need anything that might trip his wires and set him off.

"HALF MARATHON. RIGHT!"

"13.1 miles, Caleb. A long way."

"Half marathon thirteen miles. Long distance. Right!"

"Too far for me," I confessed.

"CALEB LONG-DISTANCE RUNNER!"

Two loud thumps on the rear window signaled Curtis's arrival before he climbed into the backseat. "As ol' Gorsky would say, it's colder than a well-digger's ass out there. This has the potential to be truly brutal, Leo."

"Colder than well-digger's ass," Caleb repeated, laughing. "Right!"

"Thank you, Curtis. My mother will certainly appreciate that new phrase in our house."

"My pleasure." Curtis's teeth were chattering. "Mellow out, Leo. Help me pin my bib onto my shirt. I can barely feel my fingers." He dropped four safety pins into my open palm, and I leaned over the front seat and secured his race number to his jersey.

"You ready to kick some ass today, Caleb?"

"Run half marathon. Right!"

"You're a braver man than us," Curtis told him. As the patter of sleet grew louder on the car's roof, Curtis turned to me and whispered, "I would say let's bag this, but I get the vibe that's out of the question."

"Not a chance," I warned him. "Don't even think about it."

The sun had yet to appear, and the sleet was now coming

down harder. Caleb pointed at the clock on the dashboard. "RACE START TEN MINUTES!" he announced.

I did my best to sound cheerful. "Then what are you waiting for?" I opened my door and stepped into the frigid rain. "It's race time!"

I got Caleb situated among the other half marathoners, then left him alone in a crowd of runners, talking to himself about breakfast cereals. Curtis and I headed to the 10K starting area and stood in the sleet for five minutes. We were drenched and frozen before the race even started.

Even with the hard pace, our teeth still chattered and our quads were numb after two miles. We settled in with a pack of similar gluttons for pain and managed to hammer out 5:30 miles and cross the finish in a little over 34:00—not bad given the miserable conditions. As soon as we got to the finish, Curtis continued toward his car. The sleet had subsided, but the cold rain was now coming down in buckets.

"Mind if I don't stick around for Caleb's finish?" he asked.

"No worries."

"Seriously, Leo, I feel bad, but if I don't get under a hot shower soon, there's a serious chance I'll never see my testicles again."

"Remind me why that would be a problem?"

"Go to hell, dipshit," he said, climbing into his car. "That's the type of workout that will callus you and make you stronger. Trust me."

I stood at attention in the downpour and saluted as he started his car. He rolled down his window as he pulled away.

"Tell Caleb congrats," he yelled. "He's certainly a better man than us today."

"Enjoy that hot shower!" I yelled.

I bolted to my car, pumped the heat full blast, toweled down, and got into some dry clothes. By my estimation, Caleb wouldn't be crossing the finish line for over an hour. A good brother would probably have gotten his butt out of the car and backtracked the half-marathon course and run the final portion with him for support, but there wasn't a chance in hell I was going to step back into that cold rain. I drove the car to a vantage point where I could see the incoming runners, flipped on the radio and windshield wipers, and left the engine running.

From my cozy confines I watched the endless trail of incoming runners slog their way to the finish, and I started wondering about why Caleb ran. Did he get a high like I did when he ran for miles at a time? Did he feel the same release and escape I did when I put on my shoes and bolted out the door? Or did he simply thrive on the repetition and routine? Was it no different from twirling a stick in front of his face for hours, drawing endless lines of train tracks, or building piles of grass? Maybe it was simply the self-inflicted pain he craved, like when he punched his own head or slammed his fists into the wall when he was angry. I wished that I could talk about it with him, and it pained me that I could never be part of his inner world, and that he would never enter mine.

At the 1:58:00 mark, I spotted Caleb's unmistakable gait, the awkward lope of the left leg and the skip of his right. He crested the final, gentle ascent and was approaching the long stretch to the finish. Despite the rain, I bolted out of the car and started sprinting toward him, yelling at the top of my lungs. "You've got this, Caleb! You can break two hours if you push!"

He responded and began increasing momentum, his lope turning into a gallop, his right-legged skip becoming something more like a hop.

I was now beside him, running stride for stride. "C'mon, Caleb! Break two hours! You can do this!"

He looked over at me, then looked forward and focused on the large ticking clock above the finish line.

I ran beside him, pumped my fists at him, and began a running commentary: "Caleb Coughlin might just do it, ladies and gentlemen," I yelled. "In his debut half marathon, this runner might just break the two-hour barrier!"

I used to do this when we were younger, recounting his basketball stats as he shot hoops from the same spot on the driveway again and again. It made him laugh.

"He's going for it, ladies and gentlemen!" I shouted. "Caleb Coughlin might just pull this off! This is an outstanding performance!"

Caleb's right arm cranked upward over his head, and his left pounded downward. God, it looked painful, but he focused like a laser on those large red digital numbers ticking away on the clock beside the finish line, and somehow he accelerated.

"Caleb Coughlin is going for it, but he'll have to push his limits to crack two hours!"

He gritted his teeth and sped up once more.

"He might do it, folks! He can do it if he pushes!"

With a hundred meters to the finish, I stopped and stood still in the cold rain and hoped.

"Go for it!" I yelled one final time, then watched him churn out the final paces and cross the line in 1:59:56. I looked around me for another spectator to celebrate with, but there was nobody, just a slew of weary, wet runners plodding their way toward the finish.

I met up with him as he was passing through the finish-line chute. He wasn't even out of breath. He had some poor volunteer at the finish confused because Caleb was asking the guy all about the birth and death dates of his grandparents. When Caleb exited the finish-line area, a finisher's medallion around his neck, he was beaming.

"LEO VERY PROUD OF YOU!"

"That was amazing, Caleb! Congratulations," I said as we exchanged a high five.

"TAKE CALEB IHOP. Want pancakes. See Miss Shelly."

The IHOP was a long haul clear across town to our old neighborhood, but I didn't give a rip. I tuned the radio to KEZK, Caleb's favorite, and listened to him rattle off the street names and makes and models of all the automobiles he saw on the half-marathon route. This was the best day I'd had with him in a long time, and I was going to make it last.

When I parked the car at the IHOP, Caleb bolted from the car before I even turned off the engine. He was darting for his Sunday-morning seat at the counter to chat with Shelly. I just knew her by her name tag, but Caleb knew her as "Miss Shelly," and of course he knew her life story. By the time I made my way to the counter, she had already placed two tall glasses of water before him, two ice cubes in each. Caleb was leaning over the counter, lifting his medal from his chest, and pulsing it three inches from Miss Shelly's face.

"Who run half marathon, Miss Shelly?"

Shelly had a soft, round face and wavy blond hair pulled back by a headband. She smiled and winked at me. "Oh my goodness, Caleb! Did you run that far?"

"LONG -DISTANCE RUNNER! RIGHT!"

"That's wonderful, Caleb. With my bunions, I don't think I could even run across that parking lot," she told him. "You must be hungry, sweetie. What can I get you?"

Miss Shelly knew the routine.

"Chocolate chocolate chip pancakes!" Caleb stated, before reading the menu description verbatim: "Four rich, chocolate-batter pancakes filled with chocolate chips and topped with powder sugar and whipped topping!"

"You got it, Caleb."

"Miss Shelly's husband Ryan birthday next Thursday."

"Oh my goodness," she said, glancing in my direction in awe. "Thank you for reminding me, Caleb."

"How about you, honey?" she finally said to me. "I apologize, but I can never manage to remember your name. I've got hundreds of customers, but none like your brother. That boy has a mind like a steel trap."

"It's okay," I reassured her. "I'm Leo. I'll have an order of the original pancakes and some coffee."

"Well, you two just sit tight. I'll be right back in a few minutes. By the way, Caleb, my children just loved those brownies you made for them. I'm going to make sure that the cook makes you an extra pancake."

Caleb was beaming. "Thank you, Miss Shelly!"

Besides candy, Caleb spent some of his cash on Betty Crocker instant brownie mix, usually the Original Supreme, and baked batches of brownies. He charged me a dollar a brownie. The rest he loaded on paper plates and wrapped with several layers of plastic wrap and gave to his favorite people, usually women—the woman who cut his hair at Supercuts, the woman behind the desk at the YMCA, and some of the women at the grocery store. It was at times like these that I realized Caleb had a unique ability to make people happy.

When his chocolate chocolate chip pancakes arrived, he doused them in a thick layer of blueberry syrup, then smiled and laughed through the entire meal. He reminded me several more times that he was a long-distance runner before tapping into some of his other favorite conversation topics, notably the times in my past when I had gotten into "big trouble."

"Who broke jar of zucchini relish at Grandma Grandpa's?"

"I did."

"Long, long time ago," he began with a laughing whisper, "who went bathroom behind curtains on Colgate Avenue in University City?"

"I don't remember it, exactly, but apparently I did," I confessed.

"Leo got in big, big trouble!"

"I'll take your word for it."

"Who broke Mrs. Swift window with baseball?"

"That would be my bad," I agreed.

When I pulled the car into the garage, part of me was relieved the morning was over and it had gone off without incident, and part of me wanted the time to continue. When I turned off the engine, we sat a moment before heading inside the house.

"Thank you, Leo!"

"Thanks for what, Caleb? That was a blast."

"Thank you for long-distance runner!"

Sometimes I tried to correct Caleb's grammar, but this wasn't one of those times. Besides, I wasn't exactly sure what he meant, but it felt like it was something good, something that didn't need correcting.

32.

WHEN I SAT DOWN AT THE kitchen table on the following Saturday morning, Mom reminded me curtly that Grandma and Grandpa were due for arrival any moment. She ordered me to dust the living room and dining room. I rolled my eyes and sighed. That didn't go over too well.

Mom's birthday was on March 6, a Monday, so my grandparents decided it was the perfect time for a visit. It also meant I was in for one lousy weekend.

"Listen, mister," Dad said, slapping his newspaper sharply on the table, "you've got a few minutes before your grandparents arrive to change that attitude of yours."

"C'mon," I said to him. "You don't like them either."

Dad started laughing, but it wasn't a warm laugh. "Leo, you're going to meet a lot of people in this world you don't like. But learning to fake it is a necessary life skill."

"Quiet, both of you!" Mom hollered. "I'll dust the damn furniture myself," she muttered as she stormed out of the room.

"Your mother is a little stressed at the moment," Dad whispered.

"You think?" I said.

My father tried to fold the paper neatly and place it on the table. He then arranged the salt and pepper shakers and wiped his place with a napkin. That was his idea of helping Mom out.

"If it makes you feel any better, I'm not too excited about your grandparents' visit, either. Your grandfather is fine, but your grandmother," he told me, "well, she never quite approved of me from day one."

"I've picked up on that, Dad. What exactly did you do?" I asked.

"The hell if I know. I can't do anything right in her eyes."

"I can't, either," I told Dad.

Dad laughed. "Nobody can, Leo. Just smile and try to keep a low profile this weekend. Hang out with your grandfather."

"He's not really a talker," I reminded him.

Dad didn't respond. He picked up the paper and tried to pretend he was reading when Mom came back into the kitchen.

"I could really use a little cooperation from you two," she said. "This place is a mess. Leo, I need you to vacuum the living room and dining room after you dust. And you," she said to my father, "I'd appreciate it if you could get up off your ass and wash the dishes."

Mom stormed out of the room again, and Dad and I got moving. I finished the vacuuming just as my grandparents' yellow Ford pulled into the driveway. "They're here!" I yelled cheerfully.

My mother hollered from the far corner of the house. "Leo, go help them unload the car!"

My grandparents' car was packed to the gills with boxes and bags filled with all sorts of crap.

"Nice to see you, Leo," my grandfather said with a smile. I gave him a hug.

I went to greet Grandma, but she already had her head buried in the trunk. "Let's cut the chitchat," she snapped. She turned and handed me a box that felt like it was loaded with rocks. "We'll socialize after we unload. Now chop-chop!"

Grandma and Grandpa brought their surplus of Mason jars and Tupperware containers crammed with last autumn's fruits and vegetables from their garden, plus two coolers of frozen beef from a slaughtered cow they split with Mom and Dad.

My job was to unpack the coolers of meat into the basement freezer. After that I swapped last year's empty Mason jars with the new delivery and arranged them on the pantry shelves by dates and labels. I unloaded glass jars filled with string beans suspended in cloudy green liquid, whole peeled tomatoes crammed in tight, cucumber slices fermenting in vinegar and dill weed, sauerkraut, relishes, homemade catsup—you name it. Our shelves soon looked like the work of a crazed cannibal storing his victims' innards for future meals.

Grandma and Grandpa never came simply for a visit. In addition to their annual food delivery, they carried out a laundry list of household projects. Unfortunately our house needed plenty of work. If Mom hadn't prepared a list, Grandma and Grandpa would soon be scouring the house looking for cracks in the walls, pipes that showed signs of leaking, screen windows that needed patching or replacement, clogged gutters, even car repairs. They would find something that needed to be fixed, and that section of the house would become a demolition site.

I wasn't even finished unpacking the Mason jars when I heard the noise of the hammer in the upstairs bathroom. Grandpa was already at it. This weekend he was retiling Mom and Dad's shower.

Upstairs, Mom and Grandma had newspaper spread across the kitchen table. They were busy polishing the silverware Grandma had retrieved from the dining room. "Really, Elise," Grandma said to Mom, "what in the hell happened to your husband's hair?"

"Mother, you promised." Mom sounded exhausted already.

I opened the refrigerator door and stood there for a brief moment, scanning the contents for something to eat.

"You're wasting energy, young man!" Grandma said. "Fix yourself a bowl of the green beans I brought you if you're hungry."

I closed the door and tried to make a run for it. "That's okay."

"Why don't you go see what you can do to help your grandfather," Mom encouraged me.

"If he's anything like ol' Flat Ass," Grandma said, "he'll just be getting in the way." That was Grandma's nickname for Dad.

"Would you please stop calling him that?" Mom begged.

"Your husband called me Bubble Butt first," Grandma snapped.

"That was fifteen years ago, Mother." Mom sighed. She looked at me and then closed her eyes, fatigued. "Leo," she finally said to me, "go see if you can help your grandfather."

I looked out the kitchen window and watched Dad wandering aimlessly around the yard, trying to look busy with a rake. The man was a master at escaping these situations.

It was important to Mom that I spend time with Grandpa and learn some basic skills. Grandpa could build or repair almost anything, but he really preferred to work by himself and rarely said a word. So when I "helped" him with a job, I mostly just handed him tools or helped clean up the messes he created.

"Hey, Grandpa. Anything I can do to help?" I asked as I entered my parents' bathroom. Grandpa had the floor lined with cardboard and was inside the shower, tapping the tile away with a hammer and chisel.

"Not enough room in this shower for the two of us," he said, keeping his back to me.

I considered that image a moment, and I had to agree with Grandpa.

"You don't need to stick around, Leo." I knew he was serious, but I also knew I couldn't leave. So I sat on the sink counter and watched him work for a while.

Grandpa eventually got all the old tiles off the wall. "You're still here" was all he said when he turned and stepped out of the shower. "I'm going to slip out the back and sneak a smoke before I replace the backer board." He looked at the former shower wall now littering the floor. "I suppose you can get rid of this mess."

I grabbed the whisk broom, dustpan, and a plastic bag and started cleaning. A few minutes later I heard Grandma yelling, "Bernard, I smell smoke!" My dad once pointed out that Grandma had the unique capacity to shriek each word at a different pitch.

Later, Caleb and I sat together on one side of the table, with Mom and Grandpa opposite us. Dad and Grandma squared off at the table heads. Mom had baked a whole chicken. After Caleb led the family in prayer, the bowls of potatoes, beans, salad, and bread began crisscrossing the table in all directions. Dad stood up and began hacking away at the chicken. He plunged a knife into a thigh and sawed at the joint, then used his hand to rip off a whole leg for Caleb and plopped it on his plate. That was Caleb's favorite part of the bird.

"That's *not* the way you carve a chicken," Grandma mumbled to my mother.

Dad paused and let out a loud, exhausted sigh. He slowly placed the knife on the table and sat down. "Of course it's not, Jean," he said smugly.

"What's that supposed to mean, Flat Ass?" Grandma asked.

"Mother!" Mom yelled.

"What it means," Dad said, "is there's a right way, there's a wrong way, and there's Jean's way."

Grandpa laughed. Caleb helped himself to a large spoonful of mashed potatoes and began making train tracks with his fork. "Right way! Wrong way! Jean's way! Right!" Caleb repeated in a monotone.

"Pass that chicken down here, mister!" Grandma snapped. "I'll show you the proper way to carve a chicken."

Dad slid the chicken platter across the table toward Grandma. He sat down in humiliation and sipped from his beer. Mom looked at me and rolled her eyes.

Here we go again. I kind of wished Curtis were here as my witness.

Grandma grabbed the boning knife from the table and stuck the knife's tip between the remaining thigh and back. With one swift incision she snapped the thigh and drumstick from the rest of the carcass. Then she deftly inserted the knife into the chicken's back and quickly sliced the breast meat. I thought even Dad had to admit she was pretty good with a knife. She had that bird sliced up in seconds.

"So, Leo," she said as she rationed some chicken onto my plate, "your mother tells me that you've become quite the runner."

"I'm okay, I guess," I told her.

"You get that talent from our side of the family, you know," she told me. "My brother George was a champion runner in his day."

"That's what Mom tells me," I assured her.

Dad nearly spit out his beer. "Not this again. That old tub of lard?" he said to Grandma in disbelief. "A runner? That guy could barely waddle across the room."

"Watch it, Flat Ass! My brother could outrun you any day!" Grandma said as she skipped Dad's dinner plate and served Grandpa.

Dad didn't take the bait. He sat quietly for a moment, then calmly asked, "Bubble Butt, could you please pass me the chicken?"

"Please!" Mom begged. "Can't you two just give it a rest? I swear it would be a lot better if you just didn't say a word to each other!"

"BUBBLE BUTT!" Caleb laughed.

"Caleb," Mom said. "That's not appropriate."

"Not appropriate. Right!" Caleb repeated.

Grandpa had a little smile on his face as he took a bite of his chicken leg. Mom tossed her fork onto her plate and glared at Dad.

"What?" my father asked Mom innocently. "Is it entirely

impossible that Leo might have gotten some of his running talent from my side of the family? I was quick back in my day."

Grandma couldn't help herself. "Ha! I'll race you right now. Once around the house!"

"No, thanks," Dad replied, laughing. "I don't want to be responsible if you have a heart attack."

"Niles!" Mom yelled.

"What's that supposed to mean?" Grandma said. "I'm fit as a fiddle! C'mon—Niles versus Grandma Jean. Winner gets bragging rights to Leo's talent."

I looked over at Grandpa, and we couldn't keep it in any longer. We started laughing. Then Dad gave in. Grandma was the only one who remained stone-faced.

Dad looked over at me with a coy grin. "Leo," he said, "could you please ask Speedy Gonzales over there to pass the salt to Slowpoke?"

"Niles!" Mom yelled.

"It was a compliment," Dad offered. He actually sounded contrite.

Mom got up and left the table. I finished my food, excused myself, and went downstairs to hide in my room. A few minutes later I heard Mom and Dad yelling at each other in their bedroom above me, but I couldn't understand what they were saying. I wanted to go out and run, but my stomach was too full.

I lay on my bed thinking about Dad and Grandma's dinner drama, and I started laughing again. If only Curtis had been there to see it. He wasn't going to believe this dinner story.

33.

THAT CRAZY DINNER SET THE TONE for the rest of the day. As long as Grandma and Grandpa were around, I tried to keep my head down and maintain a safe distance. An hour after dinner, I was in my room trying to write a history paper for Ohlendorf's class against the backdrop of Grandpa's buzzing and whining drill.

Dad knocked on my door. "How can you write a paper listening to that sound?"

"It presents a challenge," I admitted.

"Any interest in getting the hell out of Dodge for a while?"

"I'm game," I told him.

"What do you say we head over to Fairmount?"

"It's winter, Dad. Do horses even race in this weather?"

"They've got simulcast television, son. We can watch horses race all over the planet—Australia, for Christ's sake. It's the ultimate escape."

"Sounds like a plan," I said.

"I told your mother I needed to go to the office to get some work done. Head out the back door and meet me in the garage in five minutes," he told me.

Inside the car Dad took his phone out of his pocket, turned it off, and tossed it in the glove compartment.

"Crap," he said to me, and winked. "My battery just died."

"Mine too," I said, tossing my phone in beside his.

He started the car. "Leo, my boy, sometimes everyone needs a little break from the home front."

"Amen to that," I said.

Dad sometimes went to bet on the horses on Tuesday afternoons. The racetrack was outside the city, in Collinsville, a town across the river, a good thirty miles from home. Sometimes he took me there in the summer.

I loved the ride to Fairmount. We crossed the Poplar Street Bridge over the river, and I watched the barges loaded with coal sliding up and down the Mississippi before we skirted the edges of East St. Louis. I stared out the window and processed the change of scenery and thought about how people's lives can become so different in just twenty minutes' time.

"Your grandmother sure is a piece of work," Dad said, finally breaking the silence.

"For sure," I agreed.

"Never a dull moment in our house, I tell you."

"Never a dull moment is right," I mumbled.

The skyscrapers disappeared and the highways opened up into farmland still lined with row upon row of hacked and hollowed cornstalks.

"You still duking it out with your brother at night?" he suddenly asked.

"It's not just at night," I reminded him. "I never know when he's going to lose it."

"Leo, I'm working on it. I promise you. We're in a little over our heads with the new house at the moment. Between the payments and one thing after another needing a repair or replacement, we're bleeding money. Your mother and I are a little stressed."

"No kidding," I said.

"We also feel better knowing you're with your brother in the event that something happens."

"Whatever," I said, trying to shrug it off. "Like it would make any difference."

"What's that supposed to mean?" he asked defensively.

"Nothing." I turned my head and stared out the window, signaling I was done with this conversation. This was supposed to be a break from home, I thought, for both of us.

Every time we pulled into the Fairmount parking lot and saw the grandstand, Dad made the same dismal declaration: "This is the last stop for most horses, Leo. If a horse can't win here, it can't win anywhere."

We paid our buck-fifty admission to the track and bought a couple forms, and then Dad led me to the Top of the Turf on the third floor of the clubhouse. We grabbed a window table overlooking the track, and Dad flipped on the simulcast beside our booth. "This is the best of both worlds, Leo," he explained. "Not only are we out of the house, but we get to pretend we're there," he said, pointing toward the television.

The green caption at the bottom of the screen read, YONKERS.

The horses onscreen were pulling the jockeys around the track in these measly little two-wheel carts at what seemed a painfully slow pace. "Where's Yonkers?" I finally asked him.

"New York," he explained vaguely. "It's harness racing, my boy."

Dad never liked to bet on only one horse. He preferred races that offered exacta and trifecta betting, picking two or three horses from the eight or nine in the field and predicting their order of finish. These bets required more careful study of the race form but a higher return on the wager. Dad didn't waste any time that evening. We left our coats at the table to stake our territory, then bulleted to the windows to place a bet on the next race at Yonkers.

As we returned with our tickets in hand, Dad told me to take a good look at the men sitting around us. "You just remember something, buddy," he began, and I knew what he was going to say next: "We're here for kicks. If we make any money, it's just a bonus."

This was another one of our rituals at the track. This time Dad targeted some poor guy about his age, in a red flannel shirt, seated alone at a table in front of his own private television.

The guy was sipping beer from a plastic cup and eating a hot dog. Dad put his hand on my shoulder and pulled me close to him. "See that guy over there, Leo?" Dad kept his voice low so no one but me could hear him.

"Yeah?" I whispered, knowing exactly what would follow.

"I promise you that guy has got absolutely no business being here," he said with disgust. "Absolutely no business." He looked the guy over and slowly shook his head. "I'm willing to bet he's about to piss the rent away. Probably got a wife and kids at home right now wondering where he is."

I thought about mentioning that Mom might be doing the

same thing, but I kept my mouth shut. A waitress in a tight black skirt and shiny red top was making her way toward our table. She was giving Dad a goofy smile, but he had his head fully buried in the race form and was looking for his next bet.

"Niles?" she said. "How are you doing, my silver stallion?" She giggled. "You're never here on Saturday nights."

Dad looked up at her, momentarily startled, and then his eyes started shifting back and forth between her face and mine. "Hello, Sheila," he finally managed. "This was kind of a last-minute decision." He nodded toward me. "Sheila, this is my son Leo."

"Well, aren't you a handsome young man," Sheila said to me, extending her hand and winking.

"Nice to meet you, Sheila," I said politely.

Sheila placed her hand on Dad's shoulder. "Should I get you the regular, Niles?"

Dad nodded.

"And what will you have, sweetie?" Sheila asked.

"I'll take a Coke," I told her.

Sheila kept her hand on Dad's shoulder, then bent down closer to his ear and spoke softly. "By the time I return with these drinks, Niles, I want to know what horse I should put my money on in that eighth race." Sheila winked at me again and nodded at my father. "This silver stallion knows his ponies."

Sheila spun and strutted her way back to the bar to retrieve our drinks. Dad nodded toward the door, signaling it was time to make a quick exit from the Top of the Turf. "I know a better place where we can watch the races," he said with a sense of urgency. "Follow me."

"What's wrong with this place, and what about our order?" I asked, trying to keep up with him.

"Don't worry about the drinks. Just keep moving," he directed me. "Next race starts in two minutes. I'll get you another drink."

We headed downstairs and clear across the pavilion to the Black Stallion Room and grabbed a booth in the corner. We didn't have a private television, but the Yonkers race was showing on one of the televisions hanging on the opposite wall.

"So who's Sheila?" I probed.

"What do you mean, who's Sheila? You just met her."

"What I mean is, how did you and Sheila meet?"

"Sheila works here," he assured me.

"It seems like Sheila knows you pretty well," I said. "Are you having an emotional affair with her?"

He looked at me with a confused expression. "What the hell is an emotional affair?"

"Well," I began, "Mary says it's kind of like a crush that—"

He shook his head. "Enough!" he said sharply. "It's Sheila's job to know her customers. That's how waitresses make tips, Leo. Now if I were you, I'd keep your mouth shut and start studying the race form."

We watched the horses and jockeys trot past the grandstand on the television, and Dad made a closer inspection. The number 4 horse got excited and started kicking, and the 7 took a huge crap. That set Dad dashing back to the windows to place another bet. "If anything, he's running light now," he informed me upon his return.

"What the hell is it between you and Grandma?" I finally asked him.

He didn't say anything for a moment. "I'm not good enough for their daughter," he finally said. "Never was and never will be."

"What's up with that?"

"She's their only child," he told me. "I'm not sure if anyone is good enough for their Elise."

"You can't be that bad, Dad," I assured him.

"I've made a few mistakes, Leo."

He had to know what I was going to ask next. "What did you do?"

Dad bit his lip as the tinny bugle call on the television sounded, signaling the start of the race. "Let this be a lesson to you, Leo. If you like a girl but her mother doesn't like you, don't bother. You'll be in for a world of pain, my boy. Trust me on that. Now let's watch the race. Enjoy a little break from home."

Dad got two of the three horses right that race, but his other horse finished a distant sixth. "Shit," he muttered, tossing his ticket on the floor. "That was the one that was supposed to be the sure bet."

Dad didn't end up winning a single race. We drove home most of the way listening to some country-and-western radio station.

"How's school going, Leo?" he eventually asked me.

"Fine, I guess," I told him.

"You like Ladue more than Central?"

"Definitely," I assured him.

"Feel like this was a good move for the family?"

"For sure."

Then Dad suddenly shifted the topic. "I've been thinking over what we talked about on the ride over here."

"About what?"

"About you and your brother."

"What about it?" I asked.

"You seem a little angry sometimes," he observed.

"Am I supposed to feel guilty when I'm angry at him?"

"Christ, Leo." He sighed. "Of course not. I guess all I'm saying is, we've all got our own stuff we have to deal with, son—your mother and I, you and Caleb. Trust me on that."

We drove the rest of the way home in silence. When we pulled into the garage, Mom's car was gone.

Dad plucked his cell phone from the glove compartment and checked his messages. "Shit!" he yelled, smacking the steering column. "Shit! Shit! Shit!"

"What's wrong?"

"Your brother had another seizure," he told me. "I'm heading to the hospital. You stay here."

Grandma told me about Caleb's seizure after Dad left. Caleb wasn't breathing for several minutes. His face was still blue when the ambulance hauled him off to the hospital, and she hadn't heard anything from Mom since.

Around midnight I heard the door slam. I headed upstairs to find out what was going on. Dad came into the kitchen, went directly to the cabinet, and poured himself a drink. "I think Caleb is going to be all right," he said finally. "The doctors figured he had another 'tonic-clonic' seizure, the kind that takes over the entire brain and causes convulsions. This one was more extreme and lasted longer than that last one."

That Monday Mom spent most of her birthday at the hospital with Caleb. His neurologists ran a bunch of tests with crazy names and abbreviations and prescribed new medications with so many syllables, I couldn't even pronounce them. When Mom and Dad asked the doctors about what the outlook was for him, there were no definitive answers. The seizures might continue to be few and far between but severe, or the medicine might keep him seizure-free. If he was lucky, he might outgrow them after his teens and never have one again, or they might get worse. The bottom line was that they didn't have a clue.

Caleb came back from the hospital a couple of days later, after Grandma and Grandpa had already left. It didn't take long for Caleb to get his energy back and return to his routines. He understood that the seizures knocked him on his ass for a couple of days and he needed to take his medication, but he didn't want anything in his life to change, or anything to get in the way of the things that made him happy. I think Mom and Dad felt the same way. For all my parents' differences, at least they were in agreement about that.

34.

THAT MONDAY ALSO MARKED the first day of the track season.

Maybe it was an omen that the sky dumped a thick blanket of wet snow. The baseball diamonds, soccer fields, and track were a mess of white slush. About fifty guys gathered in the gym in a section of bleachers. I spotted some guys from the cross-country team and recognized a few of the football players and some wrestlers. Rosenthal and Stuper were there, but Rasmussen and Burpee said they were over their heads with their AP classes and upcoming mock exams, so they were going to skip track to focus on school. I looked around, kind of expecting to see Glusker, thinking he might be a guy who liked to heave heavy objects, but I was relieved to see that wasn't the case.

I spotted Curtis seated amid a few guys I didn't recognize and made my way up the bleachers toward him.

"Coughlin, allow me to introduce you to Koprovika and Isenberg. They're in my AP Physics 2 class," he explained. "I think I've persuaded these promising juniors that track and field provides them with a unique opportunity to apply the laws of mechanics and physics to human athleticism."

Koprovika was a tall, lanky guy wearing Coke-bottle glasses

who I recognized from the library. Isenberg was short and muscular, dark in complexion, and one of those guys who seemed to have a permanent five o'clock shadow. They seemed skeptical of Curtis.

"I've recruited Koprovika as a potential high jumper," Curtis continued. "Because of his body structure and keen intellect, I've encouraged him to explore the connection between center-of-mass and aerodynamic forces involved with jumping vertically," he told me as I shook Koprovika's hand. Koprovika rolled his eyes.

"Isenberg has a slightly more challenging task with the discus," Curtis continued. "He must integrate centrifugal force, potential energy, and optimum angle, not to mention endure endless conversation with Gorsky."

Koprovika cut to the chase. "We're basically doing this to put it on our college applications," he explained.

"What about school spirit and pride?" Curtis pleaded. "You two might provide us with the few points we need to avoid another last-place finish in conference!"

Gorsky went over basic expectations and the season schedule and then announced that due to the crappy weather we'd work out inside, alternating between running hallways and lifting weights.

"This is bullshit," Curtis moaned. "Only wusses run indoors."

Stuper glanced nervously at Rosenthal and nodded. "Then we'll be joining the wusses today, Curtis," Rosenthal said.

I followed Curtis outside to the custodians' building. He

demanded two snow shovels from an old guy behind a desk, who handed them over with a simple "Be my guest."

"I'll be damned if I spend the first day of track season running hallways," Curtis told me. Wearing only our sweatshirts and shorts, we spent a half hour clearing a lane on the track, then tossed the shovels and began an eight-lap warm-up.

The early-March air was still bitter cold, with a crosswind that belted the breath out of us. It stung our hamstrings and calves from one direction and whipped our faces from the other. After the warm-up, we ran sixteen 400s on a minute recovery, switching the lead each time to give each other a break from the wind. Curtis wore his watch, and after glancing at our split after the first lap, he cursed. "We're not paying attention to times today. It's only going to piss us off."

Curtis couldn't resist his obsession with data, though. I heard his watch beep at the start of each 400, and again as we crossed the finish line. He cursed nonstop because our times weren't meeting his expectations. When we finished, our cheeks and thighs were seared red and swollen from the elements.

"Between this miserable wind and the crap snow on the track, maybe we should just be happy with finishing this workout, Curtis," I offered.

He said nothing as we began an eight-lap cooldown. "Perhaps," he finally said. "But we're going to have to do a shitload better than this. Especially you."

March often delivered its nastiest weather to St. Louis. Just when you thought spring might be arriving, it would turn cold again and sometimes snow. There was even the occasional tornado. The fields, streets, and track were wet and slushy. Our shoes and feet were numb from the cold and wet, and our quads were tight and sore from the constant backsplash of slush.

Gorsky managed the large track numbers by posting the week's workouts for sprinters, jumpers, throwers, and distance runners on a large bulletin board outside his office on Mondays. While I always took a glance at the board to get an idea where we were headed, I knew Curtis would revise the plan with Gorsky to make our workouts more challenging. We'd be doing something similar to the group, he assured me, but he always tweaked it. That meant we would be going slightly farther, target interval splits a bit faster, and suffer recovery periods a bit shorter. There were days when I questioned the pain and suffering, but Curtis confirmed it would all be worth it once the season broke open in three weeks.

As much as I hated that queasy, nervous feeling I got before racing, I kind of missed it at the same time. I started looking forward to once more stepping up to the starting line, hearing that pistol crack, feeling a rush of adrenaline, and pushing myself to the limit.

35.

I WAS SLATED TO DOUBLE in the 800 and 1600 in the first meet of the track season on Saturday at the Webster Groves Dan Sebben Invitational. Curtis would run the 3200, the next-to-last event of the day. We left early from school, and athletes segregated themselves on the bus by events. Sprinters, hurdlers, and jumpers occupied the back of the bus, and throwers spanned the middle. Most guys used the journey to catch a few more winks or to zone out to music on their headphones.

Curtis and I got wedged into the front of the bus, sandwiched between Stuper and Rosenthal in the seat ahead of us and Koprovika and Isenberg behind us. I sipped from a thermos of coffee as Curtis lectured me on the nuances of track.

"Track is a completely different animal, Leo," he told me. "Guys who couldn't catch me on the cross-country course last fall can kick my ass on the oval. And I can accept that, knowing that I can still look in the mirror each night and remind myself that I am the reigning state cross-country champion," he said sagely.

I lifted my thermos to him. "Long live the king," I toasted. "You sound a little melodramatic. Shouldn't you be a little more confident?"

"Young Leo, my mission during my time on this planet was completed in November," he told me.

I laughed.

"Oh, don't you worry, Leo. Alas, I, too, will have brief, fleeting moments of glory this track season," he told me. "But my finely tuned machine was designed to conquer distances longer than the mere thirty-two hundred meters offered by a track competition. And much more challenging terrain than the flat four-hundred-meter oval."

"Is that right?"

"That I know for sure," he said. "However, young Leo, you might just have a shot at excelling at track's glory event. So I do bequeath the oval kingdom to you."

I humored him. "Tell me more, o wise one."

"The 1600. The metric mile. The marquee event for track aficionados the world over. Sprint enthusiasts might beg to differ, but runners of our ilk believe the mile is the true demarcation of athletic supremacy on the track oval, for it requires both speed and stamina."

"Qualities you think I now possess?"

"Mind you, I can certainly kick your ass in any longer distance, Leo."

"You never fail to remind me."

"But you have the tools to dominate this race. You're strong enough, and you've got raw speed."

"So why not the 800? It seems a whole lot easier to run two laps versus four."

"Don't flatter yourself," he said, laughing. "You're fast, but you're not that fast."

"Seriously, what's your real advice for today?" I asked him.

"When the gun goes off, run as fast as you can."

"That simple?"

"Yep. It's your first track race, Leo. Just run and learn."

Things were looking up in Curtis's world. The previous week he'd finally made a commitment to run at Haverford College in Pennsylvania. Although he was tempted by an offer from a small college in the Rocky Mountains, he told me he'd decided to consider his life beyond running. Haverford had a top-notch Division III cross-country program and excellent academics, a perfect match for him. The school had a pretty hefty price tag, but they managed to assemble a package for him that he couldn't turn down.

The bus dumped us out beside the track. We schlepped our bags to a section of bleachers, then ran a few slow laps to shake out the cobwebs from the bus ride.

The track oval felt like a three-ring circus. High jumpers were at one end of the tarmac, marking their steps with white medical tape, and the long jumpers did the same on a slice of runway adjacent to the homestretch. On the opposite side, pole-vaulters were gauging the precise location for their take-offs. And on the far corners, the throwers stood around concrete rings heaving shots and discs. While some sprinters executed drills over a compressed sequence of hurdles set up on the backstretch, others just hung out in the bleachers listening to headphones and tightening spikes. Some guys did nothing at all but lie on benches with closed eyes, trying to absorb a little warmth from a sun still making its way up the sky on a chilly April morning.

"Nervous?" Curtis asked.

I surveyed the scene again. "I am now. There are a hell of a lot more people here than at your typical cross-country meet."

"The track oval is an athletic stage," Curtis noted grandly. "Unlike cross-country, you're on display for everyone, my friend." He swept one hand across the entire venue. "Consider this your grand debut."

The 1600 was the fourth event, following a relay and a couple of sprints. I was a mess. The butterflies were beating against the walls in my stomach, and by the time they announced the first call for the 1600, I tasted the orange juice I drank three hours ago snaking its way up into my throat.

I was going nearly out of my mind before my race when I spotted Mary across the track. She was looking supercool but relaxed in her old faded jeans, black Chucks, and a gray hoodie. I waved and jogged over to her. "What are you doing here?"

She rolled her eyes at me. "I came to watch those big thugs over there whip heavy objects," she said, nodding toward the shot ring. "What do you think I'm doing here, Leo? I came to watch you run."

"You didn't have to come all the way out here to see me run a mile."

She stepped forward, put her arms around me, and pressed her nose to mine. "I wanted to come, Leo. Why can't you just be okay with that? I don't care if you're running for only five minutes. I like to watch you."

"Hopefully it will be less than five minutes," I told her with a grin.

She kissed me quickly. "Good luck," she whispered in my ear.

"I've got to get ready," I finally said to her before starting my last warm-up, one that included a quick pit stop behind an equipment shed to puke up what was left of my breakfast.

The meet director kept the order and the tempo of the day with clarity and precision. The announcements for first, second, and final calls for track and field events were constant. When I heard the last call for the 1600, I did one last stride on the backstretch, then jogged over to the starting line and checked in with the marshal. The morning air was still crisp and cold, so I kept my sweats on until the last minute.

They crammed twenty-four of us onto the curved line, three to a lane for a waterfall start. I looked up into the bleachers and spotted Dad sitting alone two rows in front of Mom6. My heart was pounding and my gut was churning. I reminded myself to get out quick and not get boxed in by the pack, but when the pistol cracked and the race started, it was clear that every other guy in the race had a plan just as urgent as mine. We ran as a herd, flailing knees and elbows, stretching hands, tapping and shoving shoulders and fists, in order to keep balance and hold position. After two hundred meters the pack thinned out a bit, and I was able to thread my way to the front with five other guys. A space opened and I lengthened my stride and focused on breathing. The butterflies were gone. Now I was locked in and just running.

We passed through the first lap, and the counter on the inside posted a large number three, a reminder of how many laps remained. A timer inside the rail showed the seconds that had elapsed so far: 67...68...69...70.

I saw Curtis at the turn, standing beside Koprovika and Isenberg, who was gripping his discus in one hand and a hot dog in the other.

"It's slow, Leo!" Curtis screamed. "Pick it up."

I thought the pace felt a hell of a lot faster than any cross-country race, so I hung with the pack another lap, only to be yelled at again by Curtis as we passed through the half in 2:16. "You've got to be kidding me, Coughlin," he wailed.

Part of me was tempted to tell Isenberg to smack Curtis in the head with the discus, but instead I decided to find some guts and take the lead. I waited until we completed the first curve, surged to the outside until I had a couple of strides on the pack, then slipped back in along the rail. Since no one went with me, I held my position and didn't press the pace. I stayed strong and calm as we ran the back turn, then accelerated as I strode into the homestretch. The lap counter on the infield signaled just one more to go. As we approached the final lap, the clanging bell pierced my ears. I didn't hear a split, Curtis's voice ... anything. But some of the other runners must have gotten juiced on adrenaline from the sound of the bell, because suddenly three of them swallowed me. It was like the race was starting all over again.

Before I knew it, I had slipped back into fourth. I was looking at the backs of three guys who couldn't touch me during the cross-country season. I wondered what the hell was going on, but I didn't hesitate to react. I slowed a bit to give the pack some room and then veered to the outside so I could pass again on the first turn. When I heard Curtis yell, I second-guessed myself but continued to accelerate. By the time we hit the backstretch I had a five-meter gap on the pack, but I also got slapped by a nasty headwind that came out of nowhere. I held my lead until the turn and then heard the rumble of the pack closing in. My shoulders tightened, and my legs felt like the blood inside was turning into sludge.

The pack caught me on the curb, and three runners eased by me. I could see the finish line now, just a hundred meters ahead, and I was able to dig deep enough to hang tight to the back of the bunch. But with fifty meters left, two runners dropped an extra gear and pulled away. I managed to pass one guy and finished third in 4:32.

I staggered ten meters past the finish line, bent over, grabbed my knees for support, and gasped for oxygen. "Not bad, Leo," Curtis said, lifting my arms from behind so I could stand upright.

"That didn't look like too much fun," Isenberg commented, taking a bite from his hot dog.

"It wasn't," I said, wheezing. "It totally sucked."

"Switch to discus," he told me. "Just three throws—I didn't even break a sweat."

"And you didn't make the finals, where you'd have the grueling task of throwing three more times," Curtis informed him. "Maybe you would have broken a sweat then."

Isenberg gnawed some more on his hot dog and considered Curtis's insult. "I'm content with my debut," he finally answered.

"Keep walking, buddy," Curtis encouraged me.

"I'll see you guys later," Isenberg said. "I've walked far enough today."

"I don't get it," I whined to Curtis. "I killed those guys in cross-country. Today they're right with me. And we trained all winter."

"What you learned just now is that you ran a respectable 4:32 1600. And hopefully what you'll remember is that there are plenty of other guys who can do that, too." He laughed. "Start wrapping your head around that."

I looked up into the stands and spotted Mom and Dad and gave them a simple thumbs-up that I was okay.

"How come your parents don't sit next to each other?" he asked me.

"I don't know," I told him. "How come your parents don't even show up?"

"Touché."

I gathered up my sweats, and Curtis joined me for a slow jog to shake out the lactic acid in my legs. "If you run this race twenty seconds faster, nobody will touch you," he told me.

It took a moment to process. My legs began to come back to life, but my lungs still felt roasted. "How am I going to do that?"

"Your first lap was pathetic, Leo," he reminded me. "As a matter of fact, so were the second and third." He was now laughing again. "You've just got to run faster. Go from the gun. It's as simple as that."

We jogged in silence for a few minutes. "I don't know, Curtis," I finally told him. "That really hurt."

"It's always going to hurt. How much pain are you willing to take?"

Curtis put in a far more impressive performance than I did in his season debut. Despite his sad soliloquy earlier that morning, he won the 3200 easily. Granted, the competition wasn't as stiff as in the 1600, but he still outpaced the rest of the field easily by nearly twenty-five seconds.

Track was a completely different animal. I got my ass handed to me that day in the 1600, and again in the 800. It didn't help at all that Mary had shown up to witness it.

She hung out until after the meet, wanting to give me a ride home. Curtis took our bags and tossed them in her car. "We're running back to school," he told her. "Lover boy won't be available for another hour."

I looked at Curtis, and I looked at Mary sitting comfortably in her car. "Sorry, Curtis," I told him. "You're running this one alone. I got beat up enough today."

"You're getting soft, Coughlin," he chided.

"I promise extra miles tomorrow," I said as I slammed the door.

"Leo Coughlin standing up for himself!" Mary laughed as we left Curtis in the parking lot. "Never thought I'd see the day."

"I probably should be running, but I'm trashed," I admitted.

"Let's do something," she said.

"I'm sorry, Mary, but I promised my parents I'd pick up Caleb from swimming. He's at the Mid-County Y."

She tapped her fingers on the steering wheel. By now I knew that meant that her mind was at work. "Let's pick him up now, then pick your car up at school," she offered. "I'll follow you to your house. That way we gain at least an hour."

"There's one slight glitch in that plan."

"What's that?" she asked.

"Caleb might have an issue if we arrive early and cut into his swimming time."

She dismissed my concern. "No worries. I'll handle it."

I spotted Caleb launching off the high dive, doing his signature corkscrew, when we arrived. From the balcony waiting area, I let Mary observe Caleb's routine for a few minutes. Of course, the window provided a noise barrier, so Mary missed the sound element of Caleb's performance. Still, she looked pretty bewildered. "That's quite an impressive display," she remarked.

"My father describes it as a unique combination of athleticism and performance art."

"I don't think I've ever seen anything like it."

"You're not alone, Mary. He has perfected this high-dive routine over the years, and he's made it truly one of a kind."

"What is he yelling?"

"You don't want to know." Caleb tended to scream his deepest, darkest confessions while in midflight, but I figured Mary didn't need that information.

We watched him jump a few more times.

"I'll go get him," she finally said.

"Good luck with that."

Caleb spotted Mary on the deck as he climbed out of the deep end. He ran over to her and said something while pointing to the diving board. Then he scrambled up the ladder and thundered off the board, this time without screaming. She applauded when he surfaced, encouraging him to continue.

I watched as he plunged into the water and lingered below the surface. I wondered why he loved swimming so much. Was it the moment of impact and splash? Did he simply love moving in a liquid medium? Or maybe it was because water provided him with a nearly noiseless world, where vision blurred and there were few distractions?

After Caleb's fifth jump, Mary met him at the ladder and said a few words to him. He calmly collected his towel and disappeared into the locker room. Somehow she had convinced him to cut his pool time by twenty minutes. Astonishing.

"What did you say to him?" I asked her when she returned.

"I just asked him if he wouldn't mind if we left a little early."

"That's it?"

She put her arms around me and smiled. "Leo, I don't think *what* I said had anything to do with it. I think it's *how* I said it."

"You need to teach me how to do that."

"No," she answered, wrinkling her nose. "I need for you to take a shower."

"That seems like a fair deal."

36.

ONCE TRACK SEASON GOT INTO FULL SWING and winter was gone for good, it felt awesome to fully immerse my mind and body in even more intense training. The rest of April brought a heavy dose of intervals: 300s, 400s, 600s. We always finished with a series of 150s to simulate the ends of races. Curtis insisted I needed to build the muscle memory necessary to dig deeper, reach for that last gear, and harness and unleash a kick. Even when every ounce of energy seemed to be sapped from me.

My body was strong from winter training. The countless long runs in the cold and darkness began to pay off. My skin, muscles, and bones were hardened by the snow, cold, wind, sleet, and slush. Curtis still owned me at any distance beyond the 1600, but he could no longer keep up with me during interval sessions. He decreased the recovery period, but I still outran him. So he devised workouts where he took various leads and I chased him down, and I developed new skills and strategies to apply in races.

As he promised, the 1600 did become my race. I followed his advice and ran the first two laps more aggressively and pushed the pace, and sure enough nobody had the strength left to run with me in the end. I ran 800s and 3200s to improve my speed and strength, but I owned the 1600. By mid-April I had shaved thirteen seconds off my personal best, winning the 1600 at the Kirkwood invite in 4:19.

"Not bad, Leo," Curtis congratulated me. "But your work is far from done."

We decided to opt out of the bus ride home after that meet to get in a slow seven-miler.

"Take ten or eleven more seconds off and you've got a legitimate shot at winning state," he told me.

I counted off ten seconds in my head as we continued running. The distance covered in that time seemed overwhelming. "Ten seconds is impossible, Curtis."

He laughed. "Once it gets even warmer in May and this wind disappears, you'll be a different runner. Believe me."

We took a right turn onto Clayton toward school and were rewarded with one more cold blast of April wind.

I counted off ten seconds again and again in my head as we took turns breaking the headwind on our run home.

Ten seconds seemed quantum.

37.

WHEN DAD FINALLY EXITED the interstate to Fort Leonard Wood, we still had to drive another five miles past one dismal strip mall after another. At a brief stop at a traffic light, I surveyed the local businesses: a couple of gas stations, a Chinese restaurant, a few convenience stores, the usual assortment of fast-food choices, some pawnshops, and a whole bunch of flashing red signs advertising massage parlors.

"What's up with all the massage parlors?" I whispered to Dad.

"There are about ten thousand young men on that military base. And very few women. Do I have to give you a lesson on the birds and the bees, Leo?"

"Please spare him, Niles," Mom mumbled from the backseat.

"Never mind, Dad," I assured him. "I think I get it."

The Fort Leonard Wood entrance was heavily guarded by several uniformed soldiers. Dad rolled down the window, explained who we were and why we were there, and handed over some paperwork. The soldiers gave us a stamped pass, and we were allowed entry.

Caleb had arrived the day before by school bus. Kids like him were coming from all across the state to compete in the Special Olympics, and Fort Leonard Wood was providing the venue and lodging.

I'd never been on an army base before, but it was nothing like I had imagined. Most of the soldiers we saw didn't look much older than me. They looked pretty pudgy and pasty, not exactly the prime specimens featured in those commercials that promised to sculpt your abs and sharpen your computer skills if you decided to become a member of the armed forces. And their uniforms weren't the neat, crisp, shiny numbers you see on TV either.

"Is this it?" I was in disbelief.

"What were you expecting?" Dad said. "This isn't exactly West Point."

Dad, Mom, and I passed one identical building after another. Whoever painted this place clearly didn't have too many colors to choose from. I'd never seen so much brown and beige in my life. "What was being in the army like, Dad?" I asked.

"Let's just say I wasn't cut out for the military," he mumbled. "I doubt you are either," he added.

We followed signs for the Special Olympics through a maze of roads to a large athletic field. There was a cinder track that had definitely seen better days and a set of tired-looking wooden bleachers in dire need of a coat of paint. The competition began in a half hour, and the place was starting to fill with spectators.

We took our seats as the athletes were herded into lines on the far side of the track. A small flag corps marched to midfield for the playing of the national anthem. The sound system malfunctioned, and the music got painfully loud and distorted, but everyone held their hands over their hearts and managed to keep their eyes fixed on the flag.

The athletes paraded down the track in front of the bleachers where my parents and I sat packed beside other families. They waved to the crowd while a military march piped through the sound system. Mom's eyes got all misty when she spotted Caleb. "He's come a long way," she reminded me softly as she put her arm around me. "Trust me on that, Leo."

I waved to Caleb and gave him a thumbs-up. His event started in an hour. He was running the 1600—the same event I ran, of course.

"Why don't you go give your brother some encouraging words," Dad told me. "He can use all the pointers he can get after that last fiasco."

Dad was referring to Caleb's qualification meet a couple of weeks back. He was running against another kid from his school named Kevin. The entire race, Caleb ran on Kevin's heels. Every time he'd begin to run around Kevin, Caleb would suddenly slow back down and tuck himself back behind Kevin. Something was definitely up, because Caleb was running slower than usual and should have easily kicked Kevin's ass.

"KEVIN SAY DON'T PASS! RIGHT!" he told us after the race. "STAY BEHIND KEVIN! MAKE KEVIN ANGRY! RIGHT!" Fortunately both Kevin and Caleb got to move on to this event.

I spotted Caleb on the infield, sitting next to Kevin. "I think we went over that with him, Dad. He knows he's not supposed to let Kevin win."

"It's not going to hurt to remind him again, Leo. Just go warm him up," Dad encouraged me.

I left the bleachers, walked out to the field, and asked Caleb to follow me beyond the track, toward some barracks. When I told him we were going to do a little warm-up, Caleb accelerated several strides and broke into a series of crazy hops, skips, and jumps like a wild bull that had just been released in a rodeo. I thought this might be the first time Caleb was actually nervous about something.

"You need to calm down a bit," I warned him. "Just jog slowly next to me."

"JOG SLOW! RIGHT!" he repeated.

"Try not to skip or hop, Caleb," I directed him. "Try to run like this," I said, taking long strides and slightly exaggerating the pumping of my arms. Caleb ran beside me, his form still awkward, but with the skipping and hopping toned down.

"POKE LEO'S EYEBALLS OUT MIDDLE OF THE NIGHT!" he yelled.

"Let's not talk about that now, Caleb."

"SORRY, LEO! WHAT SORRY MEAN?" he asked.

"Sorry means God not punish you," I assured him.

The last thing I wanted right now was a major temper tantrum, Caleb chasing me around a military base trying to kill me. I tried to redirect him. "When that gun goes off, go fast, but not too fast," I told him. "Stand beside me and do what I do," I said to him. "We're on the starting line, and the starter will say . . . ," I began.

Caleb loved this part. "MARK! SET! GO!" he screamed, and then began laughing.

"That's right," I said, and I was laughing too. "And you want to start about this fast," I told him, grabbing his hand and pulling him along at what I thought was a manageable pace. We ran about a hundred meters, then stopped and headed back toward the track. "And remember, Caleb, don't listen to Kevin. You run in front of Kevin. Not behind him."

"DON'T LISTEN KEVIN. RIGHT!" he repeated.

"That's right," I said. "I think it's almost time for your race." I walked Caleb over to the starting area and checked him in.

The girls' 1600 was before Caleb's race. As it turned out there was only one girl in the entire race, and she was making it very clear to everyone present that she wanted no part of it.

"Margaret does not want to do this," she said to herself.

Margaret wasn't very tall, and she didn't look particularly athletic. She had planted herself firmly on the ground, her arms crossed, shaking her head and repeating, "Margaret does not want to do this."

A burly man in jeans and an auto mechanic's shirt tried to convince Margaret otherwise. He tried to pull her up by her shoulders, but she wouldn't budge. "C'mon, Margaret, honey," he pleaded. "You said you wanted to do this. We drove you five hours to get here. We know you can do this, sweetheart! Your grandmother and auntie came clear across the state to come see this. You don't want to let them down, do you?"

Margaret just kept shaking her head. "Margaret does not want to do this," she said again and again.

Her father was clearly at a loss. I sensed he was about to lose his patience, so I stepped forward. "Margaret, do you want someone to run with you? Would that help?" I asked her.

It was like I cast a spell on her. Margaret got herself up off the ground and followed me to the starting line, still repeating in monotone, "Margaret does not want to do this. Margaret *really* does not want to do this."

I explained the situation to the starter: if he wanted to keep the meet running on time and complete this event on schedule, it was in everyone's best interest to let me run beside Margaret.

Then her father came over and put the matter in plainer words. "Our family traveled nearly five hours from Rutledge to get here, and her great aunties traveled three and a half hours from Kirksville. We'd really appreciate anything you all can do. For once in her life, I'd like for my girl to win, to increase her confidence. Even if she doesn't have to beat anyone to do it."

"I'll run beside her and help her out," I offered again. "It's going to be a challenge for her to do this by herself."

The officials agreed and we got Margaret on the starting line as she continued to chant her mantra: "Margaret does not want to do this."

"Yes, Margaret," I answered, "I've heard you, but I know you can do it. You're just a little nervous, that's all."

That little encouragement perked something in Margaret. When the gun sounded, she actually started to run, albeit very slowly. It took us nearly fifteen minutes to run the four laps around the track, and the entire way she continually asserted, "Margaret does not want to do this."

I ran beside her and tried to persuade her otherwise. "You can do this, Margaret."

The last lap took an eternity. When we hit the homestretch

and I saw the tape stretched across the finish line, I told Margaret, "All you have to do is get across that finish line and you're done."

The crowd was now standing and urging Margaret along. Margaret responded to the situation by changing her mantra. "Way to go, Margaret. Way to go," she repeated to herself in the same monotone.

I stopped ten meters from the finish line when I was sure Margaret was going to stay on course. She came to a halt for a moment and looked at the crowd and realized the ovation was for her. Her father was standing on the other side of the finish line with his arms open. Finally, Margaret smiled and ran toward him.

He put up his hand for a high five, and she slapped his open palm with delight. Her father lifted her up in a giant bear hug. He looked over his shoulder at me and silently mouthed, "Thank you."

Caleb had already been marshaled to the starting line and was standing with Kevin and five other boys. I walked over to him and asked him if he was ready.

"YES!" he shouted.

"Do you remember what we talked about?"

"DON'T LISTEN KEVIN!"

"Good luck, Caleb," I told him, and I made my way back to the bleachers and my parents. It was now dusk. The field lights came on and gave the atmosphere an eerie glow.

"How's your brother doing?" Dad asked. I think Dad was more nervous than Caleb.

"I think he's okay," I told him. "A little wound up at the moment. I gave him a plan, and I think he gets it."

The soldiers in camouflage arranged Caleb and his competitors on the starting line like horses at the gate. When the gun fired, Caleb took off in a full sprint—only he added a skip into every few strides and held his arms flush against the side of his body. He was running like he urgently needed a toilet.

"What the hell is he doing?" Dad said in confusion.

"That was not the plan," I assured Dad.

We watched Caleb take an enormous lead on the rest of the field. When he came through the first lap, I estimated he had two hundred meters on the other runners.

Mom grabbed my hand and squeezed tightly. "I'm worried he's going to collapse if he continues at this rate," she said. Midway through the second lap, that was exactly what happened.

Dad didn't say anything. We just watched as Caleb slowly began to implode. First his shoulders tightened, then he no longer lifted his knees, and finally he slowed almost to a crawl.

"Oh, no," Dad whispered.

"He might be all right," I tried reassuring them. "I've been there. If he doesn't stop, he might recover and be able to pull it off."

Caleb struggled, but he continued running and held his lead up until midway through the third lap. Then one boy who started at a sensible pace eventually caught him. They completed the third lap together and then Caleb simply had nothing left in the tank. The boy took over the lead for good and won the race easily. The rest of the pack was too far back, so Caleb was able to hold on for second place.

We made our way down to the track to take some up-close pictures of Caleb receiving his medal on the podium.

"DAD VERY PROUD OF YOU!" he shouted. "MOM PROUD OF YOU!"

"Hell, yes! I'm very proud of you, Caleb," Dad said.

"LEO PROUD OF CALEB!" he yelled.

"I'm proud of you too," I told him.

"TAKE LEO TO SIX FLAGS!" he yelled. "MY MONEY! I PAY!"

"You don't have to do that, Caleb," I answered, suddenly having a flashback of the tantrum he had last time we went to Six Flags when he found out that the water park wasn't open yet.

"TAKE LEO TO SIX FLAGS!" he repeated.

I glanced at Dad and Mom. Dad shrugged his shoulders at me like it was my call, but Mom's eyebrows were raised with hope.

"That sounds great, Caleb," I told him.

Caleb then turned to Dad. "DAD TAKE CALEB OUT TO DINNER!"

"Your wish is my command," Dad said. "Where to?"

"FISH-AND-CHIPS! Long John Silver's!" Caleb yelled.

"You bet!" Dad assured him.

As Caleb climbed into the car, Dad glanced over at Mom and me. "I'll drive. You two start praying that damn restaurant is still open."

"Aye-aye, captain," I joked, but I started praying.

38.

THE NEXT WEEK CALEB MUST have confirmed our plans to go to Six Flags a thousand times. The first thing I did when I rolled out of bed Sunday morning was check the weather on my phone: overcast with a chance of thundershowers.

Crap.

Caleb and I went to Six Flags once a year. As kids we went with Mom and Dad, but for the last four years Caleb and I had gone alone. Caleb knew exactly when the place opened, the length of time it took for travel, when the lines would begin to form. The park was a good forty-five-minute drive from the house, so we had to leave early.

Mom and Dad were practically giddy that Caleb and I were headed out for the day at Caleb's initiative. When the two of us rolled upstairs that morning, Mom was at the stove making pancakes, Dad at the table with his paper. The day before I'd finally cracked 4:18 in the 1600 at the Clayton invite and was headed to districts the following week.

"What ride will you go on first?" Mom asked Caleb.

"RIDE SCREAMIN' EAGLE!" he said, laughing. The Eagle was this classic roller coaster that went sixty-two miles an hour with three death drops. Caleb loved the thrill rides, the ones that shook and rattled his insides, the ones that plummeted from high distances, the ones with countless loops and twists, the ones that accelerated to blazing speeds, the ones that scared the shit out of most people. But he loved the roller coasters most of all. When my parents used to take us to the park years earlier, we'd sometimes wait in lines for an hour for the two-minute thrill, only to dash back and get in line for another go. Usually Caleb couldn't deal with long lines, but for some reason at Six Flags he could stand in line forever.

"And after that?"

"MR. FREEZE! NINJA! DRAGON'S WING!" he shouted. As he reeled off our agenda for the day, my stomach lurched and I began taking smaller bites of pancake and chewing slowly. While Caleb had a stomach of steel, I was prone to bouts of motion sickness. I once lost it on the Ninja and nearly sprayed partially digested funnel cakes on the man and woman in the car in front of us.

"WHAT TIME PICK MARY UP?" Caleb suddenly blurted while scraping the syrup from his plate.

I dropped my fork and looked at Mom and Dad, making a facial expression I hoped clearly communicated that Caleb never mentioned this part of the invitation. He just assumed. When Caleb blasted out of the kitchen to go brush his teeth, I launched into it with Mom and Dad.

"You know there's a chance of thunderstorms today," I told them as I took our plates to the sink.

"Only a twenty percent chance, according to Sunny Munson on channel four," Mom said calmly.

"And late in the day," Dad reassured me.

I pressed the issue. "And what if it does rain?"

"You're being a pessimist," Dad said.

"Why do you always assume that something is going to go wrong?" Mom asked.

"I think I have a right to assume that something might go wrong!" I shot back. "What if Mother Nature decides not to cooperate with Caleb's plans?"

"So? What if?" Dad asked.

Their optimism and denial began to piss me off. "I think I have a right to assume that he might want to beat the crap out of me if something doesn't go his way," I shot back. "And I don't want that to happen at Six Flags, especially in front of Mary!"

"You need to lower your voice with us right now," Dad said.

"I'm pissed!" I shouted, rinsing the sticky syrup from our plates before slamming them in the dish rack. I took a deep breath, trying to calm myself.

"Sit down," Dad said, motioning toward the table.

I stood my ground and crossed my arms. "I'm sorry," I mumbled, with little apology in my tone.

"I think you need to realize that this day is very important to your brother," Mom said.

"I think it's more like this day is very important to both of you," I argued.

"Fine," Dad huffed, balling up his napkin and tossing it on his plate. "I'll take your brother to Six Flags."

"I hope you're not trying to be serious," I told him. "Like that's an option at this point. I'm already in."

"Listen," Dad said calmly, "if it will make you feel better, I'm willing to drive out there and sit in the parking lot. I've got plenty of work I can do. If anything happens, all you have to do is call me."

Dad was throwing me a rescue net, but he was also making me feel like a coward. If I took his offer, I was being a pessimist, and I wasn't upping my game.

"No, I'm good," I told him, trying to shake off my frustration. I wanted out of the conversation. "I think you're right," I said, glancing at the time on my phone and realizing Caleb would want to get going. "Hopefully everything will be just fine."

I stepped into the den and tried to get a grip on myself before calling Mary. With Dad's line that life is always going to throw you curveballs echoing in my head, I picked up my phone and hit the speed dial. "Hey," I said when she answered, "this is probably the last call you want to get early on a Sunday morning."

"What?" she answered, sounding groggy. "What happened? Is something wrong?"

"No," I told her. "It's nothing like that."

Caleb then appeared holding a thick stack of dollar bills in one hand and his black fanny pack in his other. "PAY WITH OWN MONEY!"

"Caleb would like to ask you something," I explained, then, in a cowardly move, handed the phone to him.

"HI, MARY! GO TO SIX FLAGS! TWENTY-FIVE MINUTES. RIGHT! CALEB PAY WITH OWN MONEY!" he ordered before handing me the phone.

"You gotta be freakin' kidding me, Leo," she said, sounding pissed. "I get the feeling this is not a joke. You don't even have the guts to ask me yourself?"

"Desperate times call for desperate measures" was all I could think of to say.

"Give me a few minutes if I'm not ready when you get here," she said, and hung up.

Mom was helping Caleb tuck his fanny pack under his shirt when I returned to the kitchen. "You need to hide your money, Caleb," she reminded him.

"HIDE MONEY. RIGHT!" he repeated several times as we headed out the door.

Mary, wearing tight jeans and a smile that wasn't at all convincing, was out in front of her house waiting, her hair still wet from the shower.

"It's an all-expenses-paid trip to Six Flags," I reminded her as she got in the car. "What could be better?"

———

The line was only a few families deep when we arrived. Caleb pulled out a coupon Mom had clipped from the newspaper, and his stack of dollar bills. The whole process of getting tickets took a while as he insisted on counting out the entire $105 cost of the tickets in singles.

We trailed Caleb into the park. "You'd think he'd hate this place, with the long lines and noise," I explained to Mary, "but he loves it. We only come once a year, but he has a map of it in his mind and knows it like it was tattooed on his wrist."

Caleb's itinerary was set. So he made a beeline straight for the Screamin' Eagle, with Mary and me nearly running to keep up. "RIDE WITH MARY!" he said when we'd arrived at the Eagle.

"This is as far as I go," she said, stopping at the gate. "I don't do roller coasters, Caleb. Or any thrill ride, for that matter." I could tell by the way she glanced at me that she was lying to him, and I was confused. "You and Leo are on your own. I'll be right here when you're finished."

Unlike the Fireball and Batman rides, the Eagle is one of those old-fashioned wooden roller coasters. When it's going full speed, the cars shake intensely and you feel like you're on a runaway train that's about to derail. It begins with a steep climb toward the sky, pauses at its crest momentarily to give you a view of the entire park, and then makes a steep descent downward and races through a track lined by a forest on both sides. Caleb and I laughed our heads off the entire way. Like during his twist dives at the pool, Caleb screamed out the various wrongs he'd committed in the past. I called this routine his roller-coaster confessions:

"I POKE LEO IN EYES IN MIDDLE OF NIGHT!"

"I PUT FIST THROUGH WINDOW ON COL-GATE!"

"I DRAW TRAIN TRACKS ON DINING ROOM FLOOR!"

"I PUT CAT IN MAILBOX!"

"I KICK MR. BAIMS'S DESK! MAKE MR. BAIMS VERY ANGRY!"

After several rides, including my least favorite, the Sky-Screamer, I convinced him I needed a break, so Mary took him for a slice of pizza. While I sat on an empty bench and waited for the vomity feeling to subside in my stomach, I noticed a couple of photos poking out of the backpack Mary had brought with her to the park. One was a picture of Caleb and me side by side on the Screamin' Eagle. The other was the two of us midway through the descent on the Superman Tower of Power ride, the 230-foot free fall where I involuntarily screamed like a baby the entire descent. Mary must have bought the photos at some souvenir booth while Caleb and I were on a ride. In the first we're midway through the descent of the first drop, our mouths wide open, screaming with joy, and crazed expressions in our eyes. In the other, Caleb is wearing the same expression, but I appear a little more distraught. The funny thing is that in both photos, Caleb and I have our arms raised, trying to catch more air time, but my left hand is folded inside his right, clutched so tight that it must have hurt. I guess I was so in the moment, I didn't even realize it.

When I spotted Mary and Caleb returning with their pizza, laughing and talking, I slipped the photos back into her bag, thinking maybe she wanted to surprise Caleb and me with them at the end of the day.

It was almost dusk when we finally left the park, but despite that Caleb had gorged himself on funnel cakes, pizza, and burgers and fries over the course of the day, he insisted on one final stop.

"STOP AT TED DREWES!" he announced.

"To Ted Drewes!" Mary seconded, leaning slightly toward me. "And what the hell is Ted Drewes?" she whispered.

"You've got to be kidding me—you've never heard of Ted Drewes?"

"I've heard of it. I've just never been."

"You've been deprived, Mary. It's this frozen custard stand on Chippewa. It's legendary," I explained. "But it's always packed, and it's a pain in the ass in terms of finding parking."

The lines were already long when we arrived. "Can you get me chocolate chip and banana concrete?" I asked her as we pulled up. I pulled out my wallet to fish for some cash.

"I PAY!" Caleb insisted.

I dropped them off and found a parking place in a neighborhood about a quarter mile away. When I met them a few minutes later, two fat raindrops splashed into my concrete, and seconds later it began to pour. There was no way we'd make it to the car without getting drenched.

Mary and I stood there in a panic as it began to dump, just looking at each other, not knowing what to do.

"STAND HERE!" Caleb shouted.

He was already beneath a small overhang on the side of the building, laughing himself silly as Mary and I stood there like losers in the rain. Mary hopped up next to him and I followed.

When the rain slowed a bit, we made a dash back to the car and ate the rest of our ice cream inside during the downpour. Caleb loved water any which way. He smiled and slurped through the loud drumming of the rain.

I sighed with relief when we finally dropped Mary off twenty minutes later without an incident.

"Thank you, Caleb, for a wonderful day," she said to him, then looked at me, eyebrows raised and smiling.

"I get this feeling I'm going to owe you an enormous favor," I told her.

"No," she answered slowly. "Why don't you get that?"

She dashed from the car through the pouring rain to her front door, carrying her backpack with the pictures of Caleb and me inside.

When we finally got home, Dad was sprawled out in his recliner reading the newspaper, SportsCenter muted on the television. Caleb said a quick hello and made a mad dash to the kitchen to give Mom a retell of the day's events, while I collapsed on the couch and zoned out on baseball high-lights.

"ELEVEN O'CLOCK. DRANK COCA-COLA. TWO ICE CUBES!" Caleb told my mother.

"Sounds like your brother enjoyed himself," Dad finally said, lowering his newspaper. Caleb continued shouting his minute-by-minute account over the backdrop of running water and Mom washing dishes.

"TWELVE FIFTEEN RIDE MR. FREEZE!"

By the time Caleb reached three o'clock, Dad finally snapped. "Christ, Leo! You know it drives me up the wall when he does this." Dad sighed, slapping his newspaper on his lap. "Can you at least give me an abbreviated version of the day?"

I was going to make Dad suffer a few more minutes, but then we both cracked up listening to Caleb. "No incidents," I finally told him. "I guess if I had to sum it up in a few words, we had a lot of fun."

"THREE FIFTEEN RIDE SCREAMIN' EAGLE! AGAIN!"

"I guess I owe you an apology for blowing up this morning," I admitted, keeping my eyes focused on the television.

I was waiting for the I-told-you-so, but he didn't say anything. I glanced at him. He didn't even offer a sly smirk like he was holding the winning hand. Instead, we just sat there smiling, listening to Caleb recount every last detail from the day.

39.

I WOKE UP EARLY THE MORNING of the district race and laced up my shoes for an easy two miles. I liked a slow jog before a long bus ride. It woke me up and got my insides moving and helped me take care of stuff I'd rather get done in my own bathroom. I was almost out the door before Caleb stopped me. For a moment I thought we were going to get into it.

"Run with Leo," he said.

He'd never asked to do that before. "I'm not going far," I warned.

"Run with Leo," he repeated.

So we ran together. It was just twenty minutes and we didn't say a word, mostly because I was focused on two things—wrapping my head around the race ahead and trying to use my nervous energy to focus on some intestinal motion. I picked up the pace a bit, and Caleb hung with me stride for stride down the sidewalks beneath the blooming trees. It was actually kind of cool running with my brother by my side. When we finished our run at the top of the driveway, Caleb finally broke the silence.

"When Caleb run Special Olympics?"

"You've got to wait another year, buddy," I told him. "Unfortunately your season is over."

"CALEB LONG-DISTANCE RUNNER!" He smiled.

"You're damn right you are," I assured him. "If you keep running, you'll win that race next year," I promised him.

I held up my hand to exchange a high five. We slapped hands, a legitimate smack of open palms without an ounce of aggression. Then he started laughing and continued running down the street without me.

Dad pulled into the high school right as Isenberg and the last few throwers were lugging their equipment onto the bus.

"I'm going to pick your brother up from swimming later this morning, then make a beeline over to your meet," he told me.

"Sounds like a plan," I said.

"You ready for today?"

"I'll be fine."

"Good luck, son," I heard him say as I closed the car door and made a dash for the bus.

The district qualifying meet was held at Parkway South High School. Curtis was taking advantage of the fact that the 3200 was the second-to-last race of the day and getting some extra sleep. The solitary time on the bus gave me some welcome peace and quiet. Sometimes his nonstop race-day sermons made me even more nervous.

The scene at Parkway South's parking lot looked like tribes preparing for battle: athletes in a medley of colors from schools all over the city hauling bags, poles, discuses, and shots toward the distant oval. I was making my way to the track, gym bag in hand, when the Poplar Bluff High School bus pulled up to the curb ahead of me. A bunch of maroon sweats filed out one after another onto the sidewalk.

"You Leo Coughlin?" The voice came from behind me—a slow, thick drawl.

I turned and saw a tall, lanky guy in Poplar Bluff colors approaching me. Unlike his teammates, he wasn't wearing sweats or carrying a gym bag. He was already in his track shorts, singlet, and a pair of spikes.

It was a warm May Saturday, but still, everyone wore their sweats to a meet, and nobody put on their metal spikes until a few minutes before a race. This guy had obviously worn them on the bus, and now he was clinking down the sidewalk beside me. He was looking to engage me.

"You heard me?" he barked. "I asked if you're Leo Coughlin."

"Yeah," I told him. I was about to ask him how he knew who I was, but then realized my last name was written in big black letters on my bag.

His hair was dark and oily, with bangs that draped over his eyes, so all I could see were these flaring nostrils and lips surrounded by dark, sparse mustache fuzz. His pores seemed to expand as he breathed.

"I'm going to whip your ass today, Coughlin," he told me with certainty. His spikes scraped and clanked against the concrete with each step. I just wanted him to disappear.

"You have a name?" I asked.

"I'm Arthur Fletcher," he informed me.

Only when I put out my hand for a shake did he finally retreat.

I asked Gorsky if he knew anything about the guy.

"He's trying to get inside your head before the race," he told me. "Keep your distance." Fletcher was a decent runner, he said, but I should be able to handle him. Curtis later confirmed that if I ran a strong race, Fletcher wouldn't be a problem.

By late morning it was hot, and most athletes tried to escape the sun and lie low. The Poplar Bluff team set up camp on the opposite side of the track, near a small grove of trees. Arthur Fletcher sat underneath one tree, all by himself. Whenever I looked over in his direction, he had his arms crossed and was staring at me. He was definitely getting under my skin.

Forty-five minutes before my race, I tried to work off my nervous energy with a long, thorough warm-up. I jogged, stretched, and did a few quick strides to get my heart rate up. I liked to start well before the first call, and I timed my routine by the events preceding the 1600.

The announcements for the first and second calls were made, and like me the other 1600 runners completed their preparations. But Fletcher remained parked under that tree, legs casually stretched out, eyes like knives on me. When the final call was made, Fletcher stood up, walked calmly to the starting line, and checked in.

My 4:18 1600 time made me the top seed. It was a time I'd hit consecutively in my last three races, but the third lap still plagued me. The marshal called us to the starting line and placed us in our lanes for a staggered start. We would hold our lanes for the first turn and break on the straightaway. I was in lane four, with Fletcher three lanes behind me in lane one. By midturn we would be able to gauge each other's positions and be even for the break on the straightaway.

When the gun fired, Fletcher went by me at breakneck speed, and by the time we cut down the backstretch he had nearly fifteen meters on the field. He'd extended that lead another ten meters by the time we completed the back turn. I usually went out aggressively, but Fletcher's pace was staggering. I thought he must be out of his mind.

I went through the first lap a touch over 61 seconds, meaning Fletcher probably hit 58. He was killing it. I knew I had some work to do as we headed into the second lap, but Fletcher wasn't slowing. I closed the gap by five or ten meters, but he still maintained a sizable lead. It was either his day, and he was indeed going to kick my ass, or this guy was going to collapse. When I went through the 800 in 2:07, three seconds ahead of normal pace, I felt the sear begin to well up in my chest.

Fletcher was still a good thirty meters ahead of me as I began the third lap. I knew I had to do something, so I began to press the pace. I opened my stride on the backstretch, looked down, and just started counting my strides. I knew if I counted to twenty-five, I would have covered the backstretch, and then there'd be only six hundred meters to go in this beast. Maybe I could still take Fletcher. By the time I crossed the two-hundred-meter hash before the back turn, Fletcher was just twenty meters ahead of me. I had gained ground.

As we headed into the back turn, Fletcher looked over his shoulder and saw me. He surged slightly and increased his lead. I couldn't believe the guy still had the capacity to accelerate. I could only maintain my pace at this point. We were heading into the homestretch of the third lap, and Fletcher still had a monster lead.

The bell rang well before I crossed the line for the final lap, but it provided a much-needed surge of adrenaline. Fletcher rounded the first curve, and I saw his shoulders begin to tighten, his arms begin to rise, his head begin to tilt toward his shoulder. He was getting tired. If I could maintain my form and stride, I still had a shot at reeling him in. I was dying, but he was dying more. I focused on raising my knees to increase stride length. Now I really began to close the distance between us: with two hundred meters to go, he only had fifteen meters on me. He was within striking distance now. He looked back once again over his shoulder, and his eyes were wide. He pumped his arms furiously, but his knees were barely lifting.

I got shoulder to shoulder with him as we turned into the homestretch. As I pulled beside him, he let out a gasp and I knew it was over. I still had one gear and I let him have it. I unleashed a final sprint and crashed through the finish in 4:13.

My momentum carried me another ten meters past the tape before I collapsed on the track.

I'd run the last 800 in 2:06, including a 59-second final lap, a negative split, meaning I actually got faster as I went. It was a five-second personal best, a time that I'd never thought possible, and I had qualified for sectionals and even had a shot at state.

Curtis and Gorsky met me on the track and congratulated me. I was light-headed and having problems standing. Gorsky was laughing as he helped hold me up. "Fletcher certainly gave you a run for your money, Coughlin. And guess what? You'll get to run against him again next week."

"Can't wait," I gasped. "Where was he during cross-country?"

"Academically ineligible, I assume." Gorsky chuckled.

"You'd better go with him next week," Curtis told me. "If that dude goes out again like that, he might not come back."

I looked around for Arthur and spotted him collapsed under his tree. I jogged over to him to shake hands. He was too tired to extend his arm, but he did offer me a military salute. I then looked around for my parents, but they weren't there. It was my best race of the season, and I was bummed that they'd missed it.

Curtis gave me a lift home from school after the meet. He took a close second in the 3200, earning himself a slot at state as well, but on the ride home he was focused on me. "I told you you could run 4:12, Leo. And you did it."

"I ran 4:13," I corrected him. "And it hurt like hell."

"I think it's going to take a 4:11 to win state," he told me.

As we pulled into the driveway, I spotted Mom and Dad sitting at the kitchen table. I knew something was up.

"Give me a call later on," Curtis said.

Mom and Dad didn't say a word when I walked in the house. Dad was just staring at the wall. Mom was the one who motioned me to sit down. "Your brother drowned this morning," she managed to say as I sank down in a chair, before she began sobbing.

Dad got up from the table and made a quick move toward the kitchen sink. He vomited.

40.

I DIDN'T GO TO SCHOOL THAT WEEK. As it turned out, there were all sorts of crazy things that needed to be taken care of before a funeral, especially one that no one had been expecting. It seemed like Mom and Dad were on the phone night and day, in between errands.

Dad's biggest concern for me was what I was going to wear to Caleb's wake. "It's about time we get you a new suit," he informed me during Monday night's dinner. "I want to make sure you look decent for your brother's funeral." It was a weird thing for him to be obsessing on, but I was giving both Mom and Dad plenty of space. When my grandparents arrived Tuesday afternoon, even Grandma backed off Dad and didn't give him a hard time about anything. She kept her mouth shut and focused on cleaning the house and making casseroles and pies.

It was dumping rain on Thursday night, the night of the wake, and the roads were starting to flood. Dad's car was stuck behind a large yellow dump truck moving slowly. He was getting frustrated and cursing to himself. His neck and shoulders curled toward the windshield as he wiped the fogged glass with a handkerchief. I thought he might lose it any second. Mom sat beside him with her head resting against the window.

"I think we're headed for low numbers tonight," Dad finally said.

"Huh?" I wasn't sure what he meant.

"No one goes out on a night like this," he said. "You see many cars on the road?" He looked over his shoulder at me like I was clueless.

"Christ, Niles." Mom sighed. "It's a wake, not a damn football game."

"Just figures. Your brother never could get a break, could he?"

"Does it really matter if there are 'low numbers,' Niles?" Mom said, making air quotes. She sighed. "You know, Niles, I was the one who said . . ."

Dad exploded. "Oh no, Elise. You think I haven't thought about letting him go swimming by himself? I hope to God you're—"

"Listen!" I yelled. "Both of you need to pull yourselves together right now. Can we try to act like a family for just one night? Especially this one!"

Neither of them responded. I could feel the heat coming off my face. Mom finally reached over and took Dad's hand. "All I was going to say was that I was the one who said it might be better to do this earlier in the day—when people are less tired."

Eventually Dad hit the turn signal and pulled into Kriegshauser's funeral home. Dad parked tightly against the left side of the building facing the road, so anybody passing by would see our car. We sat there for a moment with the car running and the rain blurring the windshield. Mom began weeping.

"I'm sorry, Elise," Dad said to her. "Sorry for a lot of things."

"I'm sorry too, Niles."

Dad closed his eyes, inhaled deeply, and heaved out a sigh. "Are we ready?" he asked us. He looked at me in the rearview mirror for assurance.

"I suppose," I said.

We got out of the car, opened our umbrellas, and dashed through the pouring rain, dodging puddles.

The place was empty. Dad looked at Mom, confused. Dad and I wore identical dark-gray suits that matched the weather. Mom wore a navy-blue dress I'd never seen her in before. Despite her somber expression, she looked beautiful. I spotted our reflections in the entry-hall mirror. Yep—we looked like we were going to a funeral, and it all began to feel too real.

"Seriously, Elise. What do you think?" Dad asked my mother. "Think anybody is going to show up on a night like this?"

"I don't think you should be worrying about that, Niles," she said.

The funeral director reviewed a few last-minute details with Mom and Dad. We walked in silence down the hallway past a chapel, a kitchen, and some closed doors, until we reached an open pair of doors leading to a large room.

Here I saw Caleb for the first time since I'd left for my track meet on Saturday. He lay in a half-open casket on the far side of the room. I wasn't sure what to do. A loud clicking sound came from behind me, piercing the silence. I turned and saw the doors to the room closing inward. It was now just Mom, Dad, and me, alone in the room. I suppose you could say Caleb was there too.

Mom and Dad walked up to the casket first. Mom began sobbing. She put her head on Dad's shoulders, and he put his arm around her and held her tightly, and he, too, began to cry. For several minutes they stood in front of Caleb's coffin, gazing at him and gently whispering a conversation I couldn't hear. For the moment they seemed together, there for each other, and that made me feel good. Eventually Mom's head left Dad's shoulder, and when they turned to me their faces looked drained.

It was now my turn to approach Caleb.

He was inside a traditional casket lined in white. He looked peaceful. I didn't really know what I was supposed to do—or even think, for that matter. I felt guilty about all the times I resented him when I felt he was impossible—impossible to reason with, impossible to understand, and sometimes impossible to accept. I thought about all our ups and downs over the last few months, and I wondered about a future I would never have with him. I felt like I had to say something to him, but I didn't have any words. So I kept it simple. I put my hand on his and whispered, "Peace, brother. God love you," because those words always calmed him.

Then I walked to a corner of the room and started bawling. I couldn't remember the last time I'd wept. I was shaking, and I wanted to stop, and I wanted to be alone. I thought Mom and Dad must feel the same, because each of us had retreated to a different corner.

I was staring blankly at a picture of Christ with his arms raised, thinking about all the times I had assured Caleb that God loved him, when I felt a hand touch my shoulder. It was Dad.

He turned me around and embraced me. "I keep thinking about that scene in *The Lord of the Rings* when King Théoden discovers his son is dead," he whispered to me. "He says 'No parent should have to bury their child.' It's not supposed to happen this way, Leo. This was not supposed to happen," he repeated.

He lifted my chin and made me look him in the eye, making me feel like a baby. "Leo, my boy, your brother was my hero. When I think about the cards he got dealt, he continually amazed me with what he achieved, and I'm sad and I'm pissed because we'll never see what more he had in store," he told me as he wiped a tear from his eye. "A lot of what your brother achieved was because he admired you."

"I'm not sure—" I began to argue, but he gripped my chin once more and redirected my eyes into his.

"I know he didn't always make life easy for you, Leo," he interrupted. "As a matter of fact, I know your brother could be a royal pain in the ass."

All of a sudden I was laughing, wiping my eyes, and sniffling back tears.

"Nobody's perfect, Leo," Dad told me, holding me a few more seconds. "Trust me on that, son. But you made Caleb a better person, and he made you a better person. That's what brothers are supposed to do," he said as he let go, straightening the knot of my tie. "It's time for us to pull ourselves together and hope some people show up."

I took a deep breath and ran my hand across my hair.

Our family had lived in three different neighborhoods, and,

surprisingly, people from all those places started filing into the room. I first greeted Mrs. Andersen and her daughter, Betsy, our babysitter when I was seven years old. I hadn't seen them in nine years.

Mrs. Andersen walked up to me, placed her hand on my wrist, and started babbling like I'd just seen her yesterday. "I was reading the obituaries the other day and saw your brother's picture," she told me. "I almost fell out of my chair, Leo. I swear that whenever it snows, I look out our kitchen window and see Caleb in his little snowsuit shoveling your driveway next door." She gripped my wrist harder and started rattling off more memories about my brother.

I looked around the room for Mom and Dad. Dad was working the floor, catching up with people I thought had fallen off the map. Mom sat with Grandma on a small sofa in the corner, and guests came to greet her there, mumbling a few words before visiting the coffin briefly to pay their respects. Grandpa was nowhere in sight. I figured he had probably slipped out back for a cigarette.

I moved toward an open space in the center of the room, where Dad met me briefly. "Were you just talking to the Andersens?" he asked.

"Yeah, that was them."

"Christ," he whispered, shaking his head. "Guess word travels fast," he said. "And was that Betsy?"

"Yes."

He glanced over my shoulder, gave her the once-over. "Well, she's filled out nicely," he said.

"Jesus, Dad."

He scanned the room. "Well," he said, "time to make a few more rounds." He gave me a soft pat on the shoulder. "Let's get back to work."

I looked around the room for a familiar face. I spotted a tall man in a dark overcoat standing in the corner nearest the door. He was alone, and by the looks of him he didn't know anyone and wasn't quite sure what to do. I walked over and introduced myself.

"Jim Baims," he said to me, extending his hand to me to shake.

"So you're Mr. Baims," I said with a small grin. "I'm Leo. Caleb's brother."

He looked startled. "Please," he said, "call me Jim." He studied my face. "So you're Leo?" he asked me tentatively, like he was unconvinced. "I've had several meetings with your parents, but I don't think we've met. Caleb talked about you quite a bit. Actually, Caleb used to talk a lot about your eyes." He laughed softly. "Glad to see you still have them."

"Yeah, I still have my eyes," I said, laughing. "Just barely."

Mr. Baims shifted his gaze toward the front of the room and the open casket. "Well, I'm glad to see you're all right, Leo," he said to me. "I always kind of imagined you as a blind kid."

"There were a few close calls," I said, trying to make light of it. "But I'm still mostly intact."

I told him that Caleb used to mention his name quite a bit as well, usually when he was in a foul mood.

"I'm sorry about that, Leo," he said.

"You don't need to apologize. There was no rhyme or reason to it."

Mr. Baims smiled. "Caleb and I had our run-ins," he admitted. "We didn't always see eye to eye about how to behave in the classroom."

Dad acknowledged Mr. Baims from across the room just as I spotted Curtis and Mary standing in the doorway. I thanked him again for coming and went to meet them in the hall.

Curtis was wearing a black suit that certainly provided more dignity than his father's leisure suit had. Mary wore a simple black dress. I knew it was kind of weird to be thinking about her appearance at a moment like this, but she looked amazing, and she lifted my mood. She took my hand and held it.

"How are you doing, man?" Curtis asked. He sounded concerned, even solemn, for once.

"Fine, I guess," I told them. "I'm kind of on autopilot at the moment and haven't really had much time to process."

"Wow," Curtis whispered, looking around the room in confusion. "Who are all these people?"

"Hard to explain."

Curtis then spotted the coffin. "Whoa. You didn't tell me it was going to be open casket."

"Sorry, Curtis. My father meant to consult with you about it, but I think you were busy when he called."

Curtis flinched, and I softened. "Seriously, I think it's a Catholic thing," I told him.

The three of us walked over to the casket and looked at Caleb. Curtis was clearly uncomfortable. "I don't know what I think about the whole open-casket concept," he concluded. "Would you do it?"

"I've never thought about it," I told him.

His raised his eyebrows skeptically. "You haven't? Really?"

"A hundred percent," I told him. "Can we save this conversation for another time?"

Curtis looked around again at all the people. "One thing is for sure, Leo," he told me. "Caleb had more friends than you."

I smirked, then guided Mary to a corner of the room, where we could sit down for a minute. "How are you really doing?" she asked.

"What do you mean, how am I doing?" I asked her, gently nodding toward the casket. "The last time I saw him, he was so crazy with life, running and laughing. It doesn't make any sense to me."

"I don't think it's supposed to make sense, Leo," she said quietly, taking my hand. "My grandpa Pete always told me, 'We're all just waiting in line.' Not too upbeat, but kinda true."

"And on that note, I think I'd better get back to work," I told Mary, figuring it was better to keep moving. In the corner of the room, I'd just spotted Mr. Baims with Caleb's teacher and some of his friends from school. "Dad told me I had to walk around and talk to people. C'mon. You should meet Caleb's friends."

The four of them were seated on two couches facing each other. Caleb had been in the same class with them for a couple of years, and I had met all of them at one time or another. Scott Brewster and Kevin McCarthy sat on one side, sunken into their seats, arms crossed, chins pressed to their chests, looking somewhat confused. Juanita and James sat opposite. Juanita Daniels was the closest thing Caleb had to a romantic interest. She wasn't any taller than four feet and had these tiny facial features that reminded me of the little old lady from the *Poltergeist* movies. In terms of their relationship, I'd never heard Juanita say as much as a single word. Their connection was basically platonic, but Caleb adored her. Of the four, James and Juanita seemed the most understanding of the occasion and acknowledged me when I approached them.

James spoke first. "Your brother was quite a guy, Leo."

Juanita nodded.

"Quite a guy," he repeated. He was Caleb's oldest friend and I'd known him forever. He had a deep voice and had always spoken to me in a fatherly, almost patronizing way.

"Tell me what you'll remember most about him, James," I said. The night had been a series of brief conversations, each person telling me something kind, wonderful, and memorable about Caleb. James ended that.

"For one thing, your brother sure could get mad!" James said loudly. "Boy," he yelled, "Caleb sure could get angry!"

"Oh, yeah," Juanita agreed. "Caleb sure could get mad."

Scott and Kevin sat up, suddenly interested in the conversation.

"When he got mad, Miss Lee told us to get under the desks," James continued. "Miss Lee yelled 'Get under your desks now! Cover your head! Go get Mr. Baims!'"

"Really?" I laughed to myself. It wasn't difficult for me to imagine one of my brother's tantrums and everyone running for cover.

Mr. Baims, hearing his name, interrupted his conversation with Miss Lee and tried to redirect the group. "C'mon guys, let's tell some of the nicer things we'll remember about Caleb."

James nodded at Mr. Baims's suggestion. "Caleb was quite the baker," he recalled.

"Oh, yeah," Scott confirmed. He spoke softly without expression. "Quite the baker."

"He was a good runner—even better than me," Kevin added. "And he brought brownies on our birthdays!"

"Caleb never forgot a birthday," Scott said.

Juanita nodded in agreement. "Caleb never forgot anything!"

They told me about Caleb's lemon cakes, his musical tastes, and the time he pulled the fire alarm, but nobody could tell me about Monica and who put butter on her nose. She would remain a mystery.

I looked over at the casket once more where Caleb lay. Beneath his fixed expression, I could imagine his gleeful grin. "Well," I said to them, "I guess it's going to be a whole lot quieter in the classroom."

"That's for sure!" said James. "That is *for* sure!" Then James leaned toward me and mumbled, "I am very sad about Caleb."

It was starting to get late. I had a conversation with a couple of my dad's friends from the office, Caleb's teacher, and a few more neighbors. I said good-bye to Caleb's friends, wished them the best, and wondered if I'd ever see any of them again.

Suddenly the room emptied almost as quickly as it had

filled. I walked with Mary and Curtis to the entrance. Curtis nodded at me and slipped outside, leaving Mary and me alone.

"You need anything, Leo?" she asked.

"I think we're doing all right," I mumbled.

"Seriously?"

"I'm not sure what I need, Mary." I looked back down the hallway. "My brother is inside a box back in that room, and he's going to be lowered into the ground tomorrow," I told her. "It's all pretty surreal at the moment. He's gone."

She grabbed my hand. "I keep trying to think of something more original to say than 'I'm sorry.' But, truly, I can't think of anything. I'm so sorry." Then she started crying.

"Please," I said to her, trying not to lose it. We held each other a minute before we both pulled ourselves together. "I have to go back," I told her. "Thanks for coming. Tell Curtis I really appreciate it."

"We're here," she told me.

I nodded, then turned back inside before I finally lost it again.

The evening ended the same way it began: just my mother, my father, and me. An attendant came by again and closed the door. We looked at one another and didn't say a word, then each of us approached the casket alone to look at Caleb one last time and say good-bye. It was strange, looking down upon my brother, his eyes softly closed, his face relaxed. I thought about the last time I saw him, finishing our run together and exchanging high fives. I reached into my pocket and took out the cross-country medal that I had won at districts in October, the race of my life. I wanted to give him a gift that meant something to both of us. Before leaving the house earlier that evening, I'd grabbed it from the shelf in our bedroom. It had been displayed beside the medals Caleb had won at the Special Olympics and half marathon. For a moment I'd thought about taking Caleb's medals, but I'd decided I wanted to keep them. I slipped my medal into his breast pocket, patted his heart, and whispered good-bye.

After a few more minutes, we left the room and grabbed our umbrellas, preparing for the storm, but, when we stepped outside, the rain had stopped, and the sky was clear. I saw a sliver of the moon in the darkness, and there must have been a million stars above us.

41.

SOME TIME AGO MY GRANDPARENTS bought a family plot in a cemetery in the country south of the city, and that's where Caleb was buried. His gravesite overlooked an open field speckled with tombstones, tall willow trees, and a large lake. Watching the geese float on the shimmery surface, I thought it seemed fitting that my brother had ended up near water. The ceremony was quick and simple. A priest said a few words, and it was over. Mom took solace in my father's arms and cried when the casket was finally lowered into the earth. I stood beside my grandparents, simply too tired and numb to react by that point.

I wondered why Dad had hired a limousine to drive the five of us from the funeral home, but then I realized that none of us were in any state to drive. We were all exhausted, but it was a different kind of tired, the one when your whole body feels slow and empty.

Still, despite exhaustion, I couldn't sleep.

I lay awake thinking about what happened, and more so, how it happened. Caleb loved swimming on Saturdays, probably because the pool was mostly empty during the morning, except for lap swimmers, so he usually had the deep end entirely to himself.

I thought about him jumping off that high dive. He would

climb up the ladder, make sure the board tension was adjusted for maximum spring, and position himself at the near end of the board. Then he'd storm down at full speed and launch himself, his steps timed perfectly to get the most spring from his bounce. He would explode off the board like he was going to sail clear past the edge of the pool. I thought about him in midair, in the midst of that crazy corkscrew twist, laughing maniacally. I used to watch him with my goggles sometimes when he went below.

He was pure muscle. Underwater, he'd sink to the bottom and sometimes sit a moment on the pool floor before pushing off and returning to the surface. He'd paddle to the side of the pool, climb the ladder, and prepare for his next launch, laughing his ass off the entire time. He'd jump off that high dive for hours. I suppose his rhythms and patterns, as much as they were abnormal, became normal at that pool. So probably nobody noticed when he didn't come up after that last jump.

Mom said it was likely a seizure.

Dad said that the teenager lifeguarding hadn't done his job and there would be hell to pay. But we'd worry about that later.

Nobody was quite sure what happened. All we knew was that, from the amount of water they had to pump from his stomach and lungs, Caleb was probably on the bottom of the deep end for a long time before an old man swimming laps saw him lying there.

I imagined he had a smile on his face when he made his last splash. At least that's what I wanted to think.

When I went back to school on Monday, it was clear Rasmussen had spread the news. I mostly kept my eyes focused on the ground, trying to avoid superficial conversations, and when I did have to engage with someone, we kept it simple.

"Sorry, man," someone would mumble.

"Yeah, thanks," I'd reply.

I went back to practice and I did the workouts, but I was just going through the motions—I was unfocused and lacked any intensity to push myself. Gorsky backed off and didn't bark at me for not hitting my splits. Instead he told me not to worry, just run through it, that by maintaining a routine I wouldn't lose my fitness. Gorsky said that by Saturday's sectional qualifier, if I'd get my head back in it, I'd be ready to go.

"I'll drive you to the race tomorrow morning," Dad told me at dinner on Friday. "You'll get there in plenty of time."

I wanted to say *bullshit*. I didn't feel right talking about running a race so soon after seeing my brother being put in the ground. The wake and funeral had sucked me dry, and the nervous energy that I'd come to rely upon to fuel me was absent. "I don't know if I'm up for it, Dad," I finally said.

Dad sucked in his breath. "Leo, I know how you're feeling. I also know you've worked hard for this, and it might be what you need. Let's see how you feel about it tomorrow morning."

Sectionals were at Kirkwood, the track located behind the school smack-dab in the middle of an open field with no trees or windbreaks. When we arrived, I stepped out of the car into a warm gusty wind and a sky spitting raindrops.

"It's going to be a slow one, Coughlin," Curtis told me, stating the obvious. "You don't have to worry about killing yourself. Just be there for the finish and you're good."

I must have been out of it when Mom came and found me stretching beneath the awning of an equipment shed, trying to avoid the rain. "Leo, they've announced second call for your race," she informed me in a gentle voice. She was holding a small black umbrella and offering me a bottle of water. "Your father reminded me that you like to be left alone before a race, but you're usually jogging around by now getting ready. Are you okay?"

"I'm just trying to stay dry, Mom," I answered, standing up and running in place for a few seconds. "I'd better go sign in so I don't get scratched," I told her as I headed to the track.

When I lined up for the start, I felt nervous, but I didn't have that feeling like I was ready to jump out of my skin like I usually did before a race. I felt myself dreading the blast of the starter's pistol and the pain and fatigue I was about to feel. I glanced up into the bleachers and spotted my parents, beneath umbrellas, wearing worried expressions, and then I turned and readied myself for the start.

As Curtis predicted, the race went out slow and I felt like sludge from the start, legs heavy like the blood inside was concrete. We went through three laps at 3:22, a pace that should have felt pedestrian, but I was gassed. When the bell sounded, Fletcher took off and nobody went with him. I tucked in behind two guys from Lafayette and drafted off them down the backstretch, but in the final 150 meters they pulled away and I had nothing left. I crossed the line in fourth.

"That's good enough, Leo," Gorsky assured me. "All we needed to do today was qualify and you did that."

Curtis was less satisfied. "The good news is that you qualified," he said simply. "The bad news is, you looked like crap."

"You got lucky last week, Coughlin," Fletcher yelled to me as he jogged by. "I'm going to kick your ass again next week at state."

Maybe the only silver lining in my day was that Mary was painting sets for the spring musical, so she didn't witness the race.

I woke up the next morning and headed out to Macklin Park to run. I hadn't been back there since the race in the fall. The course looked different in the spring. The trails were still worn but were narrowed and almost covered by the fresh uncut grass. The smell of wet dirt and everything blooming filled my nose as I ran the trail skirting the bluff above the river. I tried to focus and remember the details of that race from last fall, hoping they might inspire me and get me back on track. About the point in the course where I overtook Curtis, I started feeling the life come back into my legs. I thought about the sacrifice he'd made for me that day and the proud expressions on my parents' faces when I crossed the finish line in victory. I was feeling good, so I ran the loop again that morning, just like I'd done with Curtis. Passing the parking lot, I thought about Gorsky singling Curtis and me out for that final pep talk. As I passed the playground, I remembered Dad shouting at me from the hood of the car, Mom at the picnic table, and Caleb swinging so high on the swing, the metal chains went slack. Pretty soon I was cruising, reliving that entire race—all its pains, and all its joys.

"Mary stopped by while you were gone," Mom told me as I came in the house later that morning. "She dropped something off for you."

I was way behind in school, so I made myself a sandwich and headed down to my room to try to make a dent in my homework. When I sat down at my desk, I noticed a new picture on the wall, next to Caleb's version of da Vinci's *The Last Supper*. It was the picture of the two of us at Six Flags, clutching hands and screaming while we were in free fall. Tucked inside the corner of the frame was one of Mary's watercolors, a small painting of the three of us eating frozen custard beneath the awning of Ted Drewes in the pouring rain. I'd seen two pictures in her bag that day at Six Flags, and I'd figured that she was going to give one to me and one to Caleb. I guess she'd get to keep the other.

I got up and sat down on my bed and put my head between my hands and closed my eyes. That day seemed so long ago, I thought, maybe like it never happened. Just about an hour ago, I was starting to feel good again, but now I was tearing up.

42.

DAD WAS IN THE KITCHEN, waiting for me. He made me a quick breakfast of toast and eggs, then rifled through my gym bag and made sure I had packed everything before we headed out. I guess he sensed I was pretty out of it.

Mom met me in the hallway before I left and told me she would be driving to the meet with Mary.

"Mom, it's all right," I told her. "Maybe you should get some rest."

"I wouldn't miss it for the world," she said.

We were on the road for just thirty minutes before Dad tried to coax me into talking about the race. "What's the race plan today, Leo?" he asked gently.

"I don't have one," I told him, because I didn't. "Gun goes off. I run. That simple."

Dad read my energy. I flipped the radio on and pressed the buttons until I finally found a song I could tolerate. I listened for just a few seconds before Dad punched the button again and changed the station. "Sorry," he said, sighing. "That song reminds me of your mother" was all he said.

"How?"

"Do yourself a favor, Leo, and focus on running this race."

That pretty much ended our conversation. I looked out the

window at the fields of young corn, now a foot tall above the freshly plowed earth.

The state meet was held at Lincoln University. When we arrived, the meet was already under way, and the stadium was packed. I jogged in the parking lot to stretch out my legs after the two-hour ride. Hearing the loudspeakers awakened my nerves, and now I was glad we'd arrived late. I decided not to enter the stadium but hang out by the car with Dad and listen to music for a while.

An hour before the race, I found Gorsky in the bleachers and checked in with him. Curtis was beside him. They both knew I didn't like to talk much before a race.

Gorsky smiled and placed his hands on my shoulders. "You know what to do," he said, "but you're going to need to dig down."

I looked the old man in the eyes and knew he was on my side. "Any advice?" I asked.

"Keep it simple, Leo. Just win the damn race," he said. "You've earned this. Channel your energy. The race is only four minutes. Don't be afraid."

For once in his life, Curtis didn't open his mouth. He acknowledged me with a fist pump to his heart. I left the bleachers and began my warm-up.

We were given the final call for the race well before we were even allowed on the track. They kept all sixteen sweaty, nervous runners crammed together in a tiny tent for fifteen minutes. I felt like I was going to burst out of my seams corralled in there. Finally, the loudspeaker announced our event and the marshals let us out at the far end of the track.

I was assigned lane four, and I had to walk the hundred meters in my lane to the starting line as they announced our
names. I jumped up and down and tried to bring my muscles
back to life, but my head still really wasn't in it.

I spotted Gorsky in the stands first. Although he was far
away, I saw his head nod. He raised his hand, made a fist, and
tapped his heart. Curtis was next to him, with my father sitting
alone three rows behind them. Then I spotted my mother sitting next to Mary, a couple of rows in front of Gorsky and
Curtis. I tapped my heart with two fingers and pointed to her.

The marshals gave us one last minute to warm up and get
loose. I did a final stride on the first curve of the track, then returned and positioned myself on the starting line. There were
two of us stacked to a lane, a staggered start that would break
at the turn. Arthur Fletcher was to my right in lane five. He
turned and glared at me before squaring himself for the start.
I knew that I had trained to win, and I knew that I wanted to
win. But at the moment I doubted that I had anything left in
me. Then I remembered Gorsky's words. I wasn't going to let
anyone in this race think I was afraid.

When the gun blasted, I allowed myself to get sucked into
the momentum of the pack. When we hit the turn and everyone
broke for the rail, I found myself tangled in knees and elbows.
This time Fletcher held back and let someone else be the rabbit
and press the pace. The first lap was quick but manageable. All
sixteen of us were running in a tight clump as we completed the
first lap in 61 seconds, a respectable split. Some of the spectators
stood up, thinking this might be the race of the day.

I was running in the thick of it, tucked in behind the first five runners, when I felt a foot clip my ankle. I lost my balance and spun forward onto the tarmac. Runners parted themselves, trying to sidestep my flailing arms and legs. I fell forward, tucked my head, and hit the track shoulder first and somersaulted. When I popped back up, I caught Fletcher looking over his shoulder with a little grin. He dropped his right arm for a split second on the backswing and flipped me the bird. Then that bastard took off and began to press. I rolled back up on my feet, watching the pack pull away, and I continued running. I was twenty meters behind, but now I was pissed.

I spent the second lap in no-man's-land. Trying to close the gap now would be suicidal, so I just maintained my pace and didn't let them get any farther ahead. The scoreboard clock showed the leaders through the half in 2:04. I crossed the line three seconds behind them, in last place.

They slowed on the backstretch, and I caught the last runners on the far turn. Now I had the collective energy of the group and worked off their draft. I settled in during the third lap and prepared for the finish.

As we hit the back turn into the homestretch that third time, I made my move. I surged from the back and began passing runners. When I came up on Fletcher's shoulder, he heard my breathing and looked back. I could see the fear in his eyes now. It was my turn to grin.

Fletcher and I headed down the homestretch together, positioning ourselves for the final lap. I was on the outside as the final bell rang, and I tried to squeeze Fletcher into the rail. He prodded my elbow on its backswing, and I nudged him back. Then Fletcher caught me under my arm just below the elbow and knocked me off balance again. I stumbled into the third lane but was able to steady myself. As I closed in on Fletcher's shoulder, Snell broke between us and took the lead on the backstretch. Now I was running in third place. It was a three-man race.

Rounding the final turn, I couldn't see or hear anything except the back of Fletcher's singlet and the pounding of my heart. My lungs were searing and my chest felt like it was going to blast apart. Then I saw the tape across the finish line, and I said to myself that this was mine. I unleashed my kick with fifty meters to go and finally broke the race open for good. I split the tape in 4:10 and then just kept on moving.

I really didn't want to run another step, but almost by reflex I launched into my victory lap. I slowed to a gentle trot and exchanged handshakes with a few guys on the first turn, then kept running.

I thought about Caleb and the fact that I would never have to run away from him again. I thought about the irony that my success as a runner was due in large part to him. By the time I hit the back turn, I was tired of being alone. I looked up into the stands and found Gorsky, Curtis, Mary, Mom, and Dad. Even though they were just dots in the distance, I felt their presence beside me.

By the time I hit the homestretch, I was running full tilt.

43.

I SAID GOOD-BYE TO CURTIS a few days after
school ended. It wasn't so much a "farewell" as a "so long." His
father took a temporary teaching assignment at the University
of Colorado, so he gave Curtis his ultimate graduation gift: a
summer in Boulder, where he could run at high altitude.

"Any last words of wisdom?" I asked him after we'd completed our last run.

"Yeah. Stop asking for advice," he told me. "I'll be back for
winter break, and we'll celebrate being Ladue's first back-to-
back state champions. In the meantime, just run, man. Remember Gorsky's famous words: 'cross-country is a summer sport.'
Run long." He made me promise him that I would. "Run long
and you'll figure it all out."

Mom, Dad, and I each spent the next month grieving in our
own way. Caleb's absence created this massive void of energy in
our house that seemed to suck more and more life out of us.
Mom would be slicing vegetables for dinner, then suddenly
drop the knife and run sobbing to the bedroom. Dad sat in
front of the television holding a drink and watching ESPN, the
volume nearly muted, his eyes glazed over. I went for long runs,

slow and steady, the ones where you just spaced out. Sometimes the runner's high would creep in and I'd think about things that made me laugh or feel better, but then I'd feel guilty and crappy about feeling good.

I'd eat breakfast in the morning and look out the window and see him talking to himself and making grass piles in the yard. I'd look at the clock at seven each night and hear him speaking to James. I'd lie awake and hear him pose me his riddles. I'd lie awake at night tossing and turning, wondering about the infinite what-ifs.

———

By the end of June Mom and Dad were drifting further and further apart, to the point where they barely said a word to each other. Their silent treatment with each other was killing me. Dad was sleeping in the spare bedroom, and Mom was out of the house a lot. She'd turn a shoulder if Dad tried to hold her, but she asked me to hug her at least once a day. They finally sat me down one night, and Mom told me they were going to call it quits for a while and separate.

Mary told me she thought it might get ugly when they started packing things up, so I asked my parents if I could get out of the house for a few nights while they got things sorted.

"I can't believe you're actually choosing to go to your grandparents," Mom said, placing a plate of bacon and eggs before me.

"It was Mary's idea," I explained. "It's not like we have a lot of options," I reminded her. "Besides, she wants to find out if all those stories I've told her are true."

"Oh, I think she's in for a surprise," Mom said.

"I'm hoping it's not too much of a surprise." I was trying to finish the last bites when Mary pulled into the driveway.

Mom reached into her billfold and pulled out some cash. "Just make sure Mary understands all your grandmother's quirks before you get there."

"Like the two-squares-of-toilet-paper regulation?"

She laughed and handed me the cash. "Listen, Leo. She's a part of me, and that makes her a part of you."

"That's kind of a scary thought, Mom."

"Please be nice to your grandmother. I'm still shocked she's allowing her grandson to bring a girl for an overnight. Never would have happened in my day," she said, combing my hair with her fingers.

I began to make a break for the door, but she grabbed my arm. "Leo, can you give me a hug? I could really use it."

I hugged Mom and she gave me a peck on the forehead. "I love you, Leo. I haven't been my best self this year, honey. Once your dad and I get everything sorted, I want the two of us to sit down and have a long talk. Can I take you to Charley's?"

"We can do that, Mom. I'm easily bribed by a cheeseburger."

———

We arrived at my grandparents' in the early afternoon. Like clockwork, Grandma burst through the patio door, wearing her blue cornflower housedress and brandishing her metal spatula to direct traffic like a cop, Grandpa close in tow.

"Get ready," I warned Mary. I was sure Grandma was about to rattle off a long list of jobs we had to do to earn our dinner, but she surprised me with a big, warm hug and then turned to Mary.

"Hello, young lady," Grandma said warmly, extending her hand. "Let me give you the grand tour."

Grandpa lit up a cigarette, took a long slow drag, and gazed at me for a moment before gently nodding. "How are you doing, Leo?"

"I'm holding," I told him. We nodded at each other, and that was all.

Grandma showed us inside and immediately laid down the boundary markers in terms of our sleeping arrangements. Next she ushered Mary and me to the bathroom and explained the two-square-toilet-paper regulation, provided a graphic description of what happened when the toilet clogged, and reviewed how to use the plunger.

Grandma went light on work detail that afternoon. She just told us to go pick from the garden whatever we wanted to eat that evening.

After dinner we sat on the porch and Mary coaxed Grandpa to tell stories about what he was like when he was our age. He told her things I never knew, like how he hopped trains during the Depression and made money playing card games in Chicago.

"Gambling?" Mary asked.

Grandpa winked at her. "Some might call it that. Others would simply say I was making ends meet."

"What kind of trouble were you getting into in Chicago?" she asked.

"Let's just say that I was rarely the one holding a losing hand at the card table, Mary. Sometimes that can create a predicament."

"Like what?" she asked.

"For the love of God, let go of the past, Bernard," Grandma said as she cleared the table.

"Leo, run on into the house and fetch a couple of decks of cards and that pickle jar full of pennies in the cupboard," Grandpa told me. "I'm going to teach the two of you a basic life skill."

I fetched the cards and pennies in a flash. Mom had told me all about Grandpa's antics when he was younger, but Grandma had always held him at bay. Grandpa was finally going to teach me how to play cards. Despite Grandma's objections again, Grandpa taught us several different versions of poker. We bet pennies until almost midnight.

I slept on the sofa in the living room, and Mary got the guest room to herself. The windows were open, and I fell asleep listening to that same damn bullfrog who was always looking for action.

I awoke the next morning to the distinctive sounds of my grandmother's squawking, and I feared the worst as I stepped outside onto the porch. She was standing next to the split metal drum, a small fire burning the few bits of garbage that couldn't be composted. Above her, five grumpy crows sat on the electrical wires flapping their wings, eyeing whatever could be scavenged, and making a racket.

"Caw ... Caw ... Caw," she screamed, while shaking an old rusty shovel above her at the birds.

"Caw, caw," one answered back angrily.

"It's about time you got out of bed, young man! Go wake

up that friend of yours and come back out here. You need to check the strawberry patch for those thieving turtles," Grandma ordered me. "You know what to do."

I schlepped back inside, hauled Mary out of bed, and grabbed a box from the garage. I explained the turtle situation on the way to the strawberry patch.

"Sounds like a dangerous assignment," she said. She was still a little groggy. "I'll let you handle it."

Grandma's strawberry patch consisted of three parallel rows of strawberry plants ten yards long. She barricaded its borders with a fence made from chicken wire and wooden stakes. Despite the penitentiary-like fortifications, the turtles always found a way to breach security.

We spotted five turtles right away gorging themselves on Grandma's berries. I glanced over at Mary, made a pistol with my fingers, and placed my index finger to my lips, demanding silence. I crept toward the gate and motioned with my thumb for her to cover the back fence. "You take the back in case they try to make an escape," I whispered.

I then gently released the latch and kicked the gate open. "Freeze!" I screamed. "Drop the strawberries now and nobody gets hurt!"

The turtles snapped tight into their shells. Mary and I entered the patch and plucked them up and placed them in the box.

One turtle sported a faded red 7 painted on its shell. Two others bore the numbers 17 and 35.

"What's up with the numbers?" she asked.

"You will soon find out."

We lugged the box back to the house and plopped the turtles on the porch, satisfied with our work. Grandma stepped outside and peered into the box. "No-good scoundrels," she scolded them.

She picked one up from the box. "Well, if it isn't Mr. Seventeen." The turtle poked its head from its shell and looked at Grandma inquisitively. "Why, I haven't seen you in five years." She placed him back in the box and picked up another. "Mr. Thirty-Five, I thought you might have passed away."

Then Grandma shook her head and whistled sadly. "Well, well, well, it's Mr. Seven." Mr. Seven had his head tucked deep inside his shell. "This is not your lucky day, Mr. Seven. That's three strikes, mister."

Grandma reached into the pocket of her housecoat and pulled out a little bottle of red polish and lobbed it at me.

"Put a number forty-seven on that one," she said, pointing at the quicker turtle. "And the other one fifty-six," she said decisively. "After that you two can come on inside for your breakfast." Grandma walked away with Mr. Seven, clutching him like a rock.

"What are you going to do to Mr. Seven?" Mary yelled.

She continued walking. "You don't want to know, young lady," she called back. "Hopefully there are plenty of strawberries in turtle heaven."

Mary watched in horror. "Geez, Leo! Is she serious? If I'd known she was going to murder the poor turtle, I wouldn't have taken part in this operation."

"Relax." I laughed. "I got this. It's a little game she likes to play."

After lunch that day, Grandma took us back to the garage and handed me a bucket. "Leo, you know the drill. It's time to show your friend how we make blackberry ice cream here. And take those thieving turtles with you. Remind them they'd better not come back!" she called after us. The screen door slammed behind her.

Before heading out, Mary and I returned to the garage and did a quick search. I found Mr. Seven trying to hoist himself out of a tin bucket in the corner near the lawn mower. "Today is your lucky day, Mr. Seven," I told him.

I tipped the bucket to the floor to make it look like an escape, snuck Mr. Seven out of the garage, and slipped him into the box with the other turtles. Then we headed up the trail into the forest.

The trail was canopied by the green leaves of June. "Have you ever filled a bucket with blackberries?" I asked her.

"Nope."

"It takes longer than you think," I told her.

Mary nudged me. "Lighten up, Leo. It's not like we need to be somewhere."

I led Mary to an old creek bed where we could release the turtles. She removed Mr. Seven from the box and pointed him in the opposite direction from Grandma's garden. "Seven is a lucky number," she reminded him. "If I were you, I would quit pushing your luck with that woman."

We then headed to the edges of my grandparents' property,

where the wood fence paralleled the back road and the black-berries grew thick in the open sunlight. We spent the afternoon popping every other berry into our mouths and scratching our arms on thorny vines.

Along the far trail on the property, I showed her the old pond, the one with the thick cattail grove and abandoned cabin resting on the ridge overlooking the eastern bank. We sat down on the porch just as the sun began to set, and watched the reflections of the trees turn to shadows and the pond darken with the sky.

She finally broke the silence. "Well, this isn't exactly the marine boot camp you made this place out to be."

"It's not bad," I admitted.

"I like your grandparents," Mary said.

I laughed. "Grandma has been a different person since the funeral. I swear."

I picked up a stone from the ground, threw it out toward the center of the pond, and watched the concentric ripples trickle outward. "When we were younger, this is where my brother and I used to come fishing."

I tossed another stone, this time skipping it across the water's surface. "I guess I always just figured he was going to be around forever. I remember looking at him and wondering what he was going to look like when he got old. I figured once my parents weren't around, I'd be looking after him. Sometimes I imagined the two of us as old geezers sitting in rocking chairs shooting the shit. Or me listening to him ramble on endlessly about something that didn't make sense. Then we'd climb into our car and I'd take him down to the Dairy Queen."

"Seriously, Leo," Mary said, "I often wonder if crappy things like what went down with Caleb happen for some higher reason."

"And what reason is that?"

"That's the mystery," Mary said. "One we'll never know."

"Well, that plain sucks," I told her. "Based on the last month, I feel like I'm going to spend the rest of my life thinking and wondering about him. I mean, Jesus! I swear a moment doesn't go by that I don't see him or think about him."

"Don't you think that's natural?"

"Probably," I admitted. "But I'm still wondering if we were cool in the end, or if he still resented me."

"I think you were good in the end," she said, putting her arm around me.

"Yeah?"

She put her head on my shoulder. "You're the one who has to answer that."

I woke up on the last day wanting to fish one last time in the old pond before we left. Alone.

I headed down the trail with a coffee can full of dirt and earthworms I dug up from the compost pile. I flipped the old rowboat underneath the persimmon tree and retrieved the fishing pole stashed beneath. I slid the bow into the pond, stepped inside, and with one more push on the shore glided out onto the pond.

As I floated I saw Caleb and me together in this very boat. We had come here a hundred times as kids with hopes of catching a big fish.

Eventually I guided the boat over toward the cattails, where I knew the water was deep. I put a worm on the hook and cast my line. I stared at that red-and-white bobber floating on the water and thought about the last month, the last year, my whole life. A soft wind blew, making the reflections on the pond's surface flit and change.

Suddenly I felt my fishing pole jerk and my line yank. I hit the lock, the line tightened, and the pole began to bend. I gave a quick tug. Whatever was under the surface was big.

This fish was stubborn. It fought for its life, but I was patient. I pulled slowly against its resistance, released the lock on the reel, and gathered in the line bit by bit. I knew I had this one, but when I realized that I was going to have to hold it down and pull the hook from its mouth I thought about just cutting the line. But the thought of that poor fish swimming around for the rest of its life with a piece of metal lodged in its jaw didn't seem right. I had to deal.

The fish finally appeared beneath the surface and surrendered itself. I pulled it onto the floor of the boat. It was a catfish. It must have weighed nearly three pounds—by far the biggest fish I had ever caught.

It flipped, twisted, and thrashed on the floor of the boat, its slapping tail thudding and echoing across the pond. Fear welled up inside me: I would have to touch it. The fish was still for a moment. Its belly rested on the floor and its gills opened and closed quickly, the hook deeply lodged inside its mouth. I didn't know what to do with the fish. I just knew I was alone with it.

I watched it flip and thrash again for several seconds until it became still. I thought about how Caleb had placed his hand over that thrashing fish, pinning it to the boat's floor. I slowly leaned toward it and, with my left hand, gripped it on its spine just beyond its head. I pinned the fish to the floor of the boat, like Caleb had done.

I held my hand there until the fish no longer resisted. Then, with my right hand, I reached for the hook, determined the angle at which its barb was lodged, and wriggled it free. I stuck my thumb inside its mouth, lifted the fish up, and examined my catch. The fish was still except for its blood-red gills beating calmly in the morning sun. I lifted the fish over the side of the boat and placed it back in the water. It was stunned, and it floated and hovered for several seconds on the pond's surface. Then suddenly the fish came back to life. Its tail swept slowly from side to side for a moment, and then the fish slipped beneath the surface and disappeared.

I stared into the water, looking at my reflection, and it felt like Caleb was right there beside me. I took a deep breath and shook it off. He'd always be a part of me, and as complicated as that was, I smiled and thought, we were good in the end.

I paddled back to the shore and pulled the boat in under the tree. I removed the fishing pole and wrapped the line around the pole's stem a couple of times until the line was taut, then pushed the hook's barb deep into the cork handle. I placed the pole on the ground and flipped the boat over on top of it.

As I headed down the trail and back to the house, I began to run. The dirt felt soft beneath my feet, and a little dust rose, filling my footprints. The leaves were dark and glossy in the shade. I picked up my pace a bit, relaxing into a rhythm. Just up the bend I could see light sifting in, where the path opened up. My legs knew the way.

Acknowledgements

I'm beyond grateful that my manuscript found its way to Wernick & Pratt and my agent, Emily Mitchell, whose keen insights, attention to detail, and endless commitment helped make this novel possible. Additional thanks to Charlesbridge and my editor, Monica Perez, for her comments, suggestions, and guidance in seeing this project to completion. Finally, thanks to my copyeditor, Lara Stelmaszyk, for an impeccable eye for detail as well as her astute suggestions.

Thanks also to my colleague and friend Mark Burpee, for being a patient sounding board and for providing feedback, laughs, and encouragement.

Additional gratitude goes to coaches, friends, and teammates—Coach Brusca, Coach Lockerbie, Coach Fox, Curtis, Ted, Dave R., George, McGowan, Jim, and many others I've pounded the roads, trails, and track with over the years. Your collective camaraderie, wisdom, guidance, and experiences provided a treasure of memories to draw from when I was writing this story.

Finally, my family—Mom, Dad, Marian, Michelle, Teresa, Jim, and Sue. Thank you for the support, opportunities, and humor and for sharing the experience of being blessed by Chris.

Last, my most heartfelt thanks to my wife, Dana. No words can express my appreciation for her love and unwavering support. Thank you for putting pencil and paper in my hand and continually encouraging me to just write it down.